The Rookery Killer

A Victorian Historical Murder Mystery

Book 4 of
The Field & Greystone Series

Lana Williams

USA Today Bestselling Author

Other Books in The Field & Greystone Series

Want to make sure you know when my next book is released?
Sign up for my newsletter.

One

London 1884

RUPERT COBB BELCHED AS he staggered out of the Drunken Sailor pub in Camden Town, waving to a fellow prison guard as he went. "G'night, Tretheway. See ye in the mornin'."

"Not if I see ye first!" A round of laughter followed the words, but was soon muffled as the heavy door swung shut behind Rupert.

The freezing air caused his eyes to water even as it started to lift the fog in his head. The temperature dipped low most March nights, especially this early in the month. Spring was still weeks away and felt as if it would never arrive.

He'd definitely had more than his fair share of drinks this evening, which the missus would be none too happy about. But the extra money he'd received of late was reason to celebrate and made an additional drink, or two, or even three, impossible to resist. Hadn't he given her a bit to quiet the list of complaints she always seemed to have?

Rupert blinked to clear his vision then wiped his cheek, vaguely noting how dark the street was. "Good thing I ain't goin' far," he muttered to himself as he started toward home.

A pat to his pocket reassured him the notes—three months' worth of pay—were still stuffed there, and he hadn't managed to spend them all. The security of the small lump left him with a warm feeling unrelated to the alcohol he'd imbibed, and helped to ward off the chill of the night.

Chances were he'd be able to earn a little more. Rupert shrugged his shoulders to will away the persistent niggle of guilt that accompanied the thought.

Accepting bribes...it was a slippery slope. It had been one thing to share what he'd overheard a prisoner say to a visitor at Holloway Prison, where he worked. His superiors ran a tight ship at the overcrowded institution, but no one could begrudge him sharing a little gossip he'd overheard between two women. However, Rupert had taken an even bigger risk by looking the other way when another prisoner escaped a week ago.

Because that prisoner wasn't just anyone. Miles Edgarton was considered a self-made man by some—and a notorious criminal by others. If the rumors could be believed, he had his finger in more schemes than could be counted, most of them illegal.

Rupert sighed, thinking of the questions he'd had to answer for his part in the escape. While he hoped his story of being distracted by another prisoner was believed, he didn't know for certain. A few of his fellow guards continued to eye him warily since that day as if they weren't sure whether he could be trusted.

"That's all right," he whispered to reassure himself. "In time, my part will be forgotten." He needed it to be; he valued his job as a prison guard, though it didn't pay much.

The problem was, the search for Edgarton had only grown since his escape a week ago. Everyone remained on the lookout for the man who, thus far, was nowhere to be found. Rupert held a faint hope he'd left the country.

Helping a man surely guilty of several counts of murder, though his trial had yet to be held, had been a difficult decision. It wasn't Rupert's fault that he didn't earn enough as a prison guard to provide for his family, was it? Limited opportunities arose for a man of his upbringing with little schooling and few connections.

A man had to do what a man had to do, he told himself.

And he still wore a uniform, didn't he? Rupert tugged on the bottom of his navy jacket with its shiny buttons, remembering how proud he'd been to put it on for the first time five years ago. Even his wife had looked at him with admiration that day, though admittedly rarely since.

Would his prospects improve if he left the prison and worked for Edgarton directly? That was a question that kept him up at night. It would be a terrible risk in many ways, given how volatile Edgarton was said to be. Rumors abounded of his tendency toward cruelty. Second chances were not something the ruthless man believed in.

But the man surely paid well—paid better than Her Majesty's prison service, at any rate. Once again his fingers fluttered over the lump of cash tucked into his pocket.

Rupert heaved a sigh as he turned a corner. He would have to ponder the option later when his thoughts weren't clouded with drink.

Chilled to the bone, he shivered, hurrying the last few steps to reach the sagging, worn door of the lodging house, annoyed to find it jammed shut. After three attempts, he finally jerked it open and started up the two flights of stairs, grasping onto the wall to steady himself. Half the building would now be awake with the racket he'd made.

With a frown, Rupert paused to glance around when he reached the first landing, certain the stairway wasn't usually this dark. What had happened to the sconce light that normally lit the stairs? Unease crept down his spine, but he brushed it away and resumed his climb. "Wouldn't it be nice if the landlord kept things up around here?" he whispered to himself.

Heart thumping, and not just because of the exertion of the many stairs, Rupert hesitated on the second landing to eye the long hallway which led to his rooms. Something felt amiss, but he couldn't quite put his finger on it. It was impossible to see anything in the dark. Regret for that last drink filled him even as he gathered his wits before he dug in his pocket and pulled out his key.

Shadows moved—ones he didn't remember seeing before. Nothing more than his imagination, he told himself. With determination, he started forward again, his breath coming quickly, eagerness for his bed growing—

A shadow moved again, shifting into human form. "Cobb."

Rupert frowned at the familiar tone, trying to place it. A neighbor perhaps? No—

The flare of a match as the man lit a pipe gave Rupert a brief but chilling look at the eyes belonging to the voice. The man's presence was puzzling *and* alarming.

"What are ye doin' here?" he asked, annoyed by the catch in his voice.

"Came to talk to you." The man shook out the match, and darkness claimed the scene once again.

"This time of night? What fer?" Rupert's stomach roiled. Whatever the answer, it couldn't be good.

"Your services are no longer needed."

Disappointment struck him hard, along with a spurt of frustrated anger. No longer needed? Life wasn't fair. Just when he'd thought he might be getting ahead a bit—

"Mistakes were made," the man continued in a low voice, so quiet it was difficult to hear.

"Mistakes? What mistakes?" Rupert took offense to the words. "I was careful."

"Not careful enough. There's been too much talk. Too many whispered accusations."

Rupert's eyes had adjusted to the dark once again, allowing him to see the visitor nod as he puffed on his pipe. The tobacco briefly cast an orange glow that revealed a hard glint in the man's eyes. "I didn't tell no one."

"You didn't have to. People noticed. What's done is done."

He heaved a sigh. Well, it had been impossible to resist hinting to his friends that he had extra blunt. Clearly he wasn't cut out for deception. Not with so many watching him. "Fine. But if another...opportunity arises—"

"It won't."

Rupert stiffened, prepared to argue. Only too late did he realize the man wasn't alone. Awareness of someone behind him took hold but before he could react, an arm wrapped around his neck. "Wait—"

The strong arm cut off his words, stifling his protest. He gulped for air and tugged at it with both hands, struggling to gain his freedom. He writhed this way and that, but still he couldn't draw a breath.

Panic took hold, and with arms flailing, Rupert clawed at his attacker without success. His vision narrowed and he shoved his elbow into the body behind him with little effect.

Fear slowly faded and regret took its place. He never should've taken the bribe or become involved in any of this. Should never...never have...

His limbs grew heavy as darkness took a firmer hold. His last thought was of his wife on the other side of the door, so close and yet so far. He should've given her more of the extra money.

Then it was over.

The key was retrieved, the door unlocked, and the body shoved inside where it hit the floor with a thud.

"Rupert? Is that ye?" a shrill, angry voice called out. "Late again, an' I knows why!"

Only a terrible silence answered her.

Two

THE SOUND OF WEEPING greeted Scotland Yard Inspector Henry Field as he arrived at the crime scene that morning. Never a good sign. Nor did it make examining the area—or the body—easy.

"His widow isn't taking the news well, sir," Constable Barlow murmured, gesturing toward the second-floor door in the worn and tired building.

Camden Town was a touch outside Henry's usual jurisdiction, but the death of the Holloway prison guard suspected of aiding an escaped prisoner made it Henry's business. He'd been pursuing Miles Edgarton for over a week with little to show for it—until now.

But a dead body wasn't the sort of lead he'd been hoping for.

"Her grief is understandable," Henry replied, heart heavy with empathy for the family's loss, even though he had little for the victim—if what they suspected him of was true. "Cobb was killed in his rooms?"

"That's where the body was found." The constable shrugged. "Whoever did it must've followed him home, he'd been at the pub for a drink...or four."

Henry frowned. "Did Mrs. Cobb witness the murder?"

"No. She says she heard nothing except an odd thump as if something fell. She came out of the bedchamber to find him on the floor. Thought he'd passed out until she got a better look at him and realized he wasn't breathing."

Unless the woman was a heavy sleeper, she surely would've heard a scuffle or voices in their lodgings. Perhaps the murder had taken place elsewhere. Perhaps the wounded man had made it home but no farther and subsequently died.

Henry glanced up and down the dark corridor. "Can you find us some light?" He could make out the outline of an extinguished lamp on the wall near the stairs, but little else. Even for a tenement in one of the poorer areas of the city, it was especially dark. A narrow window high on the wall above the stairs was too dirty to let in much light.

"Certainly." Barlow hurried to the lamp, reached into his pocket and pulled out a box of matches. He struck one, then turned a knob, but nothing happened. With a muttered oath that Henry chose to ignore, the constable lit two more before finally managing to light the lamp. He repeated the process at the opposite end of the hallway while Henry perused the area.

While an improvement, the lighting still left much to be desired. Still, Henry bent low to study the floor in search of possible evidence, the wailing widow impossible to ignore.

"Oh the poor man—oh, my Rupert!"

Henry discovered a burnt matchstick, which he carefully wrapped in his handkerchief and placed in his pocket, but found little else.

"Let's have a look at the body," he murmured to the constable.

The man knocked on the door, the sound not halting the weeping.

An older woman with tired eyes, a lined face, gray hair drawn into a loose bun, and an apron over her faded cotton gown answered the door. "Y-Yes?"

"Inspector Henry Field and Constable Barlow, ma'am." Henry held out his warrant card.

She barely glanced at it after looking between them, opening the door wide and stepping aside to allow them entry. "You'd be lookin' fer my daughter." The room was small and sparsely furnished with mismatched chairs and a small stove, all neat and tidy. If he'd been in any doubt thanks to the appearance of the building, his suspicions were confirmed here; poor, but proud.

Much to Henry's dismay the body had clearly been moved—laid out on a rough wooden table near the window where a slightly younger version of the woman who'd let them in sat crying in a chair at the victim's side.

With a quiet sigh, wishing he had some way to ease her grief, he approached the new widow and bent low. "Mrs. Cobb?" The woman looked up with tear-filled eyes, quieting for a moment. "I'm Inspector Field with Scotland Yard. I am terribly sorry for your loss."

The weeping recommenced.

He took the opportunity to look over the victim. Cobb wore his uniform, hands crossed over his chest and eyes closed. The red shifting to purple marks on his neck were unmistakable—he'd been strangled.

The realization was...unexpected. And puzzling.

Resisting the urge for a closer look until he requested permission, he tried again to communicate with Mrs. Cobb, keeping his tone even. "I would like to ask you a few questions."

The woman—who appeared to be in her forties, given the faint lines around her tear-filled brown eyes—dabbed at her narrow streaming nose with a crumpled handkerchief. Her gown was a similar faded cotton, much like the one her mother wore. "W-what d'you want?"

"Can you tell me what happened? What you saw and heard?"

She drew a shuddering breath. "I'm...I'm sure Rupert stopped by the pub after work, which 'e does on occasion. Never expected 'im to stay so late." She sniffed in an apparent effort to control her emotions, then blew her nose into her handkerchief. "I woke up just past ten o'clock, mad that 'e wasn't 'ome. I laid there awake for a time, then heard the key in the door. There was a sound, like...like 'e might've fell." She shook her head. "I thought 'im nowt but drunk and called out. When 'e didn't answer, I got up to see what was what and...and found 'im there."

A tip of her head directed Henry to the floor by the door. Her story made Henry decide to take another look in the hallway. That had to be where the man had been killed.

"And then what?" he asked, hoping to hear the rest of the tale before the tears inevitably returned.

"I...I-I shook 'im, but 'e didn't do nothin'. So I rolled him over onto his back." Her face crumpled. "His eyes...they just stared back at me without seein' a thing. But 'e looked frightened-like with 'is eyes so wide and bulgin'. His mouth was agape, like he was tryin' to scream. A look…" The woman's voice broke. "A look of 'orror on 'is face."

"Did you hear any voices?" he asked.

"No. Nothin'."

He glanced again at the body. There had to be more. "Did he…have anything in his hands when you found him?"

She shook her head.

"Had he mentioned any concerns to you? Any worries abou t…work or the like?" Did your husband mention that he'd taken a *bribe*? That was what Henry wanted to ask, but that seemed a little insensitive of a question for a wife whose grief felt so raw.

"Only that 'e got some extra pay for extra duties." Mrs. Cobb made use of the handkerchief again. "He gave me some, but I don't know what 'e did with the rest. Must've spent it at the pub." A hint of frustration colored her tone.

"It isn't in his pockets?" Henry intended to have a look for himself, but it was worth asking.

"They's empty." Tears threatened once again, leaving him to think the missing money was a problem. Given the run-down look of the few furnishings in the room, they…she needed every penny she could get.

"I would like to have your late husband examined by the surgeon," Henry began quietly. "His insight could aid us in the investigation."

The widow stiffened, outrage etched in the lines of her face. "Ye ain't takin' my Rupert away and ye ain't cuttin' 'im open. 'Tis an ungodly practice."

"It could help lead us to who killed him and why," Henry added, hoping she would see reason.

"I won't 'ear of it!" Her tears threatened to return.

"I can promise that he won't be cut open." Especially since he'd surely been strangled. "An examination might—"

She reached out to clutch her husband's arm. "No. Nothin' ye say will convince me." She leaned forward to look around Henry at the other woman. "Ain't that right, Ma?"

The older woman folded her arms over her ample chest and nodded. "We keep 'im 'ere."

"Very well." Henry pushed aside his frustration. "I could ask the surgeon to come here—"

"No. He might try to snatch 'im." She shook her head. "I've 'eard the stories."

Body snatchers were a rarity these days, but the very idea was enough to terrify a grieving family.

Henry glanced at the constable, who shrugged, making it clear not to expect assistance from him. It wasn't the first time Henry had encountered protests over a postmortem, nor would it be the last. Many felt such an examination was an abomination, even if it could give the family justice.

In this particular case he had a general idea of the time of death, based on Mrs. Cobb's account. And the cause of death appeared obvious. However, having Arthur Taylor, the surgeon, examine the body often led to other insights which could help solve the case.

Blast. But arguing would gain him nothing when the two women were so adamant.

"I understand," Henry agreed with reluctance. "May I take a closer look at Mr. Cobb?" He held up his hands, palms out, to show he meant no harm. "It could help us find who did this." That was assuming Mrs. Cobb, her mother, and whoever else had helped them lift the body to the table hadn't already inadvertently—or purposefully—destroyed any evidence.

Mrs. Cobb's shoulders sank as she stared at her husband, the fight going out of her. "I suppose that'd be all right." Yet she remained in the chair.

"I'm sure you'd prefer to step away while I do so," Henry suggested.

The widow clenched her hands in her lap, eyes averted, clearly reluctant to leave her husband.

"It will only take a few minutes." Henry used his most reassuring voice and hoped it would be enough to gain a few minutes alone with Cobb to perform a cursory examination. It would be the best he could get.

"If ye insist." She drew a deep breath and stood, appearing as though she didn't know quite what to do with herself.

"Why don't you and...I'm sorry. I didn't catch your name," Henry said politely to the other woman.

The older woman drew herself up. "Mrs. Mottingham. I'm 'er mother."

"Why don't you and Mrs. Mottingham step into the other room as my colleague Constable Barlow assists me?" Henry added as he gestured toward the bedchamber.

Mrs. Cobb sniffed and dabbed at her nose again before nodding. She shuffled toward her mother, who sent Henry a stern look before placing a protective arm around her daughter and escorting her into the other room.

Henry waited until the door closed behind them, noting they didn't latch it. Apparently, he wasn't to be fully trusted. Well, that was no matter. He had work to do.

He turned back to the body and moved toward the head for a closer look at the neck injury. Angry purple marks were visible above the jacket.

He loosened the uniform collar to see how far they extended. Based on the width, he would guess something other than a pair of hands had choked the man. Bigger than a rope, perhaps. No fingermarks were visible on the flesh, which confirmed the assumption.

Next he gently turned the head to have a look at the back of the neck, gaze darting over the man.

"What do ye think?" the constable asked quietly.

Henry glanced over his shoulder to see Barlow a short distance away, watching with open curiosity. The question made Henry hesitate. Prison guards weren't members of the police service, so the constable was unlikely to feel misplaced loyalty toward the victim. Still, Henry was reluctant to share many details this early in the investigation.

There was rot here; rot at the heart of the government. Bribes. Prison escapes. Traitors to justice. And all of it terribly unsettling.

"Strangled." Henry didn't add that he guessed whoever had done it had stood behind the victim and used their arm. A conversation with Arthur, the surgeon, would help to confirm it, if only he could describe this to him.

"I thought so based on those marks on his neck," Barlow said with a note of pride in his tone. "Terrible way to go, though."

Another glance at the constable showed him tugging at his own jacket collar.

Henry repositioned the head with care, then lifted the victim's hand, checking the nails, palm, and what he could see of the wrist beneath the cuff. He repeated the process on the second one. Little evidence of a struggle other than a broken nail, but that didn't mean there hadn't been one—or that the broken nail was the subsequent effect. The man worked for a living, and the nail could have been broken at any time. Damn. Had the killer caught Cobb by surprise? That coincided with Henry's idea that he'd been strangled from behind.

He gingerly opened Cobb's mouth to see his tongue swollen, another sign of strangulation. Henry had seen several other victims who'd died in a similar manner, so he was familiar with the signs. He lifted the victim's eyelids and noted both eyes were bloodshot and bulged slightly. Again, consistent with strangulation.

Next he started on the jacket, which had a missing silver button. Henry checked for tears in the fabric before searching through the pockets.

"Watcha looking for?" the constable asked inquisitively.

"Anything that might provide a clue." He met the constable's curious gaze. "Perhaps you could search the floor near the door and beyond to see if you find anything."

"Right." Barlow did as Henry bid him, bending down to scan the scarred wooden planks for anything out of the ordinary.

Henry left him to it and returned his attention to the body, working as quickly as he dared. The widow hadn't seemed inclined to allow him much time, and she could return to continue her mourning at any moment.

Nothing in the jacket pockets. He moved on to the trousers. Those were maddeningly empty as well, though one pocket had a small tear. He unbuttoned the jacket to check the inside pockets but found nothing there either.

It was infuriating.

"Must've been that escaped prisoner, eh?" Barlow asked in a low voice after finishing his perusal of the floor.

"Might have been. We can't assume." Henry sent him a stern look. "Nothing on the floor?"

"No, sir."

The lack of evidence matched Edgarton's previous murders with one exception—Benjamin Norris. That murder scene in Gravesend, courtesy of Edgarton, had contained a vital clue, though it had taken Henry some time to determine where it pointed. The golden Egyptian scarab tucked in the torn fabric of Norris's chair had been perplexing at first. Only after the investigation had taken Henry on several twists and turns had it eventually led to Edgarton.

Norris may not have caught his notice, merely an import-export shop owner, but it was the fact that he had been a competitor of sorts to a cold case of Henry's that had gained his attention, a murder case with a victim by the name of Matthew Greystone.

Henry had his own reasons—personal ones—for not wanting any loose ends in the Greystone case. Reasons he felt in his core, even if he wasn't prepared to examine them too closely.

Not until the Greystone case was officially at end.

The valuable scarab was vital evidence which would help prove Edgarton had been dealing in illegal antiquities in addition to being accused of three murders. The man had to face justice.

That was, *if* they could catch him again. The man had proven more slippery than expected with connections and assistance seemingly everywhere. Two of his other victims had been shot in the temple at close range. The third stabbed. Strangulation added yet another method to the list—if, of course, Edgarton was guilty of this one.

Given that the criminal had a significant number of men at his beck and call, Henry supposed it made sense that not all the victims had been killed in the same manner. Still, something felt off about Edgarton killing the guard now, when more than a week had passed since his escape.

Why had he waited?

As he'd told Barlow, they couldn't assume anything. Henry would have to remain objective and search for evidence in a methodical manner, as he did with all his cases. Only then could he be sure that he'd reached the truth.

Deciding he'd learned as much as he was going to from the victim, Henry cast his attention to the next step. They needed to speak with the neighbors to see if any had witnessed or heard anything. Then find which pub he'd been drinking in. Then go to his place of work...

Henry had the feeling the day was going to be a long and frustrating one, given how little evidence they had at this point.

Where could Edgarton be?

Three

O*RCHIDS ARE SAID TO exude a powerful magnetism, an allure that compels certain collectors to risk their very lives in order to procure an exotic, perhaps never-before-seen, specimen.*

The words for Amelia Greystone's latest article for *London Life*, the periodical for which she served as a special correspondent, formed in her mind from the moment she came face-to-face with one of the beautiful flowers. She took a moment to jot them down in her notebook, worried she'd forget them by the time she returned home to her desk.

"As you can see, I have amassed numerous varieties of orchids," Lord Delcourt said with a note of pride in his cultured tone. "Each one special in its own way."

The Delcourt Conservatory was one of the more impressive ones Amelia had toured, this one private and only viewed by a rare, coveted invitation. The number of orchids was impressive, but there were also many other, more traditional plants and flowers which thrived in the lush environment.

While she appreciated the lord and lady not wanting flocks of people wandering through their residence, it seemed a shame not to share the beautiful blooms with more people.

"They are lovely." Amelia nodded, risking a glance at Lady Delcourt to gauge her feelings about her husband's hobby, which seemed to border on an obsession, from what Amelia could discern.

As if sensing Amelia's unspoken question, the elegant, well-dressed woman offered a tight smile, suggesting she might not share his fascination. "William is quite taken by his flowers."

"Flowers?" The lord frowned, his bushy gray brows lowering over pale blue eyes in a thin face. "It is blasphemy to call them that."

The lady nearly masked her annoyance but not quite. Perhaps Amelia only noticed because she was watching so closely. She liked to think she was an observant person with a natural curiosity that allowed her to place a different view on the articles she wrote.

The couple began to bicker with an icy politeness that was enough to chill the temperature in the warm room, allowing Amelia's thoughts to wander.

Of late, those traits were serving her well in another unexpected hobby—that of criminal investigations. Though of course she only did so in an unofficial capacity, she did seem to have a certain talent for solving puzzles, even those involving murder.

Then again, when one's husband had not only been murdered, but the case remained unsolved for over a year, it did thrust one into a unique, if precarious, position.

And murder had somehow been following Amelia these last few months. First, there had been the ravenkeeper at the Tower of London, the man dying after she had interviewed him only days before for an article. Then came the death of two mud-larks, young children who spent their days digging for treasure along the shore of the River Thames. Then there had been that poor antiques dealer over Gravesend way, and the subsequent murders that followed...

But she hadn't navigated those cases alone. Scotland Yard Inspector Henry Field had been at her side throughout all the investigations, including that of her late husband, Matthew.

Amelia had yet to determine if her growing feelings for the handsome inspector were caused by gratitude for giving her a purpose, not to mention the closure that would surely be hers once the case of her late husband's death was behind her, or whether something more was at work. What to do about these feelings was a concern she wasn't prepared to address.

Not yet, at any rate.

With a stern reprimand at her wayward thoughts, Amelia studied the vibrant purple orchid before her, deciding the couple had argued long enough. "And what is it that you find so appealing about them?" she asked the moment there was a break in their...conversation.

Lord Delcourt stared at her as if she'd lost her mind. "One needs only to see them to know."

Amelia nodded, sharing a knowing look with his wife, who clearly had the same question—and was similarly unimpressed with the answer. "How would you suggest I describe it for the article?"

"Oh." The revised question seemed to calm the lord. "The delicate blooms. The rich colors, of course."

"Though many are white," his wife quickly added, causing Amelia to hide a smile.

"Yes, well, not all. The purple are among my favorites, though the black ones exude mystery and elegance." He strolled forward to study a black flower, reaching out reverentially to gently touch a petal. "Rarity increases the desire for any collector."

Amelia nodded, having learned that during the last murder investigation which had involved the sale of illicit Egyptian artifacts, something her late husband had dabbled in, much to her dismay. Discovering that she hadn't known him as well as she thought had been a blow to her confidence, among other things.

"The symmetry of the blooms is fascinating," Lord Delcourt continued. "Yet each one is individual and unique."

"Rather like people," Amelia added.

The lord frowned. "How so?"

She blinked, unable to grasp why he had to ask. "Individuals share similarities but have different looks and characteristics, as well as personalities."

"I suppose." His dry tone could not have made it more clear that he rated orchids above people. His attention returned to the flower. "Epiphytic orchids, the exotic types, arrived in England quite by accident, you know. It is said that an explorer sent a crate of some other kind of plants from Brazil and packed them with weeds to ensure their safe passage. When the crate was opened, the weeds had disappeared, leaving lovely purple orchids in their place. Epiphytic orchids don't require soil to grow."

"And that started 'orchidelirium' from what I understand." Amelia glanced at the lord for confirmation, noting out of the corner of her eye that the lady nodded enthusiastically.

"Hmm. I hardly think the collection of such a beautiful flower should be labeled as *delirium*." He cast them both a reprimanding look.

Amelia chose to ignore both the comment and the look. "Have you ventured abroad to collect any orchids?"

"I have been to the Philippines and New Guinea, but I should very much like to go to Colombia next. Several rare blooms are said to grow there."

She wrote down the information. "How did you find those experiences? Did you encounter any dangers while gathering specimens?"

The lord chuckled. "Indeed. Another orchid hunter—"

"Hunter?" his wife interrupted with an elegant shudder. "I hardly think that's the proper term. It's not as if you're braving tigers or the like."

"Some do." Lord Delcourt appeared almost disappointed not to have had that experience. "I suppose malaria was the biggest risk we faced, though fellow *collectors* can be a tad aggressive at times. Competition between us is fierce when it comes to particular species."

The tour continued with Amelia committing many of the details to memory in addition to taking a few notes. Her editor couldn't have selected a better person to interview than Lord Delcourt, as he was clearly obsessed—despite his denial. Of course, she would take care not to paint him in that light.

Well, not overly so.

Unlike those scandalmongers of Fleet Street, her articles were informative and for entertainment purposes. She would leave it to the newspapers to argue the right and wrong of the lengths the wealthy went to in order to collect these rare flowers.

"Do you collect other items as well?" she asked, more out of curiosity than for the article.

"I'd rather not have those details printed," Lord Delcourt said stiffly, eyes narrowed as he studied her.

"Oh no, of course not." She didn't want to make him the target of thieves. "I suppose I was just curious."

They continued walking down a row of flowers and plants, and the lord said confidingly, "Between you and me, I have a few others. A rather fine collection of paintings and a few Egyptian artifacts."

"Egyptian?" The mere mention of such things was enough for unease to take hold.

Just two months ago an acquaintance of Amelia's late husband, also the owner of an import-export shop just as Matthew had been, had been murdered at his home in Gravesend. The method matched her husband's death precisely, making it impossible not to make a connection, and rightfully so. The case involved illegal Egyptian artifacts, a practice which was more prevalent than she could've guessed.

Much to her relief, the killer had been caught—at least, temporarily. His recent escape from prison only a week ago had Amelia looking over her shoulder, causing her many restless nights. While she remained hopeful that the brigand would soon be caught, life was unnerving in the meantime.

"The artifacts are fine examples of Egyptian craftsmanship."

"Are they gold?" Amelia couldn't help but ask.

The lord chuckled as if amused by her question. "One or two. Others are painted pottery."

"I enjoyed your article about the mudlarks," Lady Delcourt said with a smile as they reached the exterior door of the conservatory where Amelia's maid, Yvette, waited quietly. "So fascinating."

"Thank you. I'm pleased to hear that." Thrilled, in fact. She enjoyed the purpose her position as writer provided, and hearing rare praise helped her believe she was good at it.

"Those poor children, forced to dig in the mud for trinkets." The lady shook her head. "I was so distraught after reading your article that I promptly asked William to make a donation to the church you mentioned."

"How wonderful." To think the story had made enough of an impression to do that put a lightness in Amelia's heart. Besides, her aunt—who had devoted herself to the charitable assistance of the mudlarking children—would be thrilled.

"Why did you choose to write about them?" Lady Delcourt asked.

Amelia hesitated. How much did she share? Yet why not tell the full truth, the entire story, with the hope it made even more of an impression?

"It is quite the tale," she began. "I was interviewing a barge captain about the annual race they hold when we discovered the body of a young girl, a mudlark, along the shore."

"Good heavens." Lady Delcourt pressed a hand against her chest, eyes wide with shock, while her husband frowned—though that appeared to be his response to anything he didn't like to hear.

"Yes, it was a terrible shock." Amelia swallowed back her emotions as memories took hold. The girl's murder had struck her hard as she'd lost her own daughter, Lily, to scarlet fever at just three years old. The death of a child was a heavy burden, something from which she would never fully recover.

But that was not a part of the tale she was willing to share.

"It was later discovered she'd been poisoned." Amelia didn't mention the role she'd played in that conclusion, given her expert knowledge of chemistry. Her interest in the field wasn't considered ladylike by many, and she was certain a lord and lady certainly wouldn't think so.

"Poisoned? Whatever for?" Lord Delcourt asked.

"An experiment for...for nefarious purposes." That was as much as she would say. If they kept abreast of news reports, after all, they might be able to piece together the information she told them with what had been in the papers. "Soon after, a second mudlark was murdered. Thanks to the hard work of the police, the murderess was found and convicted."

A murderess who had been someone Amelia admired for her own work in chemistry. She shook her head, still upset that she'd been so wrong about Mrs. Drake.

That was only one of the many things she'd been wrong about, but now wasn't the time to think of those or question whether she could trust herself.

"Murderess?" Lady Delcourt glanced at her husband. "My goodness."

"I remember reading about the case. Interesting." Lord Delcourt directed his attention to a large orchid in a vase on a windowsill, apparently done with the conversation.

Interesting? That was an understated word to describe the events. Clearly the time had come to take her leave.

"Thank you both for the informative tour, and your time," Amelia said before she was tempted to share more of the story. Too often, unsavory topics were difficult to discuss. People didn't always want to learn about what was happening beneath their noses.

"I say, is that a constable standing by your hansom cab?" Lord Delcourt asked as he peered more closely out the window.

Amelia smothered a sigh, wishing Constable Peters had remained inside the conveyance as she'd requested to avoid such a question. Yvette sent her a sympathetic look, already well aware of how she felt about his escort.

While having a police officer guard her and her home had become far too common over the last few months, she had yet to become accustomed to it. Explaining it to others was even more difficult.

"Yes." She attempted a polite smile to reassure the noble couple. "I witnessed an unfortunate situation involving an escaped prisoner, and there is concern I could be in danger until he is caught once again."

Miles Edgarton, a notorious criminal, had briefly held her against her will after discovering she'd learned about not only his involvement in the sale of illegal artifacts but that he'd killed her husband. It had been petrifying, beyond anything she could have imagined, and the new cause of her nightmares. Luckily, Henry had come to her rescue.

The thought of encountering Edgarton again terrified her, but she refused to hide at home until the brute was found. Instead, she took care of her surroundings and reluctantly had a police officer accompany her on outings such as this one.

"How frightening. You have had quite the experiences of late." Lady Delcourt reached out a hand to touch Amelia's arm in sympathy. "I can't imagine."

The urge to advise her that this wasn't the first time she'd had police protection was on the tip of Amelia's tongue, but she bit it back. Listing the numerous investigations she'd been involved in would no doubt make the lady think something was wrong with Amelia, embroiled in one case after another.

"It has been a trial, but I will prevail." She lifted her chin even as she caught Yvette's gaze again, appreciating the maid's slight nod of approval. "I must be going. Thank you again for your time."

With that, she took her leave with Yvette in tow, her gaze on the intrusive though well-meaning Constable Peters.

How much longer would it be before Edgarton was caught?

Four

"Wᴏᴛ ɪs ɪᴛ?" Tʜᴇ sharp demand was uttered by a woman through the narrow crack of a door several down from the Cobbs'.

She apparently distrusted whoever had knocked; in this case, Henry. Probably wise, in this neighborhood.

Still, he smothered a sigh at the harsh words. Questioning neighbors in search of potential witnesses was never easy, but this area of the town, where people tended to mind their own business, made it even more difficult.

"Scotland Yard Inspector Henry Field." He held up his warrant card for her to view, even though it was unlikely she could read it. "I would like to ask you a few questions."

"'Bout wot?"

"A man was murdered down the hall last night. Did you see or hear anything unusual?"

The crack widened but only slightly as her gaze shifted to better view the corridor. Apparently even the police weren't to be trusted.

The woman scoffed. "I 'ear strange things every night." After a moment's pause, she opened the door farther. "'Ow?"

"Excuse me?" Henry asked, puzzled. Ouch? Or ow—how? Not who but how? He found the question odd and wasn't sure he understood her meaning.

The woman sighed. "'Ow was 'e killed?"

"I'm not at liberty to say." The more specifics they kept to themselves, the better. He'd already requested the widow and her mother not to share details, along with Constable Barlow, though anyone viewing the body would more than likely be able to tell what had happened.

"Well, I didn't 'ear no gun or screams if that's wot ye're lookin' fer."

"That is helpful." Henry pulled out his notebook to jot down the flat number and the woman's response. "And have you observed any strangers in the area of late?"

This query caused her to chuckle, deepening the lines on her face. "I see strangers every day. Impossible to give ye a list."

"Don't you want to know who was killed?" he asked out of curiosity.

The woman shifted yet again, allowing him to see a partial shrug of a thin shoulder in a threadbare gown. "Don't matter. I mind me own business. This ain't the place t'be friendly with ovvers."

He nodded even though he disagreed. It seemed like those living in such a rough area would want to stick together. Then again, he'd never lived in such a desperate place. He didn't know the best way to survive a life in this town, but he had to think knowing someone watched out for you just as you watched out for them would be welcome.

Unless, of course, she'd been given a reason not to trust her neighbors...

The woman opened the door a fraction more, revealing a face that was younger than he'd first thought. "I 'eard 'er cryin'. The wife." She tipped her head in the direction of the Cobbs' door. "Terrible, to be a widow left on yer own."

"Yes." Henry nodded, his thoughts immediately shifting to another widow. Amelia Greystone. An image of her flashed through his mind, tightening his chest. She, too, had been left on her own.

The past year or more since her husband's death had surely been difficult, especially since his murder had not only been declared unsolved but went cold. Henry had felt that weight each and every day since Matthew Greystone's death, as it was his case—his failure. And he'd finally arrested the killer only to have Edgarton escape.

Amelia was the reason he needed to find the escaped prisoner as quickly as possible. Her life might very well depend on it, and Henry refused to let her down again.

But he couldn't think of that now. He nodded to the woman before him. "If you think of anything helpful, please let us know—"

The door abruptly closed without a reply.

Henry moved on to the next one, hoping the constable was having better luck.

The morning passed swiftly, though he had little to show for it. Either no one had seen anything, or they wouldn't say. In truth, it was difficult to know which was the case. The police were presumably not well received in this area, though Henry tended to think any outsiders would be looked upon with suspicion.

He had another flat to check before he departed, but he would need to return later as no one answered at several of the doors, leaving him to assume they were at work or the like.

After knocking on the door of the last door near the stairs on the floor below Cobb's, he waited, listening for footsteps but hearing none. He knocked again and waited, this time rewarded by the shuffling sound of someone's approach until at last the door opened to reveal a man who looked to be in his fifties, with a pockmarked face and bloodshot eyes.

"Yes?"

Henry repeated the routine of showing his card and asking the same question.

The man's gaze darted past Henry and down the hallway as if expecting someone to join them. "Last night, ye say?"

"Yes. Possibly near ten o'clock." Henry studied the man, noting his nervous movements as he shifted his feet and looked everywhere but at Henry.

"Not really." The man wiped a hand on his creased trouser leg.

Was he nervous to speak with the police because of Cobbs' death...or could it be for another reason?

'Not really' wasn't much of an answer. Henry waited a moment before adding, "Perhaps you heard voices or a scuffle of some sort?"

"Um. Well." The man frowned as he licked his lips. "I might 'ave 'eard somethin'."

Henry's interest piqued. "Oh? Can you describe it?" The man seemed to need prompting to share what he knew.

"Someone made a lotta noise comin' in 'bout that time. Then I 'eard a man's voice. Not real loud."

That was hardly unusual, even at night—and could easily have been the victim muttering in his drink. "What else?"

"Footsteps on the stairs."

"From one person or more?"

"More." He shrugged. "It were late for someone to be comin' in. Most work early 'round 'ere."

Henry turned to view the nearby stairs and pointed toward them as he retrieved his notebook. "So you heard a male voice and footsteps on the stairs near ten o'clock." The man nodded, and Henry jotted down the details, hoping to give the potential witness time to gather his thoughts. When no details were forthcoming, he prompted, "Did you hear what was said?"

"Um... I believe one of 'em said, 'It 'as to be t'night,' and the other said, 'Ye keep him talkin' and I'll take care of it'. Maybe."

Henry looked up from his notes to see the man's lips twisting as he surveyed the stairway. Perhaps his nerves were only a result of worry that someone would hear him speaking to the police. "Did they say any names?"

"No."

"Do you have any idea who they were speaking about?"

"No."

Henry glanced at the interior of the flat, visible over the shorter man's shoulder, to gain a better feel for the size of the place and whether that was possible. "And where were you when you heard this conversation?"

The man's eyes widened with alarm as if taken aback by the question. After a moment's hesitation, he gestured toward a nearby chair. "Just over there."

"I see. Had you been home long?" The answer didn't really make any difference, but the man's anxiousness was puzzling, and Henry wanted to get to the bottom of it.

"Ahh...a couple o' hours, I s'ppose. Maybe more."

"Do you often hear conversations from the stairway?"

He shrugged. "Sometimes. Thin walls." He patted the nearby wall as if to prove it.

For goodness sake. Gaining information from the man was like pulling teeth—slow and painful.

Henry tried to control his irritation. "Did you happen to look out your door when you heard the voices?"

He nodded reluctantly. "Only 'cause I was preparin' to turn in for the night. Th-There was a big man. Not tall but strong lookin' wiv dark hair."

Though the description was brief, Edgarton came immediately to mind, and the blaggard was known for cleaning up loose ends. Had Cobb been one? If that were the case, why had he waited until now to kill the guard when a week had passed since his escape? It didn't quite make sense, but that there was a connection was certainly possible.

"The other one was slimmer but of a similar 'eight," the man added in a quiet voice.

"Can you tell me anything else that might be helpful?" Henry was done trying to drag details from him.

"No."

With a quiet sigh of frustration, Henry took down the man's name and a few other details, then went to find the constable to see if he'd had any better luck.

"Didn't learn a thing, sir." Barlow shook his head. "Nobody saw nothing—the usual story."

Henry advised him they had one potential witness who had given a rough description and requested the constable to remain on alert for Edgarton as well as for rumors pertaining to the murder while he walked his usual beat.

After exiting the lodging house, Henry paused to study his surroundings. If Edgarton had killed Cobb, there was a chance he'd remained nearby, possibly to see how the investigation proceeded. It wouldn't do to be caught unaware, not in this neighborhood, and especially not with the escaped prisoner on the loose.

Not for a moment had Henry forgotten the criminal's threat when he'd arrested Edgarton. *This will be the end of your career with Scotland Yard.*

That he'd not only recognized Henry but knew his name continued to alarm him. All the more reason to stay on guard until Edgarton was in prison once again—where he belonged.

Henry's next stop was the pub where Cobb most likely had been, according to his wife. The Drunken Sailor stood on a corner a few streets away, its sign consisting of a painted sailor listing to one side with a pint in hand. The grimy windows and sagging door suggested general maintenance wasn't high on the list of priorities for the landlord. The interior was much the same but boasted patrons even at this relatively early hour when luncheon had not yet arrived. So, it was that sort of place.

Henry moved toward the bar along the far wall to speak with the barkeep, well aware of the stares tracking him. "Morning." He nodded at the man who regarded him warily especially after he showed his warrant card. "Do you know a Rupert Cobb? I'm given to understand he was a regular customer."

"The prison guard?" At Henry's nod, the barkeep shrugged. "Sure. What of him?" Then the man frowned. "*Was?*"

"Unfortunately he was killed last night." Henry waited a moment to allow him to digest the news before he continued. "I was told he might have been here prior to that. Were you working then?"

"Yeah, I saw 'im." He shook his head even as he reached for a cloth to wipe the scarred bar top. "He was with Tretheway, another prison guard."

Henry jotted down the name. Perhaps now he was getting somewhere. "Did you notice what time he left? Did anyone accompany him?"

The barkeep stared across the room as if trying to remember. "Must've been just before closin' time at ten o'clock. Walked out alone, best I can remember."

"Was it just him and Tretheway together?"

"Nah, several others sat with 'em at the table. Couldn't name 'em though." He shrugged and wiped the counter again before sending Henry a questioning look. "How...how did it 'appen?"

Unfortunately Henry couldn't answer, though he had the feeling word would spread soon enough, despite him attempting to hold back the details. "I can't say as the investigation is just beginning, but I would certainly appreciate you advising

Constable Barlow if you remember or hear anything that would help us find who did it."

The barkeep shook his head. It took Henry a moment to realize he did so in disbelief rather than disagreement. "O'course I will. Terrible news."

"How did he seem last night? In good spirits or worried? Could you tell?"

"Bought a round fer his mates, so I thought all was well. Had to be better 'an normal, he tended to be tight-fisted."

That further suggested Cobb had taken a bribe. "Did he talk about his job?"

"Only in passing." The barkeep glanced at Henry out of the corner of his eye. "Didn't seem to care for it much."

That was no surprise. Few guards did, from what Henry knew. It could be miserable, thankless work. Prisoners were never happy to be there and made that known, with the guards taking the brunt of their displeasure. The hours were long, the conditions dismal, the pay minimal. He didn't envy them. But he also knew some relished the bit of power they had over the prisoners.

Henry supposed any of those were reason enough for Cobb to possibly have chosen to take a bribe, but that didn't make it right.

As far as Henry was concerned, it reflected poorly on not just prison guards but all of law enforcement, including the Metropolitan Police. Rumors of bribery degraded all of them, degraded the public's trust. Made it only harder to do their jobs.

The police force was finally regaining ground in the public's eye after a terrible disgrace several years previously. Corruption had spread into the Yard, even among inspectors, which resulted in a restructuring of the entire service. All that was behind them as far as Henry was concerned. His focus remained on keeping it that way by doing his job to the best of his ability.

That meant finding Edgarton and discovering if he had killed Cobb.

"Thank you for your help. Please let us know if you hear anything more." At the barkeep's nod, Henry departed for Scotland Yard to provide an update to Director Reynolds.

He only wished he had more to report.

Five

A MELIA PLACED THE CAP on the inkwell and rose from the small desk she kept in her drawing room to stretch. She'd spent the last two hours recording her impressions of the interview she'd conducted earlier in the day with Lord and Lady Delcourt. A second interview with another orchid collector was in order as she wanted more than one perspective for the article, but that wouldn't occur until later in the week. Perhaps by then she wouldn't have an awkward constable in tow.

"Meow."

She turned to see Master Leopold, a recent feline addition to the household, approach. "How was your nap, young sir?" she asked as she bent to scratch his head.

The cat rubbed against her skirts, purring.

"Must have been a good one."

Leopold had joined them nearly two months ago after his previous owner, Benjamin Norris, had been murdered. Amelia welcomed his company as it was just her and the servants in the house, and the cat was a warm companion these cold spring evenings. She liked to think Mr. Norris would approve.

"Shall I stoke the fire, madam?"

She looked up to see Fernsby, her longtime butler, in the doorway. "Yes, please." She glanced out the window, noting the afternoon sun was quickly fading, and rubbed her arms. "The temperature feels as if it's already dropping."

"It is indeed." Fernsby added more coal to the fire, smiling as the cat joined him. "Come to see if I'm doing it properly, Master Leopold?"

Amelia smiled, still surprised by how well the two got on. She never would've guessed that her butler, a stickler for formality, would grow attached to the cat so quickly. His wife, who served as housekeeper, had agreed, though she spoiled the cat as much as her husband.

Even Yvette, the maid, and Mrs. Appleton, the cook, liked Leopold. The cat spent much of his days keeping an eye on them all, in between napping in his favorite chair by the window in the drawing room.

Fernsby straightened. "May I get anything for you, Mrs. Greystone?"

"No, thank you." She gestured toward her chair near the fire. "I believe I will read for a time before dinner."

"Excellent. I shall prepare a pot of tea...and I suppose a different police officer will arrive shortly to relieve Constable Peters."

Amelia knew Fernsby didn't relish the police presence on their doorstep any more than she did. If only it weren't necessary. "It is about that time of the day."

For some reason she didn't particularly care for Constable Peters. While always friendly and helpful, he was almost too much so. He had been selected as one of a small group to help keep watch because he had seen Miles Edgarton and could recognize him, but something about the constable rubbed her the wrong way.

Amelia would rather Henry helped guard her and the house. Time with the handsome inspector was always welcome. She enjoyed his company and found their conversations stimulating. He had joined her for dinner on several occasions, and she counted the days until it might be appropriate to ask him again.

Fernsby turned to depart, only to pause at a knock on the door. "I shall see who that is. Perhaps the constable is in need of something."

Leopold, his tail held aloft, trailed behind the butler, leaving Amelia to walk over to the window to look out, a frequent habit of hers. In the weeks following Matthew's death, she had occasionally spotted someone who appeared to be observing the house, though he'd never been caught. It had been most unnerving to wonder who watched her and why.

To her relief, everything looked to be in order. Tidy red-brick houses lined Bloomsbury Street with their well-kept gardens and wrought-iron fences. *The perfect place to raise a family.* That was what she and Matthew had thought when they had first moved there.

The thought had her pressing a hand to her heart at its sudden ache. Life had quickly changed, and not for the better.

Amelia drew a deep breath to hold back the wave of familiar sadness that threatened. Grief for the future she'd expected to enjoy but had been wrenched from her was never far away.

Male voices conversing drifted up from the foyer but were too quiet to make out. Probably a constable providing Fernsby with an update.

A quiet knock on the doorframe a few moments later had Amelia turning to see Henry standing in the doorway. "Good evening, Amelia." He dipped his head, his warm brown eyes resting on hers.

"Henry." She strode forward several steps, heart lifting at the sight of him, his presence chasing away the melancholy that threatened. "How good to see you." Her cheeks heated at her enthusiastic greeting, but it was true. She was very pleased to see him.

While he'd stopped by briefly on two occasions over the last week since Edgarton's escape from prison, they hadn't had a chance to truly converse.

She was still puzzled by his invitation for the lovely dinner at the Criterion Restaurant in Picadilly Circus. It could have been—after all, he might have intended...

She halted her thoughts before they ran away with her.

Unfortunately the dinner had been interrupted by a constable bringing them news of Edgarton's escape just over a week ago.

Had it been intended to mark the beginning of a new sort of relationship between them?

Amelia squelched the question before it took hold. Now was not the time. Besides, she was hardly ready to declare her feelings when she didn't know quite what they were yet.

She took a moment to study him. His well-balanced features, high cheekbones, and masculine nose made for a handsome visage. His clean-shaven jaw, as much as the hint of dark whiskers that returned by day's end, appealed to her. Thick dark brows with a slight arch in their center promised intelligence and added empathy to his features. His dark brown hair was brushed to one side and neared his shirt collar, far longer than his preference, a sign that he'd been too busy to have it clipped of late.

While the warmth in his eyes pleased her, he remained his usual reserved self. It wasn't as if he had made any declaration regarding his feelings for her.

Before she could decide whether that was good or bad, she saw something else in his expression. A shadow that didn't bode well.

Her steps slowed as she sighed. "If I were to guess, I would say this is—once again—not a social call." Disappointed, though not surprised when he didn't disagree, she gestured toward the chairs before the fire. "Would you care to sit down?"

"Thank you." He set his hat on the nearby table and, after she took her chair, sat in what had become his usual place. He still wore his black woolen coat, another sign that his visit would be brief.

"Do I want to know what's happened?" Amelia asked after drawing a bolstering breath.

"Bringing you unfortunate news is a habit I would like to break. However, I thought it best to keep you apprised of...e vents."

"I appreciate that." Ignoring the world around her didn't make it less upsetting. That was something she'd learned while grieving first her daughter, then later her husband. Better that she dealt with each situation as it arose.

"The prison guard we suspected of sharing information with Edgarton, as well as possibly aiding in his escape, was murdered last night."

"Oh dear." Amelia considered the news; sorry for the man's violent demise, yet relieved it didn't involve someone she knew better. A pang of guilt struck, tightening her throat. She was the one who'd mentioned to Henry how that same guard had seemed overly interested in her conversation with Mrs. Drake, who'd been a prisoner at the time. Was Amelia partially to blame for his murder?

"No." Henry's firm tone had her meeting his steady gaze once again. "I already know what you're thinking, and you had nothing to do with his death."

The fact that he knew where her thoughts had gone almost made her smile. "I do hope not."

"He made more than one poor choice, based on what we've learned thus far."

"That is comforting." The reminder helped alleviate her guilt somewhat, though she immediately wondered who might have killed the man and why. There seemed to be one obvious answer. "Do you think Edgarton did it?"

"I don't know." Henry's focus shifted to the glowing coals in the fire, clearly sorting through the possibilities. "Perhaps, but we've only just begun the investigation."

"Of course." She waited a moment, running her hand idly over the cover of the book she was reading while she processed the news. "Did he have family?"

"A wife."

"How terrible for her." Amelia knew firsthand the grief and difficulties the woman faced, even if their circumstances were different.

"Yes. I am returning to speak with her again and question the tenants of their building that weren't home earlier."

Amelia glanced out the window at the fading daylight. Though he hadn't mentioned where that was, she would guess a prison guard didn't make a very good living, which meant his rooms weren't in the best neighborhood. "You're not going alone, are you?"

"A constable will accompany me."

"I'm relieved to hear that, though I'd prefer Sergeant Fletcher was doing so." The sergeant, who often assisted Henry, was a large, competent man with years of experience on the force after serving in the Navy prior to that.

Henry smiled. "As would I. However, much of his time has been spent with his uncle over the past few days. I believe I mentioned his uncle was recently promoted to inspector and is now working at Scotland Yard. Fletcher has been showing him around."

"I'm sure Sergeant Fletcher is quite proud to do so."

"Most definitely. From what I can see, he seems to be taking partial credit for his uncle's promotion."

Amelia laughed. "I can easily imagine that. I do hope Sergeant Fletcher returns to working with you soon. I rest easier knowing he's often at your side." Only too late did Amelia realize she'd admitted too much, and her cheeks heated once again. Henry must think her terribly forward.

To her relief, his smile broadened. "My mother has said something similar on several occasions."

It pleased Amelia to think she and Mrs. Field were of the same mind. His admission allowed her to graciously change the subject before she said something else embarrassing. "How is your mother?"

"She is doing well and asked me to send her regards. I took the liberty of mentioning your experiment with the fertilizer, and she is eager to hear the results."

"Oh, good. The pea plants are just starting to sprout, so I should know more soon." Amelia had kept a careful watch on the row of small clay pots upstairs near the window in her attic laboratory, in which she'd planted seeds with a variety of fertilizers to see which grew the quickest and healthiest.

She enjoyed conducting experiments of all kinds, including practical ones that would benefit her household. Improving the bounty of the vegetable garden would certainly do that.

Her love of chemistry came from her father, who still served as an apothecary in a village north of London. Though she didn't care to measure out remedies like he did, his work had given her an avid interest in science, and chemistry in particular.

Dare she hope that Henry would invite her to his parents' house once again? She'd had the delight of dining with them just before Christmas and had thoroughly enjoyed it. Mr. and Mrs. Field had been warm and welcoming even as they'd sent both her and Henry curious looks. No doubt they wondered about the extent of their...relationship. At the time, Amelia had considered him a friend.

But now...

She blinked to clear her thoughts. Such concerns would have to wait until Edgarton was caught and the latest—and hopefully last—murder case surrounding him solved. "Is there anything I can do to assist with the investigation?"

She liked to think she'd been helpful with the last few, though her involvement had come with a certain amount of danger. However, she'd already been embroiled in the cases and was unable to simply sit and wait for something to happen. Aiding Henry was something she enjoyed, but she'd be the first to admit to an aversion to danger—a danger which only seemed to have increased after Edgarton had held her against her will just over a month ago. Yet neither did she care to live in fear of leaving the house.

As she'd learned, action was preferable to worry even if it didn't eliminate it.

Alarm flashed in Henry's eyes. "No need. The matter is well in hand."

"Hmm." Not that she didn't believe him; quite the opposite. In fact, she tended to think she had more faith in Henry and his skills as a detective than he did. Never mind that he'd been credited with helping to save the Queen, he still seemed to doubt himself.

Unfortunately, she couldn't think of any way to help in this particular case.

"I am happy to help, even if only as a sounding board for your ideas." Helping to solve cases by considering the facts and evidence from every possible angle was something she thoroughly enjoyed. It helped to provide her with a purpose, however temporary. She welcomed the feeling of being needed, a sensation she sorely missed since she was no longer a mother or wife.

Of course, investigations could be thoroughly frustrating as well. But if the recent months had taught her anything, it was that one must continually poke and prod until a clue came forth.

"I appreciate that." Henry nodded, then cleared his throat. "However, your safety is of primary concern, and the more often you remain home, the better. I realize it isn't always convenient—"

"It isn't," she interrupted before he could continue. "As I have said before, I am willing to curtail my activities to a certain extent, but I refuse to—to huddle at home when it could be weeks or longer before Edgarton is caught."

Henry's lips pressed tight, and she immediately regretted her words.

"Not that such a result has anything to do with your efforts," she added hastily. "But clearly Edgarton has a wide network of people on whom to rely."

"Yes, he does." Henry's expression turned pensive. "I thought he might have left the area since there's been so little trace of him in the past week."

"And then a body is reported." Amelia shook her head. "How frustrating."

"It is."

Though she knew he mustn't tell her much about an ongoing investigation, she couldn't help but try to discover more. Curiosity was part of her nature, and she liked to think it was beneficial in her role as an investigative assistant. "Do you think the other guards he worked with will be able to shed any light?"

"We have only spoken with one thus far, and he was of little help. There is another who was with him last evening, but I have not yet interviewed him. Hopefully tomorrow."

"Where was the man killed?"

Henry hesitated as if uncertain how much to say. "More than likely just outside the door of his rooms at a lodging house in Camden Town."

"And no one heard anything?"

"There's...one potential witness."

She knew Henry well enough to hear a hint of doubt in what should have been a clear statement. "Potential? As in, you're not certain if he or she can be believed?"

"Something of the sort."

When he didn't say more, she smothered a sigh of disappointment. There was no point in pushing for details he wasn't free to provide. "Well, I shall hope a clue emerges soon."

"As will I." Henry shifted to the edge of the chair but almost seemed reluctant to leave, which pleased her. "I would ask that you continue your diligence and take care, Amelia. If Edgarton is the one who killed Cobb, then we know he hasn't gone far. You might very well be in danger—just as we suspected."

Amelia nodded, careful to mask her shifting unease. Henry had enough to worry about. "We will remain vigilant."

She had no intention of allowing Edgarton to claim her as a victim.

Six

T HOUGH WEAK SUNLIGHT HAD been enough to cast shadows earlier that morning, the sky over Holloway Prison was now a dark, foreboding gray.

Henry studied the clouds, briefly wondering whether the prison somehow manufactured its own weather from the despair of those within its walls.

"Are you coming?" Sergeant Fletcher glanced over his shoulder at Henry, then paused to follow his gaze to the roofline of the prison. "Is something amiss?"

"Only the lack of spring." Henry shook off his odd thoughts and started forward, pleased his friend had accompanied him. "Let us hope Tretheway arrived for work today."

"I'm relieved I don't work here." Fletcher smoothed his impressive moustache as he walked alongside Henry. "There's a terrible feel to the place."

"Do you suppose that's a result of the architecture itself or its occupants?" Henry asked as they approached the large arched gatehouse.

"Most likely both. The place looks like a medieval fortress. One can imagine a dungeon complete with a torture chamber hidden somewhere inside." The sergeant grimaced.

"True." Henry waited while Fletcher stated their purpose to a guard. Once approved, they moved on to the heavy metal doors, which opened to let them in before clanking shut behind them.

The thought of Amelia coming to the place not once but twice had Henry shifting uneasily. Her visit to the prison had been to speak with a fellow chemist, a Mrs. Elizabeth Drake, and it had been impossible to prevent when the woman had hinted that she knew who'd killed Amelia's husband.

Mrs. Drake's relationship with Miles Edgarton had surprised Henry. Why a brilliant woman, well-known for her work in organic chemistry, had chosen to associate with a criminal like Edgarton was puzzling. Had it been the lure of his dark dealings? A power he exuded? Something only a woman would understand?

They would never know the answers to those questions. Mrs. Drake had been convicted of poisoning children and sentenced to death, the punishment swiftly carried out.

While he was relieved the threat of the murderess was over, Amelia's visits to see her had brought the widow to Edgarton's notice. But that wasn't the only reason the escaped prisoner might wish Amelia harm—that blame rested squarely on Henry's shoulders.

It was his fault. He'd requested her help to ferret out who was behind the sale of illicit antiquities. Her late husband had been involved in them and used the services of a supposed 'expert' in artifacts to verify authenticity. Amelia had met with the man, Oscar Powell, telling him that a former customer of her husband's had approached her and wished to purchase Egyptian artifacts.

The ruse had been successful in that Powell had unknowingly led them directly to Edgarton. But it had also brought Amelia to Edgarton's attention—and his wrath.

The memory of her being held in Edgarton's warehouse was enough to send Henry's heart racing. Luckily he'd found her before any true harm befell her.

But he might not have been so lucky.

That made it all the more important to catch Edgarton as soon as possible. There was always the terrifying possibility that he'd make another attempt to silence Amelia.

"Tretheway?" The uniformed warden, who sat at a wooden desk on a raised platform inside the door, glanced between them. "Yes, he's working today."

Henry showed the man his warrant card. "We need to speak with him regarding a case."

The warden shook his head. "He's guarding prisoners and can't be spared."

"Perhaps someone could take his place for a few minutes," Henry suggested, unable to believe the man couldn't be relieved long enough to assist with an official investigation. Director Reynolds had advised that the prison was conducting its own investigation of the guards on duty during Edgarton's escape, but surely they were willing to allow Henry to speak with Tretheway? "It involves Cobb's murder."

The warden's bushy brows rose. "I see. Terrible news to hear he was killed. Happened right outside his door, eh?"

Though displeased that any of the details had spread, Henry wasn't surprised. He shared a frustrated look with Fletcher before saying curtly, "We have a few questions for Tretheway."

The warden leaned forward in his chair, eyes wide as if his interest was fully caught. "You don't suspect him, do you?"

"No." Henry couldn't have Tretheway looked upon poorly because of their questioning him. "We have reason to believe he was one of the last people to speak with Cobb."

"Oh. Very well." The warden seemed almost disappointed by the answer. "I will see what I can do, but it might take a few minutes to arrange."

Though Henry visited Holloway with rough regularity to speak with prisoners, he still found it depressing. The small waiting area was uncomfortable, and he didn't want to say anything of relevance to Fletcher where his words could easily be overheard.

Over a quarter of an hour passed ever so slowly before a man in a similar uniform to the warden arrived at the small waiting room near the warden's desk.

"Ye wanted to see me?" The man was pale and rubbed the stubble of whiskers on his face with a hand that trembled. Had the murder of his friend frightened him?

Henry explained the reason for their visit in a quiet tone. "Can you describe the evening for us?" he asked, aware of the warden doing his best to listen.

Tretheway hesitated, then began. "It was as the barkeep at the pub probably told ye. We stopped by after work and had a few drinks. Cobb left on his own just afore ten o'clock."

"Did he mention any concerns?"

"He was in fine spirits. Even bought a round."

Clearly that was an unusual occurrence. "Oh? What was the occasion?"

Did Tretheway know whether his friend had accepted a bribe? Henry didn't want to come straight out and ask—not when Cobb might not be the only one on the take.

The guard shrugged. "He wouldn't say. Still counted his money careful-like, as always."

Henry and Fletcher shared a look. Apparently he hadn't been paid so much by Edgarton as to make him reckless with funds. The information made Henry think that whoever had killed him had taken the money he'd had on him—presuming of course he hadn't spent it all on drink.

Fletcher wrote down the names of the three other men who'd been at the table, all friends who were regular patrons of the pub as they lived nearby.

Tretheway tugged on his jacket collar. The gesture made Henry wonder if he knew the man had been strangled. "Do ye...do ye think I'm in any danger?"

Fletcher shrugged. "Hard to say. Have you taken any bribes of late?" he asked, a hint of derision in his tone.

Alarm shot through Henry at Fletcher's inconsiderate words. Telling others they knew of the bribes would make it more difficult to catch both those offering them *and* those taking them. This investigation just became twice as challenging. He couldn't believe Fletcher hadn't considered that.

Tretheway's eyes widened and he swallowed hard, his Adam's apple bobbing with the effort. "It's—it's true then? The rumors? That's what Cobb did?"

Henry sent Fletcher a stern look before answering the question curtly. "We are investigating the matter. Nothing has been proven, and you should refrain from speaking of the situation until we know what happened."

Tretheway removed his hat and scratched his bald head before returning the hat, seemingly overwhelmed. "Terrible. Terrible."

Henry didn't ask which part he referred to and glared at Fletcher to ensure he didn't either. The disgruntled look on the sergeant's face suggested he knew he'd overstepped. Whether he regretted it—whether both of them would—remained to be seen.

"Please keep these questions confidential," Henry advised the guard, doubtful he would. The temptation to share such news and what avenues the police were pursuing would be all too easy to give in to over a pint after work.

"Yes, sir." Tretheway nodded.

"Were there any strangers in the pub? Anyone who looked out of place?" Henry took out his notebook with the hope it would make Tretheway realize how important any information he could provide might be.

"Not that I noticed."

"Did Cobb recently speak with any guards he didn't normally associate with?" Henry asked.

The guard considered the question for a long moment. "No. Not that I can recall."

Henry asked several other questions, but Tretheway was of little help. After advising the man to let them know if any information came to mind, they took their leave.

Henry waited until they'd left the prison before rounding on Fletcher, allowing frustration to color his tone. "What was all that about?"

Fletcher scowled. "I suppose I wanted to give a warning that taking bribes is frowned upon."

"Those taking them either don't care what you think or will simply abstain until interest has died down, especially if warned that we're investigating the situation." Henry bit back an oath. "You know the prison is conducting their own investigation. Wouldn't it be better to allow them to pursue that side while we pursue our case to discover who is handing out bribes *and* who is taking them? We need both ends of this."

"Yes, sir. You're right." The sergeant shook his head. "I let my anger get the best of me. It's just that when the public hears of such things, you know as well as I that they suspect anyone who wears a uniform of doing the same."

"It does look poorly on everyone," Henry agreed tersely. "But we need to follow the evidence. Verbal reprimands won't help us find those guilty. Nor will giving potential suspects more information than they need."

"Right. I'm sorry, sir." Fletcher nodded, tugging on the bottom of his jacket as he straightened. "Where to next?"

Henry studied the area to allow his thoughts to settle. He relied heavily on Fletcher for assistance during investigations. The sergeant had a logical, calm demeanor and was normally level-headed and observant. His upset about a prison guard allowing a man they'd spent weeks—perhaps years chasing down to go free was understandable. It angered Henry, too, making it feel as if all their hard work was for naught.

But this was no time for emotions to run high.

"I would wager that several of Cobb's fellow guards were suspicious of the way Edgarton escaped," Henry advised. "The fact that Cobb is now dead will make them think twice about following the same path."

Fletcher's shoulders eased, as if he were relieved to know Henry agreed with his thoughts, if not his actions. "Indeed it will."

"Let us return to Cobb's lodgings. I would like your opinion on the tenant who claims to have seen something. It will be interesting to see if his story remains consistent."

Henry shared the details as they walked but didn't mention the man's uncertain manner, preferring Fletcher to form his own impression.

"We interviewed most of the remaining tenants last night, but no one else seems to have heard anything," Henry advised. "There are only a couple we have yet to speak with."

"Odd for a murder to take place without anyone hearing anything." Fletcher sent Henry a puzzled look. "Especially in a building full of people with thin walls and in the quiet of the night."

"I thought the same, though I suppose we must remember that Cobb had several drinks in him and was more than likely surprised by the confrontation. From the wounds on his neck, he was strangled from behind, something I confirmed with Mr. Taylor."

After doing his best to describe the scene and the victim's body, the surgeon at St. Thomas' had agreed with the assumption Henry had made. Strangulation, from behind, with something other than hands. An arm, perhaps?

Fletcher nodded. "If the man's own wife didn't hear him when she was most likely the closest, I suppose it makes sense that none of his fellow neighbors heard anything."

"Especially when she gave me the impression she was annoyed with him for staying out late. I would guess she was listening for his arrival, even if she was half asleep, but still heard nothing."

"Do you think Edgarton is our man for this one?" Fletcher asked, tipping his hat to an old lady walking along the street with a basket over one arm.

Henry did the same, debating his answer. "I don't know yet."

Fletcher frowned. "Who else would bother? Edgarton is known for eliminating loose ends."

"True." Director Reynolds had said much the same thing when Henry apprised him of the progress on the case.

"Who else could it be?"

"Why would Edgarton wait a week to eliminate him?" Henry asked, rather than answering the question. "By then Cobb could've told others about what he'd done. Why not tidy the loose end the very day he escaped?"

"Hmm. True, especially with extra funds burning a hole in the guard's pocket." Fletcher lifted a brow. "Those who suddenly find themselves with extra money but aren't used to it tend to do a bit of bragging."

"Yes, and they often enjoy showing it off by buying a round at the pub." Henry gestured for them to cross the street. "Something out of character, everyone's mentioned it."

"How certain are we that Edgarton bribed Cobb?"

"Fairly certain, though we lack direct proof as of yet. Whether he killed him remains to be seen." The remainder of the walk continued in silence, both men deep in their thoughts until at last Henry's steps slowed as they reached the lodgings. "Here we are."

"Why does it feel as if we have two pieces of a chain but no links to connect them?"

Henry smiled. "That is an apt description. Let us see if we can do just that with a few more questions."

Working with Fletcher often helped to brighten Henry's outlook. While neither of them was the optimistic sort, they managed to keep one another from despair when cases felt unsolvable. That happened far too frequently in Henry's opinion and did little to bolster his often absent confidence.

Their first stop in the building was at the door of the potential witness. Mr. Jackson answered, rubbing sleep from his eyes. He frowned at the sight of Henry with Fletcher at his side. "What d'you want?"

"A few more questions for you." Henry gave an easy smile, so as not to alarm the man, and then led him through the night of the murder. Unfortunately he didn't learn anything new.

Fletcher listened carefully, asking a few questions of his own.

Even after this second interview, Henry's opinion hadn't changed. The man still acted nervous and uncertain, though his description fit Edgarton. He repeated several of the phrases he'd used the previous day almost verbatim.

Henry remembered how dark the hallway had been upon his arrival at the crime scene. The idea of being able to see anyone walking by well enough to describe them seemed improbable. But perhaps the murderer and his accomplice had put out the lights *after* Jackson had seen them?

They thanked the man for his time and moved to one of the other flats that hadn't previously answered his knocking. The woman who answered balanced a baby on her hip while another child clung to her skirts. "Yeah?"

She hadn't heard or seen anything, and nor did the next two people they spoke with.

"That accounts for everyone," Henry said as he consulted his notes. "No one left to question. I spoke with Mrs. Cobb again last evening, but she didn't have any new information to add."

Fletcher didn't say anything until they'd stepped outside. "Why is it that I don't believe this Mr. Jackson's account?"

"You too?" Henry asked.

The sergeant shook his head. "Something is off, though I couldn't say what. He can't seem to clarify any of the details of what he heard with what he saw."

"Agreed." Henry gestured for them to continue down the street even as he kept a wary eye out. "I wouldn't want to rely on him too heavily unless we can find someone else to confirm what he claims to have witnessed."

"And yet his description fits Edgarton." Fletcher held Henry's gaze.

"Yes, though I suppose it fits many other men as well. Let's stop by the Drunken Sailor to see if any of the other men who shared a table with Cobb happen to be there."

Only one was. Yes, he knew Tretheway and Cobb. How terrible that Cobb had been killed—and right after buying a round.

No, he hadn't noticed anything amiss before Cobb left the pub. Didn't see any strangers either.

They soon took their leave.

Fletcher glanced around the busy street. "Regardless of whether Edgarton killed Cobb, I wish we could find him. It's unsettling to know he could be watching us this very minute."

Henry couldn't agree more as his nape prickled. Anyone could be watching on behalf of the murderer—anyone.

Seven

FLETCHER DEPARTED TO ASSIST another inspector and Henry returned to Scotland Yard, trying to think of a way to find Edgarton as well as determine who had killed Cobb. Whether the two were related remained to be seen.

Edgarton's house had been empty for well over a month. Sable Importers, his shipping business, had closed its office upon Edgarton's arrest. The illegal lottery he'd run had been shut down as well. The criminal was reputed to have several other businesses, but only a few were known to the police. None of his men, some of whom had been arrested during the raid on the lottery scheme, were willing to talk.

Henry nodded at Sergeant Johnson, who managed the front desk at the Yard, and walked down the short hallway to the large office with its three rows of desks. His steps slowed at the sight of Inspector Perdy, a man Henry had a deep dislike for, speaking with Edward Clarke, Fletcher's uncle and the newest inspector on the force.

He considered Perdy a subpar investigator, especially after examining his work on a previous case, and didn't care for the thought of the new inspector taking advice from him. Despite the urge to stride forward to warn Clarke to avoid any interaction with Perdy, Henry held his silence, nodded at them both, then sat at his desk. That the two inspectors stopped their conversation to watch him irked Henry.

Fletcher didn't like Perdy either, and it would surprise Henry if the sergeant hadn't already shared that opinion with his uncle. So why was Clarke openly associating with the man?

Henry shrugged away the question. It wasn't any of his affair. He had enough on his plate—too much to allow him to worry about what others did.

In truth, he didn't know quite what he thought of Clarke, and not just because the new inspector was talking with Perdy. The few times he'd spoken with the man he'd acted somewhat pompous and arrogant, unusual traits for a newly appointed inspector. The majority of recently promoted officers, regardless of their title, were eager to learn all they could from those with more experience.

Clarke didn't seem interested in doing so. Henry had offered to answer any questions the man had, and while Clarke had thanked him, the older man had also given him a condescending smile, suggesting that would be unlikely.

Perhaps the inspector was trying to act confident to make a good impression and didn't realize how his demeanor came across to others. It was possible.

Henry hoped that was the case. Fletcher had already made his admiration for his uncle clear. Clarke was Fletcher's mother's much younger brother; the two men were less than a decade apart in age and had apparently been close in Fletcher's youth. Henry didn't want to lose the sergeant's friendship or his help due to a differing opinion on the newest addition to the Yard.

He opened a new case file he'd been assigned and was reading the constable's notes on the theft of an expensive clock from a home on Grosvenor Square when Perdy approached.

"Any luck finding the murderer of the prison guard?" the inspector asked, leaning against Henry's desk and crushing some of his paperwork, another irritating habit of the man.

"Still working on it." Henry didn't bother to look at Perdy, only wanting him to go away.

"Huh. Can't find the escaped prisoner or the murderer of the guard who aided him. Seems like they'd be one and the same. Simple enough."

Henry's temper rose, but he did his best to hide it. He didn't appreciate Perdy suggesting he wasn't good at his job, but he'd heard it too many times from the idiot to take it seriously. "They might well be."

"Might?" Perdy chuckled and glanced around the room. "Anyone willing to place a wager on it?"

"Last I checked, such things weren't permitted," Henry countered as he leaned back in his chair and leveled a glare at the man. If Perdy looked for an easy target, he wouldn't find one. "Not between honorable officers on the force."

"Come now. I'm only speaking hypothetically."

"I'd take the wager," Whitlock, another inspector, offered as he joined Perdy in loitering around Henry's desk.

Henry didn't know Whitlock well enough to form an opinion of the man's character, but he was certainly starting to.

"Seems to me as if they'd be one and the same." Whitlock smirked. "That means you have one less case on your hands. You can thank us later."

Conversations like this didn't bring out the best in anyone, including Henry. Rising to take the bait of their jabs would only make him more of a mark.

But that didn't mean he wasn't tempted.

"Time will tell who the guilty party is," Henry said, keeping his tone even. "Edgarton will surely show up soon, given that we're *all* watching for him."

"Sure *we* are." Perdy grinned at the other men, including Clarke, who also joined them. "Someone has to cover your back, Field."

"My nephew certainly seems to spend a lot of his time doing just that," Clarke added with a sneer.

"Yes, Sergeant Fletcher is very good at his job." Henry tidied his notes, closed the file, and set it aside before pushing back from his desk. It was clear he wasn't going to get anything more done here. Better that he removed himself before he said something he might regret.

Though regret seemed unlikely at the moment.

"If you...gentlemen will excuse me, I have work to do." Henry put on his hat and nodded with as much politeness as he could muster.

"Yes, you do." Perdy rocked back on his heels. "Don't let this one get away from you, Field. The reputation of the Yard rests on your shoulders."

Henry lifted a brow. "I think that honor rests with all of us." He met the gaze of each of the three men in turn then strode out the door.

Why was it that working there so often brought to mind his days at school, when fending off bullies had been a daily task?

He shrugged away the thought and focused on his cases. Edgarton was his priority and might very well lead him to Cobb's killer. They could indeed be the same, as Perdy suggested, though Henry still had doubts.

And since the escaped prisoner hadn't been in any of the locations they'd searched, they needed to look elsewhere.

They'd arrested some of Edgarton's men in a lottery scheme raid over a month ago, and Henry had managed to convince one or two to share a few details about their boss. Edgarton had been born and raised on rough streets—a rookery, as the slums were called, in Whitechapel.

Wouldn't it make sense for him to return to hide in just such a place? Somewhere he had friends and possibly family? Connections to those willing to aid him, especially since he had money to pay for their loyalty...

Though Whitechapel was not a place Henry relished visiting, the time had come to poke everywhere he could think of with the hope of getting information—or gaining a reaction.

Venturing there during daylight hours lessened the risk, but not by much. Henry knew from experience that most who lived on those unforgiving streets were able to tell he was with the police even if he no longer wore a uniform. There were occasions when he donned old clothing with the hope to better blend in, but this wasn't the time.

His grandfather, Charles Field and a chief inspector, had gained fame in part for giving Charles Dickens a guided tour of a few rookeries. If his grandfather managed to navigate the slums, including Whitechapel, St. Giles, and others without incident, Henry could do the same.

Of course, armed guards had accompanied them, according to some reports, though his grandfather had never admitted as much.

Henry held tight to the thought of his grandfather giving him a nod of approval as he hailed a hansom cab and directed the driver to drop him a few blocks from Fournier Street. No point in asking to be taken closer. Cabbies avoided such areas like the plague, and for good reason.

Inspectors were not always armed, the idea being that it was less likely for the public to feel threatened by their presence. This was one of the few times Henry wished he'd chosen to carry a weapon. For now his wits would have to be enough to see him through.

He alighted, paid the driver, and paused to glance about to get his bearings. It had been some time since he'd been in this particular neighborhood, and he couldn't claim any contacts there. Perhaps he'd make some today who were willing and happy to answer a few questions.

No harm in being optimistic.

If he started his search with the intent of *not* finding trouble, perhaps it would come true. He could imagine Fletcher's scoff of derision at the idea, which nearly made him smile.

He straightened his shoulders and started forward, clearing his mind to focus on his surroundings. The rookery was not the place to be distracted.

Several factories, including a bell foundry, brewery, and tannery were nearby. The soot-filled air stung his nostrils. Workers employed by those factories lived in the dilapidated lodging houses that were cheaply constructed and had quickly fallen into disrepair soon after being built. The very poor lived here—or rather, survived, which was a more apt description. Much like people of other social classes, some were kind and helpful, others mean and cruel. They tended to take care of their own, and Edgarton was surely considered one of them.

But no man could make a fortune without angering a few people. Edgarton was said to be ruthless, proven true by the trail of bodies he'd left behind. Maybe Henry would be lucky enough to find one or two of those Edgarton had betrayed who'd be willing to talk.

Dumped rubbish littered the streets and alleyways, and the stench mingled with the smoke, making something as simple as breathing unpleasant. He couldn't help but take a moment to appreciate that he at least, could leave in a few hours. Living here would be a trial on every level.

A question winged through his mind, enough to have him halting mid-step, his heart suddenly pounding frantically.

Had he been born on a street like this one?

Henry gulped in the unpleasant air to stave off the question and looked about with fresh eyes. Though he'd always wondered where—and who—he'd come from, never had it struck him quite like this.

He had discovered his adoption quite by accident at the age of twelve. The news had been a blow, and not just because he adored his parents. From a young age, he'd been set on becoming a Scotland Yard Inspector just like his father and grandfather. Learning he wasn't a true Field had cut him off at the knees for a time and left him floundering to understand who he was without that foundation.

While he had many questions, he hadn't been able to ask his parents any of them.

He still hadn't.

Would he ever?

Henry shook his head. Now wasn't the time to ponder the matter. Most definitely not.

He started forward again, forcing the unpleasant image of Edgarton into his mind. With intent, he studied those he passed by.

"Oi! 'ello, 'andsome." A young woman dressed in little more than rags, leaning against a brick building, stepped forward with an unsteady gait. "Lookin' fer a good time?" She wiggled her eyebrows suggestively and smiled, careful not to show her presumably decrepit teeth.

"No." Henry smothered a wave of sympathy for her plight. The problems in this area were too numerous for one person to solve. It would take an act of Parliament, and even then, not everything could be improved.

"C'mon, now," she persisted as she drew a faded shawl of an indeterminate color around her, quickening her pace to walk alongside him and taking care to bump against him. "Ye know ye want to."

He stopped to look at her. "I don't. However, I am in search of information."

The smile vanished as her brow furrowed, clearly not pleased with the news. "Wot about?"

"I'm looking for someone. Miles Edgarton."

Wariness flashed in her eyes; possibly due to the name being familiar, or perhaps she realized he was with the police. It was difficult to say which might be the case. Henry waited for an answer while she seemed to mull over her options.

"Can't help ye none with that." She smiled again, a hint of discolored teeth showing. "But I can with a bit of...pleasin'."

"No, thank you." He dipped his head and handed her a shilling before striding away, ignoring her call to come back.

Several other prostitutes lingered along the walkway, but apparently, they'd heard his response to the first one and didn't bother to approach.

In general, the police didn't bother with prostitutes unless a member of the public complained. While it was illegal to solicit, such cases were difficult to prove, taking time and resources better spent on more serious crimes.

Henry continued on, passing by soot-coated buildings with dirty, broken windows. A few had empty lines strung between them, waiting for laundry. The people on the street looked as tired and tattered as the structures. Several stared at him with guarded interest and others with outright hostility.

He ignored them, his focus on finding a person in a trade who might be willing to answer a few questions. Eventually he came to a cart selling sausage rolls and paused to order two. He reached into his pocket, the weight of gazes from onlookers heavy on him as he pulled out a few copper coins. He did his best to hide how much he had on his person to avoid finding himself the victim of theft later—or worse.

"Here ye go," the grizzled seller said, holding out the steaming sausage rolls.

"Thanks." Henry added an extra shilling to his payment. "I'm also in the market for information."

"Oh?" The man, middle-aged and favoring one leg, showed little interest in offering any.

"Happy to pay for it."

"Hmm." His scowl suggested that didn't change his mind.

"I'm looking for Miles Edgarton. Do you know him?" Henry took a bite of the hot roll while he waited for an answer.

"Maybe." A wariness darkened his eyes.

"Any idea where I can find him?" Henry asked carelessly.

"I don't think ye want to." The man shook his head as he adjusted the sausage rolls in the warming pan with a long-handled spoon.

"Perhaps, but I need to." He set another coin on the worn cart, doubtful it would help to tip the scale in his favor.

"If he don't wanna be found, money won't help." The man left the coin where it was, even as he looked at it with a hint of longing.

Henry took another bite as he considered how to proceed. "If I were to linger on this street, might I come upon him?" He nudged the coin closer to his reluctant informant.

"More than likely." With a glance around to see who watched, the sausage roll seller palmed the coin with a smooth movement that, had Henry not been watching carefully, he might have missed.

"Might that happen this very day?" Henry asked, excitement building.

"Hard to say."

"Is there anyone else along the street who could help?"

The man hesitated, keeping his eyes on his work. "Always good to lift a pint t'see what's what." The man tipped his head down the street then turned away, apparently having said as much as he was willing to.

Henry took the hint and strolled nonchalantly down the street, starting on his second sausage roll. The food was surprisingly good, and his stomach reminded him that he hadn't eaten since breakfast. He took in the rest of those on the street but didn't see anyone among the closely packed squalor who looked eager to talk. Better that he moved on in search of a pub, as the man suggested.

Children played on the street as they had no other place to do so, seemingly oblivious to the squalor around them. There certainly weren't any parks in the area. Their cries added to the clamor of passing carts and passersby. The buildings leaned against one another as if in need of support just as much as those who lived there.

It didn't take long for Henry to find a pub, but it also didn't take more than a glance to question the wisdom of going inside. The place looked rougher than most he'd ventured into. Blast. If only he'd thought to bring Fletcher with him. After a moment's hesitation, Henry reached for the door, reminding himself he hadn't come all this way for nothing.

He wasn't a small man by any means and liked to think he could hold his own in a fight. Of course, that was assuming he wasn't outnumbered.

Such worries could wait until a situation arose.

He hoped one didn't.

The interior of the pub was as rough as the outside, the lack of cleanliness giving him pause as much as the hard look of the patrons, many of whom glared at him with distrust and barely concealed malice.

He nodded at them anyway and approached the long, ale-stained bar, where a large man with a full gray beard cleaned glasses.

"What can I get ye?" he asked.

"The house ale, please." Somehow, it seemed unwise to ask questions without making a purchase. Besides, the sausage rolls had made him thirsty.

The bartender poured a glass and slid it his way.

Henry paid and took a sip, pleased to find it of decent quality. "I'm looking for a Miles Edgarton. Do you know him?"

"Aye, I know of him." The barkeep went back to polishing glasses, though based on the color of the cloth, it wouldn't do much good.

"Any idea where I can find him? I can make it worth your—"

"No." The man stepped away, swiftly ending the conversation.

Henry turned with his glass in hand to survey the premises, hoping someone else might be willing to answer his question.

But even after several minutes, no one approached or even met his gaze, though they'd more than likely heard his question. He sipped the pint and quietly sighed.

Where did he try next?

Eight

T HE SIGHT OF DELICATE sprouts reaching for sunlight in the row of small clay pots in her attic laboratory had Amelia smiling. Even the lateness of spring could not daunt them. The tiny seedlings were stronger than they looked.

She liked to think the same description applied to her.

Her experiment involving various types of fertilizer was progressing nicely. Each of the five pots contained a different additive that she'd mixed into the soil: crushed eggshells, tea leaves, ammonium nitrate, one with eggshells and tea leaves, and the last pot was plain soil with no additions. No obvious winner had come forth as of yet, but she was confident one would soon be revealed.

She retrieved a clean beaker and carefully measured water to pour into each container. It was imperative that she treat them all the same in order to determine which fertilizer worked the best.

The laboratory was her favorite place in the house, and more hers than any of the other rooms. Working in the large space up in the attic brought her happiness and, more importantly, peace. The focus required to conduct experiments cleared her mind as nothing else did. It allowed her to set aside problems for a time, and often when she returned to them, a solution had come to mind.

Her late husband had been amused by her interest in chemistry but had not necessarily understood it. That was an apt description for many parts of their marriage, she supposed, as she had felt the same way about some of his interests. At least, the ones she'd known about while he had lived. In recent weeks, she'd been forced to face just how much they'd grown apart prior to his death. Now she wondered if they'd ever enjoyed a true union.

Amelia's disappointment in him, his activities, and herself for not realizing what was happening were all pains she continued to work through. In all honesty, the situation had shaken her trust in herself. How could she not have known what was going on beneath her nose—with the man with whom she'd shared a bed?

That question kept her awake many nights. Was she so selfish that she hadn't seen it? So focused on her own wants and needs that she hadn't noticed what Matthew was doing, and more importantly, why?

She didn't know, which left her wondering if she would be better off remaining alone for the rest of her life. The idea of hurting anyone else, being hurt by anyone else, gave her pause. Perhaps she wasn't equipped to be a wife.

Did she even want to be one again? She wouldn't deny that she enjoyed her newfound independence now that she was growing accustomed to it. She could do what she wanted when she wanted, orchestrate her own life, run her own household...yet loneliness often threatened. Evenings with Henry had shown her how much she enjoyed the company of others, especially his.

A quiet sigh filled the silence of the room—her own, of course.

That was another disadvantage of being alone so often, other than the servants. She tended to hold conversations with herself. Luckily, most of them were silent.

Amelia held a beaker of water but paused mid-pour as her thoughts continued to swirl. What did she want? What did she hope for in the coming years?

The question was one she had only recently started to explore. Perhaps that was a result of finally knowing who had killed Matthew and why.

He reached too far.

So Mrs. Drake had said when Amelia had visited her at the prison. What that meant, or if it was even true, were questions for which she might never have answers.

She shook her head and returned to watering the pots. Dwelling on the past served no one. Surely she had enough answers now to let it go and move forward with her life.

Without Lily. Without Matthew.

The sharp ache in her chest was familiar, almost an old friend. Would there ever be a time when it eased? Another question she couldn't answer.

Amelia blew out a long, slow breath and refocused her attention on the experiment. One day at a time was as much as she could manage right now. Anything more felt overwhelming and uncertain.

Voices echoed through the house from below. She paused to listen, a familiar feminine tone making her smile. With quick movements she finished watering the last pot, tidied her workspace, then hung her apron on the peg by the door.

The sight of her aunt reaching the landing below warmed her. "Good afternoon, Aunt Margaret."

Her aunt was the younger sister of Amelia's mother and had moved to London just before Christmas. Amelia enjoyed having a family member nearby and knew her aunt felt the same.

"Amelia. How good to see you." Her visitor lifted a brow. "Were you finished in your laboratory? I am happy to keep you company up there if you're still working."

"I'm finished for now." Amelia descended the stairs.

Soon she would need to determine another experiment to conduct. Anything to keep herself busy and filled with purpose. Why was it that the idea of doing so felt discouraging, rather like an uphill, never-ending task? Yet having something to look forward to each day was imperative, something she frequently struggled with since Matthew's death.

"I'm so pleased you called," Amelia said as she reached for her aunt's outstretched hands, happy to have someone to distract her from her circling thoughts.

"I am sorry to have been absent for the last week." She released Amelia and turned toward the drawing room. "It's funny how quickly life passes by whether we want it to or not."

"It is." She followed her aunt, eager to hear what had kept her so busy. "Tell me, what have you been doing?"

"Fundraising efforts with the church, of course. That has involved several meetings which I attended, and they took more time than expected. We have received several donations after your article in the periodical."

Warmth spread through her at the thought. "I'm pleased to hear that."

Aunt Margaret had stayed with Amelia during the mudlark investigation and soon after became involved in the efforts of a church that was now aiding the children by offering housing and education. Most were orphans and needed a helping hand to have a chance for a better life.

Two of the mudlarks, Agnes and Pudge, held a special soft spot in Amelia's heart. To know they now attended school and no longer had to worry about where they would spend the night, or where their next meal would come from, was a relief.

However, those changes required money. Her aunt had thrown herself into the church's efforts to help the girls and the other mudlarks with great success. Amelia helped on occasion as well, where she could from her widow's income.

"And how are Agnes and Pudge?" She had visited them just before Edgarton's escape and looked forward to doing so again once the man was caught.

She bit her lip, hating that she was now defining her life as before and after that day. Not for long, she reassured herself. Henry would find the escaped prisoner soon, and the heavy weight shadowing her would be gone.

Please let that be true.

"They are well, but before we delve into the topic, tell me I imagined that a constable is lingering outside." Aunt Margaret's eyes narrowed as she met Amelia's gaze, a look of evident concern on her face.

"I wish I could. The police *are* watching over the house again." Amelia hesitated, wondering how much to share.

"You're not involved in another investigation, are you?"

"I'm not." That much was true. Helping to find Miles Edgarton or whoever had killed the prison guard, wasn't anything she could lend assistance with.

Her aunt eyed her beadily, clearly not entirely convinced. "Well, that's a relief. Then why is a constable necessary?"

There was no hiding it forever. Arguably, Amelia should have told her when it had happened. "The...the man who was accused of killing Matthew, who is also suspected of murdering at least two others, escaped from prison just over a week ago."

Her aunt's gasp filled the room. "I read about an escaped prisoner in the paper but didn't realize who he was." She glanced about as if expecting to see a sign of him. "How terrifying. Why don't I stay with you until he's recaptured?"

"That is kind, but there's no need." Amelia shook her head. She loved her aunt but didn't want her underfoot again. She tended to treat Amelia as a young woman in need of supervision, not a widow with her own mind and opinions. Their relationship was much more cordial when they lived under separate roofs. "I don't truly think he will come in search of me. My testimony is only a small part of the case against him." At least, that was what she continued to tell herself.

"I'm surprised he hasn't been found by now. What are the police doing?"

"They have mounted an extensive search, but the man managed to build a criminal empire by the sound of things. He has numerous contacts all over the city and surrounding areas, as well as abroad. It's been difficult to determine where he might be."

Before Amelia could further defend the police, Henry, in particular, a 'meow' caught their notice.

"Master Leopold," she said with a smile as the cat rubbed against her skirts. "Have you come to greet our visitor?"

"What is this?" Her aunt stared at the feline in surprise. "You have a cat guarding you, too?"

Amelia laughed. "I suppose I do." She hesitated to explain how he'd come to be with her when it involved another murder investigation. Aunt Margaret was going to think her life revolved around murder cases...though in many ways, Amelia supposed it did. "An...acquaintance died and left him to me."

Aunt Margaret sent her a questioning look. "You've not returned to deep mourning—a close acquaintance?"

Amelia sighed. "Benjamin Norris, the man Matthew and I knew,who was murdered in Gravesend, had the cat."

"Oh. I see." Her aunt appeared taken aback by the news.

"None of the man's relatives wanted him, so we took him in." Amelia rubbed the cat's soft fur, feeling her tension ease. "He has been a delight."

"And Mr. and Mrs. Fernsby don't mind?" The disbelief in her aunt's tone made Amelia laugh.

"Much to my surprise, no. He is very well behaved." At least, they'd managed to keep him out of trouble thus far.

Leopold looked up at her and purred as if to thank her for saying as much.

"That is most definitely a surprise." Aunt Margaret shook her head. "Nor would I have guessed you'd enjoy having a cat in the house."

"I wouldn't have either, but it is working out quite well to have him here."

Her aunt removed a glove and reached out tentatively to touch the striped feline. As if to show his approval, or perhaps to better direct her touch, he rubbed his head against her fingers. "Goodness. How soft he is."

"It's rather therapeutic to have him here." Amelia didn't mention how welcome a distraction he'd been for the entire household. Even Yvette, the maid, had warmed up to the cat, despite the hair he left on the furniture.

"I can see his appeal and am pleased you have the company." Her aunt straightened and watched Leopold cross the room to the window and hop onto his chair before returning her attention to Amelia. "There is a matter I wanted to discuss."

"Oh?"

"You mentioned before that it might be possible to notify the authorities to watch for the return of my...my former gentleman friend." Aunt Margaret lifted her chin in defiance against the rogue. "I do believe I would like to pursue that."

Amelia nodded in approval. "I'm pleased to hear it. I applaud your decision."

"I don't know if it's possible to make him return the money I lent him, but I would like it back." She brushed her skirt as if to wipe away nonexistent lint, a hint of color high in her cheeks. "It has taken me some time to overcome my embarrassment over the matter."

Amelia's heart softened, as it always did whenever she considered the man who had promised much, but ultimately robbed her maiden aunt. "You have no reason to be embarrassed. You were being kind and helpful, and he took advantage of that. He's the one who should be embarrassed."

"You're right." Aunt Margaret sighed. "Yet it's not easy to remember, especially in the middle of the night."

Amelia could certainly relate but didn't say as much when she didn't care to share her own doubts and worries. Not today. "It would probably be best if you spoke with Inspector Field personally to explain the details. If you would like me to be there when you do so, I would be happy to lend support."

"Thank you." Her aunt nodded. "If you would be so kind as to mention it to him, I would appreciate it. Just send word as to when I should meet him." She hesitated, her brow puckering. "I won't have to venture to Scotland Yard, will I?"

Amelia imagined Inspector Perdy speaking with her aunt and nearly shuddered. "I would be happy to advise Inspector Field that you'd prefer to meet elsewhere."

Aunt Margaret nodded, clearly relieved. "Perhaps we could meet here if you're agreeable."

"Of course."

Amelia liked the idea of her aunt taking action against the man who'd not only taken her money, but hurt her, injuring her confidence and sense of self. Perhaps this step would bring her aunt some peace. Amelia knew how important that was.

Besides, it would be a pleasure to arrange such a meeting, as it would provide another opportunity to see Henry. The thought lightened her heart...perhaps more than it should.

Nine

Henry's patience stretched thin as he lingered at the pub. Another sip of the ale confirmed it was quite tasty, but enjoying it wasn't his reason for venturing to Whitechapel.

Further consideration of the situation left him resigned to giving the suspicious patrons more time to decide if they would speak to him before he departed. A glance at the bartender suggested he was being watched closely, so he requested another drink, certainly no hardship when it was of good quality.

He would find someone else along the street to speak with if no one came forward. There was a chance Edgarton would hear about his inquiries, but that could prove fortuitous. While it might be dangerous to stir the pot, action of some sort was needed to force the man from wherever he was.

He couldn't stay hidden forever.

Though tempted to approach the table where a few men nursed drinks as they conversed in low voices, he decided against it. They'd surely overheard him speak with the bartender and knew the reason he was there. If they had anything to say to him, they would have already spoken.

After a painfully long quarter of an hour, Henry decided nothing would be discovered there, so he finished his drink and, with a nod at the barkeep who'd kept his distance, took his leave. Aware of gazes following him, he paused outside to look up and down the street, then picked a direction and walked, taking his time with the faint hope a patron from the pub might follow him with information.

No one did.

Was that because they knew nothing about Edgarton, or were frightened of him, or did their loyalties run deep? With a sigh, Henry continued on and soon came upon an old man selling matches. The man's cloudy eyes suggested he didn't see much, but Henry bought some matches and hoped he might be helpful.

"Do you know Miles Edgarton?" Henry asked as he pocketed his purchase.

"Who doesn't?" the man responded.

Henry didn't tell him he was one of the few to admit it. "Has he been around of late?"

"Oh, sure. Though 'e keeps to the shadows these days." The man looked Henry up and down, his murky eyes clearly better than Henry had thought. "Are ye 'oping to put 'im back in prison?"

Henry smothered a sigh. Even if he hadn't bothered trying to hide that he was a police officer, he'd rather not be recognized so easily. "I am. He will have his day in court to share his side of the story." Never mind that Henry didn't think the escaped prisoner had a chance of being proclaimed innocent, no matter what he said.

"Wish ye luck wiv 'at." The old man shook his head. "Ye'll need it."

"Any idea where I can find him?"

"No. But there's always the chance 'e'll find ye." He laughed, leaving Henry to wonder whether he jested or told the truth.

The idea of Edgarton approaching him seemed doubtful, but had Henry taking a closer look around as he continued down the street. The man's words were a good reminder to watch his back. He did exactly that, pausing several times along the street to give anyone who wanted to speak with him the chance to do so. Still, nothing. Nobody.

The afternoon was passing quickly, and he couldn't linger much longer if he wanted to leave before dark, a challenge of these March afternoons. He walked by an alleyway only to slow his pace at the sight of a man pressed against the side of a building, looking decidedly nervous.

"Lookin' fer Edgarton?" the man asked in a quiet tone.

"Yes," Henry said, hope building as tingles rushed down his spine.

"Ye didn't 'ear it from me, but he sometimes stays with Betty Knox over on Dorset Street. I've seen him comin' in and out several times the last few days."

"Who—" Before Henry could finish the question, the man turned away and hurried down the filthy alley.

Henry frowned. It wasn't much of a clue, but it was more than he'd had before. Entering a lodging house in this neighborhood by himself was too risky, no matter how determined he was to find Edgarton. For all he knew, the information could be a trap, designed to lure him in. He'd have to return with a few constables to see if what the man had told him was true.

But first, he needed to scout out Dorset Street. He paused to request directions from passersby as he walked and soon located it. His hope faded as he stared at the numerous tenements lining the street. Lord, there had to be thirty or forty of them, at least. He had no idea which one this Betty Knox might live in.

Though tempted to take a closer look or ask around to narrow the search, he didn't want Edgarton to learn he'd been on the street where he was hiding. If only he had informants in this part of Whitechapel...

The thought had him glancing about, wondering if any of the desperate people along the street might be willing to aid him.

A young lad in an oversized coat caught his eye, reminding him of Charlie, one of the mudlarks who'd been murdered. Approaching the boy with the chance to earn some money seemed like a fitting tribute to honor the orphan Henry hadn't been able to save.

"Interested in work?" Henry asked with a lifted brow.

The boy, who now examined him, looked a bit older than Charlie. He wiped his nose with a tattered coat sleeve as he eyed Henry from head to toe, a wary look in his brown eyes. "D'pends. Wot ye need?"

"Information."

A light of interest gleamed in the boy's thin face. "Wot sort?"

Henry explained that he needed to know which building Betty Knox lived in, what room, whether a man was staying with her, and if so, for the boy to keep watch until Henry returned in the morning. "The man is dangerous," he warned, misgivings tugging at him even as he spoke. "You'll need to take care to remain out of sight and even more care who you ask about him or Betty Knox."

The boy studied the numerous buildings as he considered the request for a long moment. "An' 'ow much?"

Henry handed him a shilling. "I'll give you two more if you're here when I return in the morning, and another two for the information."

"Wot if I can't learn more?"

"Find out what you can. Keep watch anyway," Henry suggested in an undertone. "And above all, take care."

"Fair 'nough." The lad palmed the coin with a smooth motion.

"What's your name?" Henry asked, deciding he liked him already.

"Marcus."

"Pleased to meet you, Marcus." Henry offered his hand. "I'm Henry."

The boy studied it with surprise before clasping it firmly. "Pleasure, Mister 'enry. I'll see ye come mornin'."

Before Henry could say anything more, the boy darted away, quickly disappearing from sight, leaving him to wonder if that would prove true.

With one last glance at the row of buildings on Dorset Street, Henry started toward Scotland Yard. Prickles ran along the back of his neck. So he was being watched, then. He halted several times to look for whoever followed him but without success.

Though the urge to leave in haste took hold, Henry pushed it away and walked at a comfortable pace. He hoped his frequent perusals of the street told whoever followed him that he knew of their presence.

However, he would readily admit to feeling relieved when the streets of the rookery gave way to cleaner ones with friendlier people. He finally located a hansom cab and returned to Scotland Yard, which was mostly deserted at this hour—including, Henry saw with pleasure, the men who'd annoyed him earlier.

Even the Director had left for the day, which meant Henry would have to wait until morning to tell him what he'd learned. He left a note requesting Fletcher's assistance for the next day and departed for home, a restless energy gripping him.

Though tempted to call on Amelia to ensure all was well, even Henry could see that it would merely be an excuse to see her. He couldn't—shouldn't—drop by unannounced yet again. How could he pursue a relationship with the lovely widow when Edgarton was at large and remained a potential threat to her? That truth didn't reduce his longing to see her in the least.

An errant thought occurred to him and Henry slowed in the middle of the pavement, a pair of ladies moving around him and staring at his sudden change of pace.

"Bother." He changed direction and started toward her home. Well, didn't she deserve an update on progress? Shouldn't he advise the constable who watched over her to remain vigilant? And perhaps Amelia should be reminded to take care—she did tend to take unnecessary risks.

"And yes, all those are excuses," he muttered to himself. Was it so wrong to want to spend a few minutes in her company and make certain that she's well?

Luckily, he didn't say the last part aloud. Holding conversations with himself was only one of the reasons he was determined to expand and deepen his friendships. Clearly he needed to work harder on that.

Within twenty minutes Henry had arrived at her house, reminded the constable on duty to take care as they were on the lookout for an escaped prisoner capable of terrible deeds, and knocked on her front door.

"Inspector Field, welcome." Fernsby opened the door wider with a smile.

"Thank you. Good to see you, Fernsby. All is well here?" he asked quietly.

"It is indeed. No issues to report."

"Excellent."

The butler reached for his hat and gloves, and with a sigh, Henry handed them over. It looked like he couldn't help himself. "I won't be staying long." Whether he told himself that or Fernsby, he couldn't say.

"As you wish, sir." Fernsby set them aside to help remove his jacket. "Mrs. Greystone is in the drawing room, I believe."

"Very well." Shoving aside his guilt, Henry instead focused on the warmth of anticipation at seeing her that poured through him.

He paused in the drawing room doorway as she rose from her desk, her expression one of welcome. She wore her usual gray gown of half-mourning, but that didn't diminish her attractiveness. His stomach jolted in response. His feelings for Amelia were growing deeper by the day.

"Henry, what a nice surprise. I'm pleased you stopped by." She studied his expression briefly as if to ascertain whether he came bearing more bad news.

How he detested that. If only—

"May I pour you a drink?" She glanced at the clock on the mantel. "Are you done for the day?"

He wished he could act on the potential lead for Edgarton, but it wouldn't be too long to wait; morning would be here before he knew it. Or so he hoped.

"I am, though I wouldn't want to impose." Would she tell him if he was? "I only intended to ascertain if all was well."

A ridiculous excuse, when he could've checked in with the constable and Fernsby to know that.

"Oh, it's no imposition. I'm happy to see you." Amelia met his gaze, her warm smile easing his guilt to a more manageable level, not to mention his restlessness. "Shall we enjoy a drink and a visit?"

Yes, I would like that very much. And dinner. And conversation all evening.

Luckily, he didn't allow that to slip out...or mention how his heart settled just from being in her presence. "If you have the time." He glanced at the books and papers on her desk. She liked to stay busy and was an avid reader in addition to her other interests. "You've been working?"

"Yes, on my latest article about orchid collectors." She turned to the sideboard where the crystal decanters awaited. "I'm pleased to say it's coming along well."

The cat meowed as it trotted into the room, seeming to ask what he'd missed.

"You have quite the talent for making such things fascinating. I look forward to reading it." Henry bent to greet the feline and scratched behind its ears, appreciating his greeting as it made him feel like part of the household—a dangerous thought. "Hello, Master Leopold. And how are you?"

The cat meowed some more in answer and rubbed against Henry's legs before moving to greet Amelia. She bent to pet it, murmuring a few soft words of praise.

Leopold made himself at home on the rug before the fire to groom his fur while Amelia finished pouring their drinks.

"Are you finding your research on orchid collecting interesting?" Henry asked after they'd settled into their chairs, eager to hear about her day and welcoming the distraction from his own.

"It is. I had no idea there were so many kinds, or how rare some are." She took a sip of her sherry as she met Henry's gaze. "However, it never fails to amaze me what lengths some people will go to in order to collect the rare and unusual."

"Whether it involves Egyptian artifacts made of gold or flowers," Henry suggested with a wry smile. He drew a slow breath, enjoying the moment. The lightness in his chest and the pleasure buzzing through his system had nothing to do with the glass of whiskey in his hand.

"Exactly." Amelia nodded to emphasize the point, her expressive brown eyes shining with delight. "I knew you'd understand."

He blinked, realizing just how much he was in over his head with the lovely lady across from him. Would he have had the courage to share some of his feelings the night they'd had dinner at the restaurant before the constable came charging in to tell them of Edgarton's escape?

Or should he take that interrupted moment as a sign from Fate that this—whatever it was building between them—wasn't meant to be?

Or worse...was it all one sided? Did she consider himself anything more than a friend she'd met under unfortunate circumstances?

"You'll never believe this," Amelia continued, reaching out to briefly touch his arm in her enthusiasm. "Lord Delcourt—the man I interviewed for my orchid piece—he also collects Egyptian artifacts."

"Oh?" Henry did his best to focus on the conversation rather than her touch. "Did you have the chance to see them?"

"No." Her lips tightened as if she was disappointed by that fact. "I dearly wanted to ask him if they were obtained legally."

"But you didn't, did you?" Henry had to ask, worry filling him. Her propensity to press for information had proven dangerous in the past.

"No." Amelia heaved a rueful sigh as she sat back in her chair. "I didn't think you would appreciate it, nor would my editor, if the lord or his wife mentioned that I showed too much interest in that area of questioning."

"I don't suppose. I will make a mental note of his interest though, in case something more on the issue arises." A customs officer had taken over that arm of the investigation, so he hadn't heard of any recent developments.

"Lord Delcourt says a few collectors have risked their lives to find rare specimens. Orchids, I mean." She shook her head, clearly in disagreement with their efforts. "Why do some find the need to possess such things?"

"I have no idea. The fervor they experience can be alarming and lead to, shall we say, unfortunate behavior."

"Very true. Collectors have actually engaged in physical altercations with one another in order to secure an orchid. Can you imagine?" The disbelief in Amelia's tone amused him.

"I'm afraid to say that I can."

She heaved a sigh as she took another sip. "Enough of orchid collectors. How was your day?"

The genuine interest in her eyes warmed him. He liked to think she asked because she truly wanted to hear about his day and that it didn't necessarily have anything to do with Edgarton. Was that possible?

"Uneventful. Pursuit of potential clues with little to show for it." Henry didn't mention the lead on Edgarton when nothing might come of it. Much could happen during an ongoing investigation. Nor did he share his irritating conversation with Perdy, though she held the man in the same poor regard as he did, having experienced his ineptitude firsthand during the raven-keeper's case, their first one together. Neither did he mention that he'd ventured to Whitechapel, or his intention to return there on the morrow. It would distress her.

"No additional signs of Edgarton?" Amelia asked lightly.

"No signs at all," he gently corrected. The man seemed to have vanished—unless the lead he'd received proved true and Marcus managed to locate him.

"You still doubt he was the one who killed the prison guard?" Her brow furrowed as if she found that puzzling.

"I don't know." Henry's gaze shifted to the cat curled in a ball on the rug before the fire, envying him his peaceful slumber. "I have difficulty determining a motive for him to have done it."

"You think if Edgarton wanted him dead, he would've killed him during the escape, or immediately after."

"Right. Of course, it's possible that even though Cobb took a bribe, his loyalty to Edgarton was in question. He may have been loose lipped, which earned him Edgarton's wrath."

"That sounds logical."

Then why couldn't Henry accept as much and declare Edgarton their one and only suspect? He didn't know. In this case, he worried his instincts were leading him astray. He'd always had that worry; that because he wasn't a true Field, an adopted son into the family line, that his instincts were untrustworthy, unreliable. That he could never go with his gut.

With this case, he felt as if he took one step forward then two steps back.

"If not Edgarton, who else?" Amelia asked.

The question had Henry shifting in his seat. He didn't want to disappoint her, but he didn't have an answer. His ineptitude frustrated him more than he could say. He dearly wanted to put this investigation behind both him and Amelia...yet Fate seemed to have other plans.

Ten

T HE LIGHT IN HENRY'S eyes dimmed, making Amelia wish she could take back the question. It had clearly made him uncomfortable, a reaction she'd never intended. Besides, what did she know about investigations and motives and suspects? Being involved in a few cases over the last few months hardly made her an expert.

Henry was an experienced detective with an excellent record of solving cases and bringing criminals to justice. She'd witnessed his skills firsthand on several occasions, after all.

Once again her curiosity had overcome good sense, and she'd pressed too far. Now she worried he would take his leave when that was the last thing she wanted.

"I didn't mean to suggest—" she began.

"Not at all." He shifted again, then shook his head. "I only wish I had an answer."

He must have a suspicion of some sort or a reason for his uncertainty about Edgarton's guilt in the guard's murder. She pressed her lips tight to keep from coaxing it from him. As much as she enjoyed discussing cases and helping to solve the puzzle they presented, this might not be the right time to push for more.

Besides, Henry could not spill all Scotland Yard's secrets in her drawing room. The man had pride in his profession, a pride that was admirable.

Instead, she searched for a way to ease the sudden tension now gripping the room. Or did it only clutch at her?

"I continue to wonder who else had something to gain from Cobb's death," Henry finally said, making her almost giddy with relief.

"Is there anyone else suspected of taking bribes? Another prison guard perhaps?" she asked hesitantly, even as she told herself that he would've asked if he wanted her help.

"None as of yet, but officials at the prison are looking into the matter. Whether they will apprise us of those efforts is unclear."

Amelia waited a moment to see what more he might add, disappointed when he remained silent. "I'm pleased you don't jump to conclusions in your eagerness to solve cases." She smiled when he met her gaze, wanting him to know how much she admired him, though she could not articulate such a feeling in words.

"I won't say it's not tempting as the pressure mounts to provide an answer."

"I'm sure, which makes your restraint all the more impressive. Do you think Edgarton has left the area?"

"He might have. However, from what little we know, it seems more logical for him to stay near where his businesses and connections are. Which makes it imperative that you remain alert," he advised with a pointed look.

"I will." She didn't add that she thought it unlikely Edgarton would bother to seek her out when he had the entire police force searching for him. It wasn't as if she'd witnessed him killing Matthew; she'd only heard that information secondhand. Of course, she'd helped to connect him to the sale of illicit artifacts, and there was the fact that he'd briefly held her against her will, threatening her very life...but still, her role in his arrest seemed minor compared to others. Edgarton's crimes were many.

"Good. I'm counting on that." His smile eased the seriousness of the subject.

Nerves took hold as another question came to mind, and Amelia clasped her hands in her lap, debating whether she dared to ask it. She was surely being overly forward and too needy, entirely unseemly for a lady of her status.

And yet the words slipped out even as she told herself not to voice them. "May I invite you to join me for dinner?"

Drat. Where was her self-control? Heat filled her cheeks as if she were a young woman rather than a widow still in half-mourning attire. Her heart pounded as she attempted to smooth her expression, hoping her longing to spend more time with him didn't show.

She valued his friendship and not just because she was lonely. He was an interesting person with intelligence and a dry wit that she enjoyed. He was respectful and honorable. Just because he happened to be a handsome man she found attractive didn't mean inviting him to stay for dinner was wrong. They were both adults and had to eat, did they not?

And that was as many excuses as she was willing to offer to herself for now.

"I have no doubt my cook has made more than enough, as she always does." Amelia attempted a casual smile.

Henry hesitated, lifting her hopes. "I shouldn't."

Which promptly dashed them again. "I understand, though I would hate for Mrs. Appleton to think you prefer your landlady's meals over hers." Yes, apparently she would resort to such ploys if necessary. What on earth had she become?

Henry chuckled, his gaze meeting hers, the warmth in his brown eyes stealing her breath. "Nor would I." He gave a single nod. "I would be pleased to join you, if you're certain it's no bother."

And she realized in that moment that more than friendship brewed within her. While not entirely new information, neither was she willing to consider what the emotions bubbling inside her might mean.

Not this evening, at any rate.

"Then it's settled." She rose before he could change his mind and walked to the bell pull, stepping out of the room to the top of the stairs to catch Fernsby before he climbed them. He made enough trips up them throughout the day. A few moments later, the butler walked into view. "Fernsby, Inspector Field will be joining me for dinner."

"Excellent, madam. I have already set another place." The elderly man's nod of approval was much appreciated.

"Oh. Thank you." Somehow the news flustered her further.

Amelia returned to the drawing room, taking a moment to admire Henry's profile as he gazed into the fire. The strength in his visage appealed to her, as did his handsomeness. With broad shoulders and a thick chest, he was in fine health. Her gaze dropped to his long fingers, which loosely held the whiskey glass. What might it be like to twine those fingers with her own?

Oh, dear. Definitely more than friendship if she was noticing his hands.

"I...I thought it might rain this evening based on the clouds I saw on the horizon earlier," she said, determined to divert her thoughts as she rejoined him.

"The scent of it is in the air."

Amelia couldn't help but smile as she retrieved her glass of sherry. "That is something my father would often say. I'm rather amazed you were able to notice, given the soot-filled air of London."

"I suppose when one spends as much time walking the streets as I do, one can soon recognize the subtle changes."

"You've always lived in London then?" While he spoke of his parents and grandparents with fondness, she didn't know much about his past other than a few brief stories shared during the dinner at his parents' home.

"I have, though we often ventured to the country in my youth to visit one cousin or another during the summer." His gaze held on her. "What of you?"

The conversation continued cheerfully and easily after Fernsby announced that dinner was ready. Amelia enjoyed every minute of it and appreciated the deepening connection between them, especially when it involved things other than murder.

"I can easily see a younger version of you in your father's apothecary shop," Henry said after the soup bowls were cleared. "Cleaning bottles and handing change over a bench taller than yourself. He must be very proud of you."

"He is, though some of my first experiments alarmed him."

"Do tell." Henry lifted a brow, amusement shining in his eyes. "What did you do?"

"I was fond of making things foam and always mixing chemicals in his shop to find the best results. One nearly exploded, though I will say that particular foam was spectacular."

Henry's laugh had her joining in, and Amelia reveled in it. He didn't do that nearly often enough. Then again, so often their conversations involved investigations rather than childhood antics.

Fernsby returned with the next course of Sanders, as her father called it, also known as shepherd's pie, made with minced lamb mixed with gravy and layered with mashed potatoes.

"This looks delicious," Henry said.

"A simple but hearty dish, and one of my favorites." Amelia's family had often enjoyed it during her childhood, especially in the winter months.

"I already struggle to compliment my landlady's meals," Henry said with a shake of his head. "After the delicious dinners I've enjoyed here, I will be forced to resort to lying."

"Your secret is safe with us," Amelia replied, delight sparkling within her that he liked the dishes.

Henry's eyes widened when Fernsby eventually brought in dessert, a pudding ideal for this time of year when fresh fruit was so difficult to find. "Cabinet pudding?" he asked.

"It is, sir." Fernsby smiled as he cut slices, set them on plates, and served them.

"Another of my favorites," Henry declared.

"Mrs. Appleton's artistry is at work again," Amelia said as she admired the careful arrangement of preserved cherries, candied peel, and ginger that lined the molded pudding.

The cook was as adamant as Amelia about not allowing anything to go to waste. Custard and a dash of brandy completed the pudding, a fine way to use stale sponge cake.

Henry clearly savored every bite. "It's been an age since I've had this."

"Oh? I would've thought your landlady made it, at least on occasion."

Henry leaned forward as if to impart a secret. "She does, but it doesn't taste anything like this. Her custard is quite inferior, to say the least."

Amelia laughed. "Mrs. Appleton will be beaming for the remainder of the week when I tell her that."

The evening was pure joy as far as Amelia was concerned, and she didn't want it to end. But she knew Henry had work the next morning, and his day would undoubtedly start early.

"Do you have a busy day tomorrow?" she asked, enjoying the last few sips of her wine.

"Yes, I do." His expression tightened, eyes sharp with interest, making her think he had a specific task in mind. "What about you?"

She nearly scowled in disappointment when he didn't share it. How sad that she was living vicariously through Henry's work. It wasn't as though she didn't have plans. They just never seemed as interesting as his.

"I have more work to do on the orchid collectors' article. I'm debating whether an interview with another collector is necessary to provide a full view of the hobby."

"Always helpful to have more than one source, I'm sure." He frowned. "Do take care if you decide to leave the house."

"Of course." The reminder of her supposedly precarious safety dimmed her happiness, or perhaps Henry's impending departure was to blame.

"Thank you for a delicious meal and a fine evening," he began as he pushed back from the table.

"Thank you for joining me." She set her napkin on the table, only to remember her promise to her aunt. "Oh, I nearly forgot. There is something I wanted to speak to you about."

"Oh?" His eyes darkened, making her briefly wonder what crossed his mind.

"My aunt had an unfortunate situation occur with a gentleman friend. She lent him money, only to have him leave the country." She winced. "It was a significant sum, so I suggested she consider speaking with you about it to see what could be done, if anything."

"I see." He slowly nodded, seeming to process the information. "I would be happy to offer what assistance I can. Is it possible for me to speak with her?"

"Of course, but could we have that meeting here? She isn't eager to venture to Scotland Yard."

"Understandable. Just let me know a convenient time."

"Thank you," she said, pleased he'd agreed. And that she would see him again soon for that reason if nothing else.

"My pleasure." He stood. "I have an early start, so I shall say good night."

"Do take care, Henry." She moved around the table to join him, holding his gaze. His work frequently held risk, but pursuing a murderer as heartless as Edgarton made it even more dangerous. Though she wanted the escaped prisoner behind bars, she didn't care for the idea of Henry himself confronting the criminal again.

"I will." He hesitated, his manner uncertain, sending a mixture of curiosity and anticipation coursing through her. At last, he dipped his head. "Good evening, Amelia."

And then he left, leaving her wondering what he had considered saying or doing...before he changed his mind.

Eleven

THE MORNING DAWNED GRAY and rainy, but Henry's spirits remained high as he rose early and quickly dressed. How could he feel otherwise after receiving a possible lead on Edgarton *and* enjoying another wonderful evening with Amelia?

The unexpected urge to brush his lips on her cheek had startled him last night. No doubt such a gesture would've startled her as well. He was getting ahead of himself. The past had to be put to rest before he could consider anything resembling a future with her. Besides, he remained uncertain whether she would welcome such an overture. She might be satisfied with their friendship and desire nothing more.

He dearly hoped that wasn't the case.

After a hearty breakfast of coddled eggs and sausage, courtesy of his landlady, whose culinary skills were incomparable to Mrs. Appleton's, he returned to Whitechapel.

With luck, Marcus had followed through with Henry's request and would be waiting with information and a hand outstretched for his shillings. With even more luck, Edgarton would remain unaware that he'd been under unofficial surveillance.

Dorset Street was even less inviting this dreary morning. Those walking by mostly ignored him, going about their business despite the rain. He paused near the place he'd spoken with Marcus the previous afternoon, rain dripping off his hat's brim, but couldn't see the lad anywhere.

Disappointment speared through him. Had he misjudged the boy? He couldn't begrudge Marcus the single shilling if he had taken it without doing as Henry requested. It had perhaps been too much to ask of a lad, though Henry thought his young age made him less noticeable to someone like Edgarton.

"Ye're up and about early."

Henry turned with a smile to see Marcus approach, his cap pulled low over his brow, the collar up on the same worn coat as yesterday. "Wanted to see how you fared."

The boy nodded. "Well enough." He tipped his head toward the tenements. "She's in the last one on this side of the street, though I don't know which room." He scowled. "If ye'd given me a bit more time—"

"And the man?" Henry interrupted, hardly able to contain his rising excitement.

"Yeah, 'e's there, too." Marcus returned his attention to Henry. "Rumors say he's in a 'eap o' trouble."

"He is." Henry pulled out another coin. "You've done an excellent job. Can I ask you to watch another hour or so until I return, then I'll pay you the rest? I want to know if the man leaves, and if so, where he goes."

"I 'spose." He eagerly pocketed the money, the movement an unspoken agreement that he was more than happy to do so. "May'ap I can figure out wot room by then."

"That would be helpful, but don't take any unnecessary risks. And whatever you do, don't let him see you."

"Right." He studied Henry with narrowed eyes. "Ye're a copper then?"

"An inspector." Henry waited for the derogatory remark which so often came from the public.

"Fancy that." Marcus nodded, a gleam of unhidden admiration in his eyes. "Ain't never met one of ye before." He tipped the brim of his filthy hat. "I'll see ye soon."

The small show of respect warmed Henry. "Yes, you will. Thank you, Marcus."

Henry departed for Scotland Yard, already anxious to return for Edgarton. Luckily, the rain slowed to a drizzle, but he was already damp and chilled. March was proving stubborn in holding back spring.

Despite the detour to Whitechapel, he still arrived relatively early to the Yard. He greeted Sergeant Johnson at the front desk and continued down the hall, noting Fletcher had yet to arrive.

"Field?"

Henry turned as he reached his desk to see John Reynolds, the Director of Criminal Investigations, approach. "Morning, sir."

"I received a message from the customs office, and they want the Egyptian scarab found at the Gravesend crime scene."

Henry nodded, relief seeping through his chest. "It will be good to have it off our hands."

"Took them long enough," Reynolds said, shaking his head. "Can you retrieve it from the evidence room?"

"Certainly. But first, I have a lead on Edgarton," Henry said, lowering his voice, though he couldn't have explained why.

"Oh?" Interest shone in the Director's brown eyes framed by his spectacles. "That is excellent news. What is it?"

"I was in Whitechapel yesterday and given the address of a lodging house on Dorset Street where Edgarton is rumored to be staying with a woman."

"Quite a different location than his previous home, eh? What's your plan? Do you intend to conduct surveillance in the area?"

"I found someone to watch it during the night to narrow down the exact location so I could return with reinforcements this morning. My contact was able to confirm Edgarton is there with the woman, though he isn't certain which room they're in. I intend to gather a few men to bring in Edgarton." Henry looked forward to that moment, as well as giving Amelia the good news.

"Good work, Field." The Director looked around the office where only a few officers were beginning their day. "How many men do you need?"

"Two or three should be sufficient. I'd rather not bring more when doing so will only bring unwanted notice and sound the alarm. Fletcher and I would both recognize Edgarton. Perhaps bringing a couple of the others who have also seen him might be wise."

"That's a rough area for so few officers, but I suppose you'll be outnumbered no matter how many you bring."

"True."

Reynolds considered it for a moment before nodding. "Take Fletcher, Peters, and Stephens. They were all there the night of Edgarton's arrest."

"Yes, sir." Henry glanced around the room to see that only Peters was present at the moment. "The others should arrive shortly. I'll get the scarab while I wait."

"I look forward to hearing the results." Reynolds returned to his office.

Henry made his way to the evidence room toward the rear of the building where a sergeant was posted nearby to oversee all who entered.

"Morning, Miller," Henry greeted him.

"Inspector Field."

"I need the Egyptian scarab to take to the customs office. They've requested it be sent over."

"Certainly, sir." The younger man pushed the large ledger book forward for Henry to sign, along with the date and time, and the reason for his visit.

Out of habit, Henry perused the entries above his own, noting that Perdy and Clarke had visited the evidence room the previous day. Hopefully they were both making good progress on a case if they'd accessed the evidence room.

Miller took the key attached to his belt and unlocked the heavy reinforced door, which squeaked open, the hinges sorely in need of oil. Henry stepped inside the cold, dim space. Thick stone walls muffled sounds from the street and helped keep the room secure. Iron bars lined the single narrow window for further protection. No one had ever gained entrance, the evidence carefully stored to bring about justice.

Two gas lamps penetrated the gloom of the room with their low steady glow, revealing a row of lockable cabinets and shelves lined with evidence boxes neatly marked with case numbers in white chalk. A few items too large for the evidence boxes were wrapped in brown paper and also carried luggage labels with case numbers and dates.

In the center of the room was a waist-high table with a bound ledger book open on its worn surface. Previous ledgers were stored on the shelves beneath it, the chain of evidence visible and accessible to everyone on the force. Henry located the entry containing the scarab and noted that he was taking it to the customs office, along with the date, while the sergeant observed him. No one was allowed in the evidence room alone, not even the Director.

Miller unlocked the drawer where the scarab had been placed and stepped back. Henry opened the drawer and reached for the familiar cloth bundle only to stiffen in confusion.

It was empty.

Certain he had to be mistaken, he lifted the fabric and shook it out.

Nothing.

With a sinking sensation in the pit of his stomach, his pulse now thrumming in his ears, Henry bent to look in the drawer to no avail.

Nothing was in it.

"Is all well, Inspector?" Miller asked politely.

"No, it isn't." Henry's thoughts raced as he glanced about the room, trying to imagine where it could be. "The evidence isn't where it should be."

"That can't be," Miller exclaimed as he peered past Henry into the empty drawer for himself. "It has to be here somewhere."

Could it have fallen out? Perhaps it had been placed in the boxes either side of it by accident—mistakes were made, of course, and his heart pounded as he desperately looked in the other evidence boxes for it with Miller looking over his shoulder. Next the two men searched nearby shelves. But no scarab.

Henry stilled, his mind desperately working. His name was the only one next to the thing. He'd been the last person to have it.

Yet there was no doubt the valuable piece wasn't where it should be.

"Field?" Fletcher called from the doorway. "I saw your note and—" The sergeant glanced at the cloth Henry held before looking back at him. "What is it?"

"The scarab isn't here." Dread settled in the pit of Henry's stomach. He couldn't understand where it had gone. "At least, not where I left it."

"It must've been misplaced." Fletcher stepped into the room and opened a cupboard to review the contents. "Easily done, someone must've moved it."

Henry hoped that was the case, yet the terrible feeling gripping him suggested otherwise.

"I saw you put it in the drawer myself, sir, though that was some time ago," Miller said worriedly as he opened another drawer to search a second time.

"I haven't seen the scarab since returning it here, as noted in the ledger, after having its authenticity verified at the British Museum well over a month ago," Henry advised.

The golden scarab was easily the most valuable item in the entire evidence room, not just because of its metal but also because of the history it represented and its craftmanship. They had to find it. Absolutely had to.

Fifteen minutes later, they still hadn't found any sign of it.

Henry was sick to his stomach, trying to conceive of how this was possible. The rules for entering and exiting the room were strict. No one could access it without the sergeant on duty. The officer was the only one other than the Director who had a key.

But the scarab was still nowhere to be found.

"Inspector Field, sir?" Miller flipped a page of the ledger back and forth, studying it closely.

Hope leapt. "Yes?"

The constable pointed to a line on the previous page. "There's another entry for the scarab. It says you took it out a week ago."

Hope died. "I didn't do any such thing."

Fletcher paused in his search of another cabinet to join Miller. "Are you sure, sir? It does look like your handwriting, though the notation isn't on the proper page. Such things happen to the best of us. Minor details slip my memory all the time."

Henry strode forward to have a look for himself, but there was no question in his mind. He had not been in the room even once this week, he'd had no reason to be. What was going on?

He studied the line Miller pointed to. The entry bore his name and looked similar to his own signature, but it certainly wasn't his. "That isn't my writing—nor my signature."

Miller continued to study him silently as if willing him to change his answer or to suddenly remember that he had, indeed, taken the scarab.

Yet Henry couldn't oblige either of those wishes. "That is *not* my signature, and I wasn't in here."

"We need to report this to the Director." Miller closed the book and tucked it under his arm, clearly intending to take it with him. "All three of us."

Henry smothered an oath, retrieved the empty cloth the scarab had been wrapped in, and followed the men out, waiting impatiently as Miller carefully locked the door behind them.

The situation cast him in a poor light. Someone wanted others to believe he had taken the scarab. But who? And where was it?

No matter how many times he reassured himself that he had nothing to worry about since he hadn't done anything wrong, it didn't help.

Edgarton's vow the night of his arrest rang through Henry's mind once again, painful now in its accuracy. *This will be the end of your career with Scotland Yard.*

Henry wouldn't allow that to happen. He was innocent and somehow, he'd prove that.

Twelve

T HE NEXT HALF-HOUR PASSED at a snail's pace. Director Reynolds was furious to learn of the missing scarab. Henry felt much the same and didn't appreciate the questioning looks directed his way by his fellow officers. That Perdy and Clarke were among them, muttering together and casting him distrustful looks, made the situation worse.

Reynolds and Miller closeted themselves in the Director's office and reviewed the ledger at length. The evidence room was examined, revealing no sign of anyone breaking in. Nothing else was missing—only the scarab. Those who'd accessed the room in the past few days and happened to be at the Yard were called in and interviewed sharply.

None of that revealed any clues.

Henry did his best to mask his upset while he waited. He refused to show any guilt when he'd done nothing wrong, but in truth, he was shaken. Deeply so. It was clear someone in the department had taken the valuable piece—it could not have gone any other way.

And whoever that was wanted Henry blamed for it.

His faith in those he worked with each day was also shaken. Ever since he could remember, he had trusted and respected those who worked to serve and protect the nation; his father, his grandfather, all the men who proudly wore the uniform and took the oath. He looked around the room with fresh eyes, realizing everyone was a suspect, even those he knew well and had always trusted—including Fletcher.

"I just can't believe it," the sergeant kept muttering, clearly beside himself. "Where could it have gone?"

Was his apparent upset only an act? Henry hated that the question even crossed his mind.

"Nor can I." Henry shifted his shoulders in an attempt to ease the tension there with little success. He drew a steadying breath, then another, feeling the weight of continuing stares and whispered comments.

Even worse, the search for the missing evidence had delayed the plan to catch Edgarton. Marcus could only watch so long. The fugitive might be gone by the time they arrived in Whitechapel at this rate.

Of course, Perdy seemed to relish the opportunity to look down upon Henry and now spoke quietly in a corner with Duncan and Clarke, sending pointed looks in Henry's direction.

For a brief moment, he wondered if Perdy had managed to arrange the theft...but without any evidence to prove it, he couldn't share the suspicion.

"Surely there's something more we can do," Fletcher suggested as he paced the aisle before Henry's desk.

Henry couldn't agree more. "I'm going to ask Reynolds to allow us to proceed with the search for Edgarton. Waiting here isn't helping anything."

The Director and Miller had been going over the blasted ledger long enough. He pushed to his feet and strode to the Director's closed door to knock smartly upon it.

"Yes?" came Reynolds' muffled reply.

Henry opened the door to see Miller and the Director looking at him, the ledger before them, along with a page of meticulous notes. The coolness in Reynolds' expression was something which hadn't been there before. Henry didn't care for it.

"I'll continue the search, Director." Miller stood and quickly departed, brushing past Henry with a glare.

Henry ignored him and returned his attention to his superior. "Sir, I'd like to proceed with the plan to return to Whitechapel to look for Edgarton." He gestured down the hall toward the evidence room. "I'm not doing any good here."

Reynolds studied him for a long moment, and if Henry didn't know better, a glint of suspicion shone briefly in his eyes. Dare he hope it was merely a trick of the light as it glanced off the man's spectacles? Any other option didn't bear thinking about.

"Hmm. I suppose you have to proceed." The Director removed his glasses and rubbed the bridge of his nose before putting them back on. "I am still trying to decide what explanation to give the customs office."

"Not an easy task." Henry considered his next words carefully, forcing himself to inhale slowly. "Sir, I want to state once again that I did not take the scarab and was not involved in any plan to do so." He desperately wanted the Director to believe him, regardless of the evidence. "I can't imagine what happened to it, but that is not my signature nor my handwriting in the ledger." He drew another deliberate breath, wishing he knew what the Director was thinking. "I realize the situation doesn't reflect well on me or the force as a whole. For that, I'm sorry."

He hated to think of the Field name being associated with a wrongdoing at Scotland Yard—and the police force certainly didn't need another smear on its reputation.

Reynolds tapped a finger on the notes before him. "This is… We need to get to the bottom of this as quickly as possible."

"Yes, sir." Disappointment speared through Henry even though it was ridiculous to want the Director to immediately absolve him of any wrongdoing. That wasn't possible until they discovered precisely what had happened—and who had done it. "If you prefer for me to remain here while the evidence room is searched again, I will do so."

The Director sighed. "Let us pursue the escaped prisoner. Resolving at least one of our problems would be helpful."

"Thank you, sir." He turned to go.

"Field?"

Henry looked back, heart hammering.

"Don't take any unnecessary risks. Whitechapel is a dangerous area, and I don't want any of my men injured."

"Understood." Henry nodded, wishing Reynolds would show a little more faith in him. He returned to the main room and advised Fletcher, Peters, and Stephens of the plan. They all stood, gathering their coats and hats.

"And where do you think you're going?" Perdy rose from his desk to glare at Henry. "Seems like you should remain here until the missing evidence is found."

"The Director thinks otherwise." That was as much of an explanation as Henry was willing to provide, well aware that several other inspectors were listening. No doubt they thought the same. Blast. Was this to be his life until his name was cleared?

Perdy shook his head, watching as Henry donned his coat and hat. "If it were up to me, you'd be in a holding cell, Field."

Henry studied the others, wondering if they thought the same, relieved to see most shook their head—though whether in disagreement with Perdy, or the Director's decision to let him continue with his duties, he wasn't sure. His gaze shifted to Fletcher, who glared at Perdy as if prepared to march over and throttle him. Henry drew a breath of relief to know he'd earned the respect of some of his fellow officers over the past three years.

"Doesn't help that we heard you were at Mrs. Greystone's most of last evening," Perdy continued, a smirk on his face. "That doesn't look good on you either, Field."

"One has nothing to do with the other," Henry replied, not appreciating his remark or that one of the constables on duty at Amelia's had felt compelled to share what Henry did in his free time.

"Hard to believe associating with a lady involved in a prior case is wise," Whitlock added quietly. "It reflects poorly on you."

"I appreciate your concern, but I have done nothing wrong. The truth will soon come out. Meanwhile, duty calls." Henry spoke quietly, meeting some of the other men's gazes with the hope of making it clear he wasn't guilty of anything. Then he led the way toward the door. "Let's go."

He started in the direction of Whitechapel at a brisk pace, needing to work off some of the energy that gripped him. Only after they'd crossed the next street did he slow down to search for an omnibus to take the four of them.

Within a few minutes, they were seated together on the upper level of one. Due to the coolness of the day, the majority of passengers rode on the lower level, which offered shelter as the horses pulled the omnibus along.

Henry cleared his throat, deciding he needed to address the issue of the missing scarab. The uncomfortable silence demanded no less. Better that he spoke about it so they could focus on the mission before them. They didn't need distractions. Otherwise, someone might end up hurt.

"I did not take the scarab, nor do I know who did." He held each man's gaze, part of him daring them to say otherwise, his temper after Perdy's words still running hot. "I intend to do everything in my power to discover who did, as they clearly intended for me to take the blame." He glanced briefly at the passing scenery, shaking his head before returning his attention to them. "If any of you believe me guilty and don't want to join me for this mission, tell me now. You can return to the Yard without recourse."

Fletcher met his gaze. The frustration in his expression suggested he'd been holding back his opinion until now. "We'll find out who did this and we'll make them pay. Perhaps Edgarton has something to do with it since it was evidence against him. In which case, bringing him in will help solve both cases."

The uncomfortable knot in Henry's chest loosened. "Yes, it might."

"It must be some sort of mistake," Stephens said as he frowned. "After all, it doesn't make any sense that you'd take the scarab. Why would you take evidence, weaken the case? Not when you've been pursuing Edgarton for so long."

Their comments made Henry wonder if he'd assumed the worst and that more than a few of those he worked with believed him.

"We'll get to the bottom of it, sir." Peters' easy smile seemed out of place, given the seriousness of the situation. "I am certain of it." A hard glint flashed in the constable's eyes, though Henry couldn't decide if it was from determination...or something else.

Secrets, lies, treachery, theft...Henry faced them every day. He just hadn't expected to find them in his own office.

He had yet to decide whether he fully trusted the constable, but perhaps now Peters felt the same. There was no time like the present for them both to gain a better feel for each other's skills.

The mission might provide a true test for all of them.

"Thank you," Henry said after a moment. "I appreciate your support. Now, let's see if we can find Edgarton." As the bus lumbered toward Whitechapel, Henry shared what little he knew. "A lad has been watching the tenement but doesn't know which room Edgarton might be in, so we will have to search the building from top to bottom."

"And if Edgarton is there, how do we proceed?" Fletcher asked.

"Use whatever means necessary to arrest him and bring him in," Henry advised. "He is likely to be armed and known to carry a pistol but might also have a knife. Do not underestimate him. He is dangerous." Henry paused, thinking how the man must be feeling by now. Dangerous. Anxious. Determined to stay free. "Chances are he's desperate to keep his freedom."

"Being on the run for this long has to have him on edge," Stephens suggested. "Hopefully that will give us an advantage."

"It might," Henry agreed. "Our safety is the top priority. Stay in sight or shouting distance of one another at all times. We don't want to spread too far apart. Chances are the moment we enter the building, Edgarton will be aware of our presence."

"Yes, sir." Peters bobbed his head.

"One of us will watch from inside the front door and the other inside the back. I'll start the search on the top floor and work my way down. It's taken more than a week to have the chance to recapture him. We don't want to muddle it." Most definitely not.

Thirteen

The omnibus dropped them a few streets away, and by the time they arrived on Dorset Street, they had a basic plan. Fletcher would watch from inside the rear entrance and Peters just inside the front while Henry and Stephens conducted the search.

Those nearby watched them walk past with narrowed eyes, leaving Henry to wonder if one or more kept watch for Edgarton. That was no matter as he intended to move quickly before anyone had the chance to warn the man. Yet he hastened his pace just in case.

Once again, Marcus found him first. "'e's still there. No word on which room, though."

"Good work." Henry paid him, the money well worth it.

"Pleasure doin' business wi' ye." The boy dipped his head with a grin.

Henry hurried toward the three-story, dilapidated building and, after a nod at Fletcher and Peters, continued up the stairs with Stephens following behind. If he were Edgarton, he'd rather be on the top floor to better keep watch on the street below. Whether his guess proved correct remained to be seen—but if Edgarton was in the building and heard them and tried to flee, Fletcher or Peters would catch him.

On the third floor, Henry knocked on the first door. The constable moved to the next door to knock on it while Henry waited for a response.

Henry's nerves stretched taut as he listened for footsteps or voices from behind the door. Unfortunately, he heard nothing. After a few moments, he tried again.

Someone answered the door Stephens knocked on, and Henry braced for action.

"Betty?" the woman within replied. "Nah, no one lives 'ere by that name."

Would she tell them if it was true? She tried to shut the door, but Stephens placed a hand on it to stop her.

Henry quickly joined him, wanting a closer look at her and the room if possible.

She didn't look particularly nervous or worried by the sight of a uniformed constable at her door and insisted she didn't know anything, so Henry moved on to the next door to try his luck there.

They repeated the process until they reached the back of the building with little success. Few people answered—though it was unclear whether they weren't home or chose not to answer the door.

Henry turned to suggest to Stephens that they move down a floor when the first door they'd tried opened, and a sleepy looking Edgarton stepped out with a yawn. He looked much different from the night he'd been arrested. He'd lost weight and wore worn, ill-fitting clothing, but it was definitely Edgarton.

Everything within Henry stilled. This was it.

The man's eyes widened as he caught sight of them, then he raced down the stairs with Henry and Stephens in close pursuit.

"Halt! Police." Henry yelled as he gave chase, though he didn't think for a moment Edgarton would comply. Hopefully his shouts warned Fletcher and Peters below to be on guard given the thin walls of the building.

Edgarton moved quickly, despite his sleepy appearance, skipping several stairs to jump onto the landing and causing the flimsy handrail to crack.

Henry jumped down too, leaving Stephens to keep up with them. "Halt!" Henry called again at the top of his lungs, willing Fletcher and Peters to be prepared to stop the fleeing man.

Peters was the unlucky person at the front entrance and though he braced himself to stop Edgarton, the criminal pushed past him with little effort. "S-Stop!" the constable called as he tried to right himself, managing to step directly into Henry's path.

"Move," Henry ordered with a yell and shoved him aside to pursue Edgarton.

He had to catch the fugitive—he had to end this.

From the shouts behind him, Henry presumed Stephens and Fletcher had encountered the same problem, with Peters being more of a nuisance than help. Blast it all—how had it already gone so wrong?

Edgarton sprinted along the busy street, easily dodging those in his way. He darted down an alleyway with Henry chasing after him, hoping one of his men was near enough to see where they turned and follow.

The cobblestones beneath Henry's feet were slick with grime and the rain. More than once, he caught himself on a building to keep from falling as he ran. Edgarton turned at the end of the alley and Henry did the same, already fearing the other officers would be too far behind to follow their crooked path—but that couldn't be helped.

The escaped prisoner glanced over his shoulder as if to see if he'd lost Henry, only to run faster when he realized he hadn't. Then Edgarton darted around a corner. When Henry rounded it, the man was nowhere to be seen.

Henry slowed his steps, out of breath as he scanned the area. The man had to be hiding somewhere nearby. The street was busy and noisy with people, carts, and wagons, all going about their business. With so much to see, it was difficult to find anyone.

A glance over Henry's shoulder didn't show any of his men arriving as of yet, but he couldn't wait and risk losing Edgarton.

He continued forward, not bothering to ask anyone when it seemed unlikely they would offer aid. Businesses and shops lined the street and it was impossible to know whether Edgarton had entered one. Henry didn't want to risk a thorough search of any for fear Edgarton would slip away while he was inside.

Blast it all—he needed a hundred men, not three, and still that might not be enough!

He examined the people on the street to see if any hinted at where the man was hiding, while he continued to look for a sign of him. The thought of returning to Scotland Yard with Edgarton in hand was a heady one, something that would help regain his own credibility with both his peers and the Director.

He had to find him.

Besides, Henry couldn't dismiss the idea that Edgarton had something to do with the missing scarab, though it seemed unlikely he would've risked entering the Yard to take it.

There had to be a connection between them of some sort. Henry need only determine what—or who—it was.

A narrow, dark corridor between two tall buildings drew Henry's interest—it looked like the perfect place for Edgarton to hide. Henry hesitated, looking around to see if any other options were visible, but he had to make a decision. He couldn't just stand here, waiting for Edgarton to throw himself into the waiting arms of the law.

Henry peered down the length of the alleyway, but the shadows of the towering buildings concealed anything that might be waiting there. All he knew was that it looked to be an ideal place to hide, one he would use if on the run.

With a deep breath, he started down the length of it, moving carefully in the dim light, feet slipping on the damp earth. Worry prickled that he'd made an error and that the prisoner was fleeing at this very moment, but Henry continued forward, blinking as his eyes adjusted to the dimness, hoping he'd made the correct choice and that the other officers weren't far behind.

They had to catch him.

He'd ventured halfway down the dark lane when shouts from the street had him turning to listen. Had one of his men spotted Edgarton elsewhere while Henry wasted time here? The worry had him rushing toward the entrance.

He had nearly reached the street when movement out of the corner of his eye caught his notice—a man in a doorway.

Henry reacted a moment too late. An arm, strong and desperate, snaked around his throat from behind, and the image of Cobb's bruised neck jumped into his mind. He tugged on the arm with both hands as hard as he could. He was not going to die that way—

The sight of a knife blade before his eyes had him stilling.

"Damn you, Field," Edgarton's voice sneered. "You should've left well enough alone. Left *me* alone. I am not the only one involved, you idiot."

It took a moment for the growling words to sink in. "What—do you—mean?" Henry managed, the hold on his neck making it difficult to breathe, let alone speak.

"Take a look closer to home, Field. Do you think I got where I am without help?"

Was he talking about the Yard? Was someone there on his payroll? "The—scarab," Henry bit out, desperate for air. He jerked on the arm with little effect then threw a punch over his shoulder, striking flesh.

Edgarton grunted then tightened his grip, preventing Henry from doing it again and making stars pop in the corners of his eyes. Yet to Henry's surprise, he didn't feel the pierce of the knife in his flesh. "Exactly. That wasn't me—and I didn't kill Cobb, even if he did die like this." He flexed his arm, briefly cutting off Henry's air.

"Then—who?" Henry managed between gasps, filled with disbelief. Why should he believe anything the man said? He would've asked, but speaking had become impossible when he couldn't breathe.

"You'll figure it out. I have enough problems to worry about without solving yours."

With his vision quickly narrowing, Henry struggled harder against the man's hold. Unable to break free, he went limp, hoping the weight of his body would break Edgarton's grip.

A moment later, he was sitting in the muck of the alley gasping for air, throat aching, as he heard footsteps running in the opposite direction. His thoughts swirled with what Edgarton had said, even as frustration mounted that he'd lost the escaped prisoner.

Damn. What more could possibly go wrong today?

Fourteen

A MELIA STARED OUT THE window of her laboratory, unable to concentrate, discomfort twisting in her stomach. The sight of the constable walking up and down the street below only worsened the feeling.

The gloomy day was barely half over, and already she felt restless—and she placed the blame solely at Miles Edgarton's feet. She couldn't help but think that if he were back in prison, she wouldn't be in this state of limbo where she could neither go forward nor backward. Instead she was simply waiting, her life on hold once again. It was exhausting to stay on guard, constantly be looking over her shoulder, wondering what might happen next.

Where could the man be?

From what little she'd learned from Henry after the murderer's initial arrest, Edgarton was a self-made man, having come from a rookery. His house and businesses had been searched for stolen artifacts then locked tight. He clearly couldn't return to any of them.

The police had arrested a few of the employees at the shipping business and several of those involved in the lottery scheme had been charged with crimes. They'd also questioned his servants but learned little that was truly useful from them. And anyway, anything they said could be lies, couldn't it?

Henry had said he didn't know if Edgarton was still in London, but *someone* had to know *something*. Surely any family he had lived in the area if he'd been born and raised there? Without additional details, it must be difficult for the police to know where to look.

There was one person she knew who was acquainted with Edgarton—Mr. Oscar Powell. Matthew had supposedly used the man's expertise to verify the authenticity of some of the items he'd sold. Only recently had she learned that Mr. Powell, who also served as the Director of the Wexley House Museum, had gone further and assisted Matthew in sourcing the illegal antiques.

That involvement had caused Mr. Powell to be investigated for his involvement, but to her knowledge, he had not been arrested. Whether that was because he'd chosen to provide evidence against Edgarton or hadn't been guilty of a crime, Amelia didn't know.

Her fingers tapped on the worktable in her laboratory, breaking the silence. Though she knew the man had been questioned at length after Edgarton's arrest, she doubted the police had spoken with him since the prisoner's escape. The connection between Edgarton and Mr. Powell had been tenuous at best. But perhaps a visit with Mr. Powell—with the constable along, of course—could prove helpful.

Pleased to have something productive to do, even if Henry almost certainly wouldn't approve, she tidied the worktable, returned her apron to the peg by the door, and went downstairs.

She collected her cloak and other things from her bedchamber, then continued down to find Fernsby.

Well aware he would be concerned for her safety, she thought through her plan again. The chance of experiencing any danger was slim, and if the constable accompanied her, that would lessen the risk even more. Mr. Powell didn't seem the violent type, and the fact he hadn't been arrested reflected his limited involvement.

Of course, convincing Fernsby of that wasn't easy.

"Are you certain such an outing is necessary?" the butler asked, his pained expression making his opinion on her plan clear.

Amelia drew herself up firmly. She appreciated his concern for her safety but needed to feel useful in some way. "No," she answered honestly. "But what if Mr. Powell could help? We would be able to rid ourselves of having the constable sooner rather than later, and...and Matthew's killer would be brought to justice."

He sighed, a subtle sign he wished for the same thing she did. "Allow me to send for a cab and advise the constable of your intention."

"Thank you, Fernsby."

Twenty minutes later, she was riding in the hansom cab with Constable Dannon standing on the small step next to the driver.

She was pleased Dannon was the one accompanying her, if a police officer had to. He'd helped guard the house during the ravenkeeper case; she liked him and had faith in his skills.

Unfortunately, she couldn't say the same about every officer she'd come to know over the last few months.

It didn't take long to arrive at the Wexley House Museum, a large three-story house in a quiet residential neighborhood. At Henry's behest, she'd visited the museum a few weeks ago to tell Mr. Powell that one of her late husband's clients had contacted her about obtaining Egyptian artifacts. That had been a lie, admittedly—but immediately after hearing it, Mr. Powell had led Henry to Edgarton, which helped to prove he was involved in the crime.

Trepidation stirred within her at the idea of conversing with Mr. Powell again, but he was the one who'd been in the wrong, not her. Whether he was willing to speak with her remained to be seen. He might very well request she leave. Hopefully Amelia could convince him to answer a few questions before that.

Though the errand would be challenging, she need only remember how good it had felt to have uncovered justice for Matthew and how relieved she'd been after Edgarton was in prison. She wanted to feel that way again: to be able to sleep peacefully at night and not continually look out the window for trouble during the day.

And perhaps she could do something to make that happen.

With a lift of her chin, she gathered her confidence as Constable Dannon offered a hand to help her alight from the cab.

"There is a chance I will be asked to leave," she advised the officer in an undertone, feeling it was only fair to warn him.

"Oh?" The constable's brow furrowed. "Shall I insist otherwise?"

"No. I'd understand if Mr. Powell doesn't wish to speak with me after our last conversation created more than a few problems for him. You never know, he might welcome the opportunity to improve his standing with the police."

"I see." The constable paused, eyes narrowed. "Actually, I don't. What exactly would you like me to do?"

In truth, she would prefer he waited in the cab, but that was unlikely to be accepted. Perhaps she could use his presence in some manner. "If you could nod a time or two in support of my questions...my inquiries, that would be helpful."

Constable Dannon only looked more confused, but instead of offering additional insight she continued up the steps to the door, preferring not to explain the situation in full.

She didn't want to alarm the constable by advising him ahead of time that she was trying to help search for clues regarding Edgarton's whereabouts. Hopefully the officer would catch on quickly enough if Powell could be pressed into telling anything he knew.

That, or else this would be a wasted trip.

"Allow me, Mrs. Greystone." The constable hurried forward to open the door.

"Thank you." She was counting on those same good manners to aid her in the next few minutes. As polite as the constable was, he was still likely to interrupt her when he realized her intent.

A familiar chime sounded from the depths of the large house, which had been converted from a home to a museum to display the late owner's collection. She had the constable's presence to thank for not being nearly as nervous for this visit as she had been for her last one, when she had ventured in alone.

The foyer looked similar to what she remembered, the walls lined in wood paneling and the floor covered in a rich black and cream tile. The same musty smell as before had her nose twitching.

"Would you look at that?" Constable Dannon moved to examine a nearby knight's suit of armor that stood in the corner. With great interest, he reached out a tentative finger to touch the pommel of the sword propped in the knight's metal glove. "Never seen the like of it."

"Please do not touch the exhibits," a male voice commanded from above them.

Amelia turned to see Mr. Powell descending the stairs.

"Sorry sir," the constable murmured with an apologetic look.

She returned her attention to Mr. Powell, rather enjoying the dismay that tightened his features when he recognized her.

"Oh. Mrs. Greystone." His steps slowed. "What a...surprise."

An unpleasant one, she would guess. "Mr. Powell. I trust you are well."

"Er..." The museum director glanced between them, clearly perplexed and most definitely concerned by their presence. "Yes. Quite. Quite. And you, madam?"

"Well, thank you." She chose not to introduce the constable, preferring that Mr. Powell wonder at the reason for his presence even as her heart raced. "For the most part, at any rate." She fluttered her lashes as she dropped her gaze to the floor. Such antics had worked well during her previous visit. Would they again?

"Oh?"

She returned her gaze to Mr. Powell and leaned slightly forward. "I'm sure *you* have heard the concerning news."

"News?" His face flushed as he again looked between her and the constable, appearing thoroughly confused by not only their arrival but what she was saying. "Concerning?"

"Of Miles Edgarton's escape from prison." Surely the best way to manage the situation was to act as if the man had duped and betrayed both her and Mr. Powell.

"Um." Mr. Powell's eyes widened, clearly uncertain how to respond.

She glanced around the foyer as if the criminal might be lurking in the shadows. "Has he contacted you?"

"Me?" The man's voice squeaked, and his eyes nearly bulged from his head.

"No?" Amelia pressed a hand to her chest. "Thank goodness. I'm sure he is as unhappy with you as he is with me."

Constable Dannon's head tilted as he listened, clearly intrigued by the conversation. Well, that was fine—as long as he didn't disagree with what she said.

"I-I—" The man blinked rapidly as if panic was setting in. His one-word answers were rather entertaining, but she hoped to learn more from him.

"I can't imagine how he managed to escape." Amelia shook her head, took another step closer, and lowered her voice. "You may have heard that he's suspected of...killing my late husband."

She didn't have to pretend distress or the tremble in her voice.

Amelia drew a steadying breath. Even saying that weakened her knees. This wasn't a game; she couldn't forget for a moment what Edgarton had done. He'd taken Matthew's life, along with many others, forever changing her own.

Mr. Powell's throat bobbed alarmingly as he swallowed, then he slowly nodded. "I...I did hear something along those lines."

Once again Amelia gathered her thoughts, remembering her purpose. "I can't help but wonder where he could be." She lifted a brow. "Do you have any idea? Perhaps he spoke of other people he worked with? Did he ever mention his family?"

"We weren't friends, you understand." The older man rubbed a finger along his upper lip where a tidy narrow moustache resided.

"Of course not." Amelia shook her head. "Why would you be friends with a criminal? I just thought he might have mentioned something in passing during a conversation. You spoke on numerous occasions, did you not—before you knew of his ignominy, naturally?" She had to believe that as he'd gone to the man's home to speak with him about her request for the artifacts. That suggested a certain amount of familiarity.

"I did." His chest puffed out with self-importance. "I knew him for several years."

"Oh?" Amelia nodded but held her silence with the hope he would add more.

"Did—" Constable Dannon began only to halt when Amelia sent him a warning look. He quickly shook his head when Mr. Powell looked at him. "Never mind," he muttered and took a step back, his attention returning to the armor.

"You were saying?" Amelia prompted the man.

"Well." Mr. Powell hesitated, a bead of sweat appearing on his brow. "I don't remember him mentioning much about his personal life."

"Surely he shared a few details. Did he collect any of the Egyptian artifacts?"

"A limited number. Mr. Edgarton seemed to find it amusing that the wealthy enjoyed collecting them, but he didn't share the same level of interest."

She nodded again to encourage him, willing him to remember more. She had to be close to something.

"He preferred more practical items, though he had several wonderful paintings in his house."

Probably stolen along with the artifacts, Amelia thought but kept her opinion to herself.

Mr. Powell stared across the foyer, eyes narrowing as he tried to remember. "He wasn't married, but he did mention his mother once or twice. She favors pearls, and he was always looking for unique pieces for her."

"She lives here, in London?"

"Yes, though he never said where exactly."

Amelia did her best to hide her disappointment and offered an encouraging smile instead.

The man returned her smile awkwardly. "He still has ties to Whitechapel, where he was born, and visited often prior to his arrest."

"Perhaps his mother lives there still," Amelia murmured.

"No, he moved her into a fine house with servants, something that seemed to please them both."

Had the woman known how he'd paid for her new life? Had she taken pride in her child just like every mother did? Did she think him a respectable, legitimate businessman, not realizing how ruthless he was?

It was odd to think of Edgarton having a soft spot for anyone, even his mother. But no one was entirely evil or entirely good, for that matter. Everyone had shades of both within them.

What had driven him to the path he'd taken?

"Did he mention his father?" she asked out of curiosity. Surely the more they learned about him, the better.

The moustache twitched. "His father died when he was ten, but he didn't have much good to say about him, only that he was harsh and drank too much."

Edgarton's childhood likely hadn't been easy if he'd grown up in Whitechapel, Amelia could not help but think, but that was no excuse for what he'd done.

"I have to wonder if he would keep his mother fairly close if she was alone."

Mr. Powell's eyes lit up. "I think you're right. I remember him saying her house was within walking distance of his, though I can't think of anything else he said."

"He didn't mention the street?" She needed more, something specific that would truly help Henry find him.

"No. I wish I could be of more help." Mr. Powell heaved a sigh. "It is unnerving to think he could make an appearance at any moment."

"Especially when he knows where to find you." Amelia held the man's gaze to allow him time to consider that truth. The same was true for her, of course, but a part of her wanted Mr.

Powell to be as worried as she was. "If you happen to remember anything else, I would certainly like to know—and the police would appreciate hearing about it, too."

"We would indeed," Constable Dannon added when she sent him a pointed look. "The sooner he's off the streets, the better. Safer for us all."

"Yes, of course." Mr. Powell nodded. "I will give my previous conversations with him further thought."

"I'm pleased to hear that. We will wish you a good day." Amelia turned to go, with Constable Dannon stepping forward to open the door, but the museum director's forthcoming words stopped her in her tracks.

"Do take care, Mrs. Greystone," Mr. Powell said quietly. "Mr. Edgarton wasn't pleased to hear your name when I mentioned it prior to his arrest."

Amelia turned to glare at the fussy man. "I can't say that I appreciate you mentioning it to him. A rather ungentlemanly thing to do, in my opinion."

Mr. Powell's mouth gaped even as his cheeks turned an unflattering shade of pink. Constable Dannon's low chuckle confirmed that she'd struck her target.

With that, she turned on her heels and departed, hoping never to see Mr. Powell again. Whether what little he'd shared would help was unclear, but it couldn't hurt, and she liked feeling useful.

Even if his final words were an unnecessary reminder of just how much danger she was in.

Fifteen

"**A**RE YOU ALL RIGHT?**"** Fletcher arrived in time to see the escaped prisoner fleeing around the corner. "Was that Edgarton?" he asked breathlessly.

Henry nodded in answer to both questions, his throat sore, his lungs tight. The sergeant tore down the dark corridor, nearly losing his footing as he rounded the same corner in hasty pursuit. The rain had returned, a steady drizzle that made the alley even more slippery.

Pressing an unsteady hand against the brick building, Henry gained his feet, legs trembling, all too aware of his aches and pains, especially his throat. Thank goodness Edgarton hadn't used the knife. The thought made him grateful that he could stand.

He considered it a miracle Fletcher had located him, given the winding path he'd taken while giving chase.

But it wasn't over. As long as he had breath in his body, he would use it to find Edgarton, injuries be damned. He paused long enough to retrieve his hat, taking one more hoarse breath, and then ran after them as fast as he could manage, silently cursing the burning in his throat.

"Watch it!" a man shouted when Henry nearly plowed into him as he made it to the street.

"Sorry," Henry muttered, searching for sight of Fletcher and Edgarton as he continued in the same direction he'd last seen them.

"Inspector Field!"

Henry turned to see Stephens nearly upon him. He gestured for the man to hurry and pointed ahead.

Without a word, Stephens sped his pace to a sprint and quickly disappeared among the passersby.

Henry followed, frustrated that he couldn't match the younger man's pace—not with his body weakened from the attack and his lungs desperate for the air which had been denied them. As fast as he could manage, he wound through the young and old walking along the street, watching for his men and Edgarton. The prisoner was clearly adept at finding places to hide, so he kept on guard for exactly that—but the man grew up here, he knew every alley and crevice. How could he compete with him?

Henry had crossed two streets when he found Fletcher and Stephens on a corner looking about, both out of breath.

"Anything?" he asked, his voice raspy.

"I lost him." Fletcher shook his head, his frustration obvious. "For a moment, I thought I—" He looked at Henry as he spoke, eyes widening as he stared. "Your neck. What happened?"

"An encounter with..." Henry cleared his throat, causing it to burn like the devil. He tugged on his shirt collar, but that didn't help the pain. "Edgarton." His voice was so hoarse that the name was barely recognizable.

"Sir?" Stephens looked him over incredulously from head to toe before his gaze held on Henry's neck. "Are you certain you're well?"

The examination made Henry aware of the cold dampness of whatever muck he'd fallen into, sticking to his clothing in several places. The stench wafted up to him, strong enough to convince him not to examine it too closely.

"He damn near choked you to death," Fletcher accused, eyes dark with worry.

"If that had...truly been his intent...I'd be dead," Henry managed. "He had a knife but didn't use it. He gave more of a warning...of sorts." That was what he preferred to believe. Otherwise Edgarton wouldn't have bothered to speak to him.

"Hell of a warning. You could've ended up like Cobb." The sergeant touched a hand to his own throat as if easily able to imagine how it must've felt.

"I didn't." Henry detested how hoarse he sounded and how shaken he felt.

"Did he say anything?"

How much did he share about what Edgarton had said? The man's oblique warning that someone with the police couldn't be trusted echoed in Henry's mind. The very thought made him ill, even though he'd already had that suspicion when the missing evidence had come to light.

But he couldn't distrust everyone—and he refused to believe Fletcher was involved.

"Only..." Henry swallowed, his voice slowly returning. "Only that I should leave well enough alone. That he didn't do this without help, and I should look closer to home."

Henry considered the most likely candidates, Perdy coming immediately to mind. Fletcher's uncle, Clarke, was a close second. Wasn't it interesting that Edgarton had escaped soon after Clarke's arrival at Scotland Yard? Then there was Whitlock, another inspector Henry had reservations about. But he didn't want to say too much in front of Stephens—and besides, he might be wrong. Was this his professional life now, flinching from shadows?

"What's that supposed to mean? Was he talking about the prison guard helping him escape?" Fletcher frowned, clearly puzzled.

"I don't know. Perhaps. Or maybe someone at the Yard." Henry shook his head, still frustrated, chest still tight. "I only wish I'd seen him before he grabbed me. I was halfway down that corridor when I heard a clatter from the street and thought I must've missed him. So I headed back toward the shouts. Edgarton was hiding in the doorway. I missed him on the way by."

"No wonder, as dark as it was." Fletcher frowned. "We should have a doctor look at your neck."

"It's fine." Henry didn't say that he felt as weak as a kitten or that he was more unsettled than he cared to admit. At least his tongue didn't feel swollen, something often seen in the victims of attempted strangulation.

Victim. He detested thinking of himself as one. That he'd allowed Edgarton to get the better of him annoyed him—and anger felt preferable to fear.

With a deep breath he started forward, continuing to study the noisy, bustling street on the unlikely chance the man lingered nearby. "Where did Peters get to?"

"When I last saw him, he was limping along behind us as we left the tenement." Fletcher stretched tall to look over the area. "I suppose we should return in that direction to see if we can find him."

They found the constable waiting for them on the next street corner.

"Must've twisted my ankle when the fugitive shoved me," Peters muttered apologetically, his cheeks shamefaced. "Hurts like hell. Thought I'd be more help watching for Edgarton from here, where I could see several street crossings, but I haven't seen him."

Would he have told them if he had, Henry wondered. There was every chance Edgarton had come by that very spot after leaving Henry and eluding Fletcher.

Damnit. He couldn't operate alone, he had to trust.

Though perhaps not completely.

"What happened?" Peters looked between them and finally appeared to notice the marks on Henry's neck. His brow furrowed, his expression similar to Stephens' when he'd noticed them. "Did he try to kill you?" The constable asked as he took in Henry's appearance.

"It seems he doesn't wish to return to prison," Henry advised wryly, his voice still a rasp.

"He nearly took your voice." Peters shook his head, seeming astonished. "You're lucky he didn't take your life too."

"If you don't mind me asking, how did you get away, sir?" Stephens asked as he frowned at Henry's throat. "He's a bull of a man."

"Played dead." It wasn't glamorous, but it had been effective.

"How do you mean?" Stephen's brow further furrowed.

"He had a hold of me from the back." Henry bent his arm and held it near his neck to demonstrate. "I went limp, a dead weight. It forced him to let go or follow me to the ground."

"Huh." Fletcher nodded with approval. "Clever. I'm not sure I would've thought to do that. Not in the heat of the moment."

"You would be surprised what comes to mind in those moments," Henry answered. He'd experienced more than his fair share. "Let's...let's have another look at the rooms Edgarton was staying in."

Though he was more than ready to find a place to sit down for a few minutes and have a cold drink, he couldn't miss the opportunity to learn more about where the escaped prisoner had been lying low.

"Filthy coppers!"

A smattering of uncomplimentary shouts followed them as they walked along, a reminder that the police were not well liked in the rougher areas of the city. Perhaps that had happened when Henry had raced past the first time, but he hadn't heard them, too focused on pursuing Edgarton.

A pursuit which had not ended well.

"I'm relieved not to be part of H Division," Stephens muttered. "This wouldn't be an easy area to police."

"No, it wouldn't." Henry had sent word to the chief inspector of the Leman Street Police Station, the main station for

Whitechapel, to be on the lookout for Edgarton directly after he'd escaped.

"Agreed," Fletcher said. "Though I suppose it's like any other beat. One gets to know the warehouses, shops, and pubs along the way and the people who frequent them."

He was right; and it was those connections that could help make a constable successful in preventing crimes.

"I doubt Betty Knox remained home after our previous visit to her building," Henry advised in his raspy voice, "but we will have a look around to see what we can find." He quickened his pace. It wouldn't do to dawdle, no matter how poorly he felt.

They soon returned to the run-down building. Henry searched for Marcus nearby but didn't see the lad anywhere. He gestured for Fletcher to accompany him upstairs, leaving Stephens and Peters to keep watch outside.

As he'd suspected, no one answered their knock on the door that Edgarton had emerged from.

Fletcher tried the knob and found it unlocked. "No harm looking inside, eh? We'll say it stood open if asked."

Well, Henry wasn't opposed to bending a few rules, especially in cases like this when they had probable cause. He followed Fletcher into the miserable rooms, unable to imagine living there.

Two wooden chairs and a scuffed table sat in the front room, along with an empty crate turned upside down, which apparently served as another table. In the back, a sagging bed stood in one corner with ragged bedclothes strewn over a dirty mattress. Paint peeled from the walls, or perhaps it had been wallpaper years ago. It was difficult to know. A bit of rag was stuffed into a hole in the wall to keep out the cold, but it hadn't managed to prevent the damp. The windowsill was crooked, suggesting it would be impossible to open even if one wanted to.

"Rather homey, eh?" Fletcher asked in a quiet voice, a scowl on his face. "It does appear as though a woman has recently been here."

Henry followed Fletcher's gaze to a faded striped gown hanging on a peg near the bed and a brush on the bedside table. Other than a few items of clothing, there was nothing that offered a clue about Edgarton and certainly nothing to search.

The place was more than depressing and spoke to Edgarton's desperation that he would stay there, when compared to the fine house he'd lived in previously. But he hadn't had much choice, had he?

"Did Edgarton say anything else?" Fletcher asked as he studied Henry.

He hesitated, debating what more to add. While the sergeant might feel loyalty to his uncle, his years on the force couldn't be ignored. He'd earned Henry's trust. "He seemed to know the scarab was missing. And he said he didn't kill Cobb."

Fletcher's gaze dropped to Henry's neck. "And should we believe any of that?"

"At the very least, we will take it into account."

"Terrible to think someone at the Yard has sunk to that level." Fletcher shook his head. "Who could it be?"

"It's up to us to determine that answer." Henry glanced around. He'd seen enough. "Let's go."

Fletcher nodded and led the way out the door only to turn back, his concerned gaze holding on Henry. "After we're safely out of Whitechapel, let's send the constables back to the Yard to make reports while you and I have a meal and a pint. You look like you could use both."

The idea sounded more than appealing, considering how much his throat burned, but duty came first. "We must update Reynolds on our efforts first and see if anything was discovered about the scarab in our absence." Henry dreaded telling Reynolds of the failed attempt to recapture Edgarton. The Director would not be pleased.

Less than a half-hour later, Henry and Fletcher were sitting in the Director's office, telling him of the near miss.

"Blast it." Reynolds looked between them. "I won't say I'm not disappointed."

"As are we, sir," Henry advised, shifting in his seat as his superior's attention returned to his presumably bruised neck.

"I'm relieved you weren't injured any worse." The older man frowned. "Shouldn't you have a physician look at that throat of yours?"

"It'll be fine." Henry could still talk and swallow, even if doing either hurt.

"We were close, sir." Fletcher shook his head. "Next time, we'll have him."

"Will there be a next time?" Reynolds lifted a brow.

Fletcher wisely held his silence, as did Henry. He had no intention of making promises he couldn't keep.

The Dhirector blew out a breath into the silence, rubbing a hand along the back of his own neck. "First a prisoner escaped, then evidence is discovered missing, now we've lost a chance to recapture the prisoner. These issues reflect poorly on us all. I can only imagine what will happen if Fleet Street decides to make the same list into a story."

Henry wished once again that he'd returned with good news, his stomach twisting. "As is always the case, someone has to know something." How many times did he tell himself that over the course of an investigation? "We will continue to pursue all potential leads until we solve these cases."

"At the moment we're opening more cases than closing them." Reynolds was clearly frustrated. He shook his head, only to hold up a hand to stop Henry from saying anything further. "I know you are doing all you can. I certainly don't like what Edgarton told you." He stared across his office, seemingly deep in thought. "Keep what he said between us three for now. I will continue to search for the golden scarab while you look for Edgarton."

Henry held back from voicing his own concerns about certain individuals within the force, especially when one of them was Fletcher's uncle. Who could be trusted? Did he dare do some digging of his own to see what he could discover? In truth, he wasn't comfortable leaving it to others when his own integrity was in jeopardy.

But how would it look if it were discovered that he'd started investigating those he worked with?

When the Director picked up his pen and returned his attention to the papers on his desk, Henry stood, deciding they'd been dismissed. Fletcher did the same.

"And Field?"

"Sir?"

"Do something about that damned throat. You sound terrible."

"Yes, sir." Henry didn't think there was much he could do to ease it, though he appreciated the Director expressing concern about his wellbeing.

Take a look closer to home, Field. Do you think I got where I am without help?

Who would aid the criminal mastermind—had possibly been doing so for some time? Why had he chosen to tell Henry any of what he had instead of killing him?

Somehow Henry needed to find Edgarton, locate the scarab, and discover who within the police force had tried to frame him for the missing evidence.

There wasn't a moment to lose.

Sixteen

THE NEXT FEW HOURS left Henry frustrated, a dog chasing its tail. Despite the urgency filling him, there was only so much he could do.

While he'd been in Whitechapel the evidence room had been thoroughly searched, and all officers with their names recently in the ledger interviewed. Unfortunately the scarab had not been found, nor was there any obvious clue as to who had taken it.

He'd given a brief version of his encounter with Edgarton more times than he cared to, which only made his throat hurt more—but given the marks on his neck, it was nearly impossible to avoid. Those who happened to be at the Yard had shown sympathy, with the exception of Perdy. That was no surprise.

Luncheon with Fletcher had been brief as the sergeant's uncle had requested his nephew's assistance on a case, so Fletcher had been pressed for time and had left early. Henry hadn't minded since swallowing was painful, even if drinking a pint had temporarily helped.

Henry returned to the Yard and spoke with several other inspectors to try to determine a list of unofficial suspects regarding the missing evidence. It was unfortunate that the few officers he'd spoken with didn't have any ideas. Leaving the matter to Reynolds to look into didn't sit well, but he hoped the Director was having better luck than he was.

Shifting his focus to finding Edgarton, Henry ventured back to Whitechapel mid-afternoon, this time by himself. He kept a careful watch for both Marcus and Edgarton as he walked. The lad had proven helpful, and he wanted to hire him again, if he could. Trouble was, the lad would be impossible to find—

"'eard things didn't go yer way this mornin'," Marcus said, appearing at his side out of nowhere just off Dorset Street.

"Certainly not as I'd hoped," Henry said in his raspy voice.

The lad's eyes widened as he caught sight of Henry's neck. "I'll say. That 'ad to 'urt."

Henry didn't bother to agree. "I'm still searching for the man and would be happy to pay for any information that leads to his arrest."

Marcus nodded. "'appy to keep my ears open and an eye on the place 'e was stayin' at."

After paying him and reminding him to be careful, Henry continued on his way, questioning the few people he came upon who were willing to speak with him, though they were few and far between. None of his inquiries provided any new information about Edgarton or Betty Knox.

As the day drew to a close, the chill sinking through his coat, he returned to the Yard to update his notes on Edgarton's case file, wishing he had more to add to it.

"Message for you, Field." Sergeant Johnson handed him an envelope.

"Thanks." Henry studied Johnson's expression to gauge his reaction to the events of the day. Much to his relief, the sergeant didn't act any differently toward him.

Despite his concerns, it seemed clear that few at the Yard believed Henry had anything to do with the missing scarab—despite Perdy's attempt to convince them otherwise.

Henry glanced at the envelope, ridiculously pleased to recognize Amelia's neat feminine script. He quickly scanned her request to stop by after he was done for the day to meet with her aunt regarding the stolen money that Amelia had mentioned previously. Amelia also noted that if he were otherwise engaged, she would arrange another time for him to meet with her Aunt Margaret.

Henry touched his neck, tempted to refuse. He would rather not explain what had happened, especially when he didn't want to worry Amelia. However it would take days, if not longer, before his injuries were less noticeable. Perhaps it would be best if he shared the news now.

She wasn't the only one he needed to speak with—his father was still well connected and well respected within Scotland Yard and would soon learn of the day's unfortunate events. Better that he told his own version of the tale before someone else did. The task was not one he relished. What would his father's reaction be?

His unease was ridiculous when Thurmond Field had always been supportive, but that didn't alleviate Henry's concern that he would disappoint him. No matter how many times Henry told himself his adoption didn't change the love his parents had for him, he couldn't forget that they'd given him his surname, rather than being born with it.

The disconcerting thought had Henry pushing to his feet. The day had already proved to be a miserable one. Why not get it all over with the hope of putting it behind him and make a fresh start on the morrow?

"Rough day, eh?" Duncan, a fellow inspector Henry admired, paused before his desk.

"That's an understatement." Henry braced himself as he met the older man's gaze, prepared to see the same questions in his eyes that a couple of his fellow officers had, even if they hadn't asked them.

Instead, sympathy warmed Duncan's brown eyes as his gaze held briefly on Henry's throat. "Edgarton is a nasty one."

"He is," Henry readily agreed. "Just as you warned me."

Concern tightened Duncan's expression at the sound of Henry's raspy voice. "I heard you returned to Whitechapel again this afternoon."

How had Duncan learned that? "I did. You might say I'm determined to find him."

"I suppose I would feel the same." Duncan glanced away before looking back at him. "My money's on you, Field. Let me know how I can help."

Surprise filtered through Henry, the other inspector's words welcome, especially after his own doubts about what the other officers thought. "Thank you. I appreciate that."

Duncan frowned. "Can't imagine who took the scarab." His narrowed gaze swung around the mostly empty office. "Makes you look at everyone differently."

"Yes, it does." Henry hesitated to say more, but one thing was already clear—he couldn't solve the cases on his own. He needed help, and that meant trusting selected others. Should he follow his gut, which suggested Duncan should be one of them?

"Any ideas?" the man asked, one brow lifted as if sensing Henry had more to say.

"Ideas, yes. Proof, no." Henry shook his head, hesitant to be the first to name names. How could he, with no evidence?

"Ideas are where queries start in my experience." Duncan leaned closer and lowered his voice. "Perdy?"

Henry smiled with barely veiled relief, pleased to know he wasn't alone in his suspicion. "Well, he's never liked me. Doesn't take much imagination to think of him doing something to cast me in a poor light."

"He's envious of you. That makes him worth watching."

Henry nodded, a reprieve from today's tension washing through him. He wasn't seeing things, then. "Do you know much about Whitlock?"

"Not nearly enough. Something seems off about him. Nor do I care for the new one."

"Clarke?"

Duncan nodded, seriously. "I have always liked and respected Fletcher, but I can't say his uncle has made a good impression."

"Good to know I'm not the only one who feels that way."

"Why don't I do a little poking around? See what I can discover about the three of them. They've been a bit too friendly with one another of late."

Henry drew a quick breath, relieved—and touched—by the quiet offer. The moment made him realize just how alone he'd felt the last few hours. "I'd appreciate that."

"If you start asking questions, everyone will know what you're up to. Better if someone else does it."

"Agreed." Henry had learned as much earlier that day.

Duncan nodded slowly. "It might prove advantageous if I act friendly with them instead of you. I should learn more that way."

"Understood." That didn't mean Henry liked it. But he couldn't deny a tiny light of hope building within him to think of Duncan helping him.

"Meanwhile...watch your back, Field." With that, the other man walked away.

Seventeen

With Duncan's warning ringing in his ears, Henry reached for his coat and hat, tucking Amelia's message in his pocket before donning his gloves and making his way toward her home.

The threat of rain remained, making the evening a dark one. The brisk air helped clear his head but he kept a careful watch as he walked, willing to admit at least to himself how jumpy he felt.

It was interesting that Duncan knew of his return to Whitechapel when he hadn't told anyone. Who was watching him? Fletcher had left with his uncle before Henry, so even he hadn't known, though he'd advised Sergeant Johnson as he'd left.

In the future he needed to take better care and have someone accompany him. The events of the day had made him foolhardy, and he couldn't allow that to happen again. Recklessness would gain him nothing other than more bruises on his neck—or worse. Neither could he watch his own back all the time.

Henry arrived at Amelia's without incident, spoke with the constable patrolling the street who had nothing to report, then greeted Fernsby warmly when the butler opened the door.

"Another brisk evening, Inspector," Fernsby said as he took Henry's things. "However before we know it, spring will arrive along with warmer temperatures." His movements paused as he noted the marks on Henry's neck, but he said nothing, though he appeared concerned.

"The reminder of spring coming is appreciated," Henry replied with a smile, deciding not to explain what had happened. His instincts, instincts he wasn't going to examine too closely, told him to share it with Amelia first. "It still feels too far away based on the current weather."

"Indeed. Mrs. Greystone and Miss Baldwin are in the drawing room, sir. I believe they were hoping you might stop by."

"Thank you." Though he'd already known her aunt would be there, he couldn't stop a pang of disappointment that he wouldn't have Amelia to himself.

Then again, this would only be a brief visit for business rather than pleasure. Seeing her on any given day was welcome, no matter the reason.

He paused in the doorway of the drawing room to see Amelia and her aunt conversing lightly in the chairs before the fire.

"Henry." Amelia stood with a welcoming smile. "I thought I heard you arrive."

He took in her attractive, tidy appearance in her usual gray gown, noting the moment she noticed his neck. There was no point in trying to hide the marks when his hoarseness would give away the injury. "Good evening."

"What happened?" Amelia stiffened, concern tightening her expression at the rough sound of his voice. "You are injured!"

"A bit of a problem in Whitechapel." He attempted a reassuring smile, hoping it was enough to satisfy her curiosity for now. He'd prefer not to say too much in front of her aunt, though in truth he was hardly sure how he would choose to explain it even if Amelia had been alone.

Her lips parted as if she intended to ask for details. Then, seeming to guess his thoughts, she hesitated. "Are you all right?"

"A bit bruised, and I seem to have temporarily lost some of my voice, but otherwise quite fine." He held her gaze, touched by her inquiry but wanting to reassure her that he was well.

Based on the way she continued to study his neck, he wasn't wholly successful. Then Amelia glanced at her aunt as if remembering her presence before meeting his gaze again. "I am relieved to hear that."

"It's good to see you again, Inspector Field, though I'm sorry to hear of your injury," Miss Baldwin said politely.

"A pleasure as always, ma'am." Henry bowed, the movement making him realize how stiff he was from the struggle with Edgarton. "Have no worries. I will live to see another day," he jested. The flare of alarm in Amelia's expression suggested it fell flat.

Bother. No doubt levity about such matters was ill-advised, given her husband's murder.

Uncertain of what to say to comfort her with Miss Baldwin watching them closely, he turned to the older woman, deciding it best to move on to the matter at hand so he could leave them to enjoy their evening. "Mrs. Greystone mentioned you had a bit of trouble of your own of late."

"I did, yes." Her attention shifted to Amelia. "My niece has convinced me to inquire whether it is possible to take action regarding the issue."

"If you would share the details, I will see what I can do."

"Please have a seat, Henry." Amelia gestured toward the chairs before the fire but didn't take a seat. "Proceed without me, Aunt Margaret. I will return momentarily."

She hurried from the room, leaving Henry to wonder why as he turned his attention to Miss Baldwin.

The older woman licked her lips, appearing nervous as she began the tale in a slow, halting voice until palpable anger at being duped took hold, speeding her story. "Mr. Walter Tinton and I met through a mutual friend. We spent time together starting late last summer for several months, afternoon tea, walks, that sort of thing, and we seemed to have much in common. He was so friendly and...and complimentary."

A mixture of emotions crossed the older woman's face, and it seemed clear she'd been flattered by his attention. Sympathy tugged within Henry. If this tale was going where he thought it was going...

"He didn't directly ask for money, but he made several comments that made it clear his situation was precarious. He was an accountant and had recently been forced to leave his position. He expected to receive his wages any day, but it had yet to arrive. When I offered to lend him the money, he acted so grateful. It was understood that it was a loan. I never expected him to leave the country without repaying it."

Amelia returned with Fernsby who held a tray. "I took the liberty of having some peppermint tea with honey prepared. It needs a few more minutes to steep, though. Then I expect you to finish all of it."

"Thank you." He never failed to be touched by her thoughtfulness.

"Of course," she said with a smile. Then she reached to pat her aunt's arm in a show of support.

The conversation continued and Henry wrote down the man's name, previous address, and description in his notebook, along with the other details she shared. He paused to sip the tea Amelia poured, already able to feel its soothing effect. With a few carefully worded questions to Miss Baldwin, he did his best to separate facts from supposition.

"What do you think?" Amelia asked. "Can anything be done?"

"It's obvious he took advantage of your kindness." He cleared his throat in an attempt to improve his voice, but it only made it hurt more. Another sip of the tea helped. "We will send telegrams to towns near the Channel to advise officials in the area to be on alert for him if he chooses to return. Unfortunately, without witnesses to verify your verbal agreement, the issue of the money will be difficult to prove. It would be your word against his."

Amelia's gasp of protest had him quickly continuing. "However, the man could certainly be brought in for questioning the moment he returns to England. It is surprising what someone might confess to when brought to a police station and questioned by an officer. Mr. Tinton might even be inclined to return the funds to avoid future problems."

"Good." Amelia gave a decisive nod. "I hope the scoundrel is frightened enough to tell everything and agree to return Aunt Margaret's money—and who knows how many other women have similarly suffered."

"Though I can make no promises, I think you're doing the right thing by coming forward," Henry advised Miss Baldwin with a nod of agreement. "After all, he might make a habit of stealing money, or undertaking worse." He didn't add that unmarried women of a certain age were often preyed upon by thieves, regardless of whether they had funds to spare. That would hardly help bolster the poor woman's confidence.

"I hadn't thought of that." Miss Baldwin lifted her chin, the light of relief in her eyes. "Then I'm very pleased I reported his shameless actions. I...I suppose I thought I was partly to blame since I willingly gave him the money."

"You lent him the money fully expecting to have it returned," Amelia countered, obviously on her aunt's side of the situation.

Henry appreciated her staunch support; he had also been lucky enough to be on the receiving end of it. That was only one of her many qualities he admired. No doubt her aunt appreciated it, too.

"I suppose I should have put something in writing," her aunt suggested.

"That would have been wise, but it's understandable why you didn't," Henry reassured her. "You meant it as an agreement between friends. First, we shall attempt to find him and then see what he has to say for himself." After addressing a few of her other concerns, he soon stood to take his leave, feeling fatigue set in. "I must be on my way."

Amelia rose too. "Your workday isn't yet over?"

"I have another stop to make." He didn't mention that it was to see his parents to advise them of his day. The last thing he wanted was for her to know just how awful today had been.

"As always, I'm impressed by your dedication." Amelia smiled. "Allow me to walk you to the door." She glanced at her aunt. "I will return directly."

"Of course." Her aunt stood, smoothing her skirts. "Thank you again, Inspector Field. I appreciate your help."

"My pleasure. I will keep you apprised of any developments. Good evening." He followed Amelia down the stairs to the empty foyer. There wasn't any sign of Fernsby.

Amelia turned to face him, her gaze dropping to his neck. "Henry," she whispered, "are you certain you are well?" She lifted a hand to gently touch the side of his neck as she took a closer look. "That must be terribly painful."

The feel of her fingers on his skin did much to alleviate any ache. "It is rather sore." His voice croaked worse than it had previously.

"What happened?" she asked, eyes dark with concern as she clasped her hands before her.

He hesitated, not wanting to worry her. But perhaps doing so would help her remain vigilant. He could attempt to fight off the bounder, but if he attacked Amelia... "I came upon Edgarton in Whitechapel. Unfortunately he caught me from behind."

Amelia gasped. "Oh, dear. That could've ended disastrously."

"Luckily, it didn't." That was as much of an agreement as he could offer. "Neither did I manage to catch him." That was what truly rankled.

She bit her lip, her manner suddenly hesitant.

"What is it?" he asked.

"I visited Oscar Powell at the museum today."

"Amelia." He touched her arm, alarmed by the idea. "Why—that was dangerous."

"I took Constable Dannon with me."

"Good." Yet he hated to think of her putting herself in danger. Was one constable enough to keep this woman safe? "Did Powell have anything of interest to say?"

An officer had questioned the man soon after Edgarton's escape, but Amelia had proven herself adept at inquiries of that sort.

"Not really, but I thought it was worth a try." She sighed. "He said Edgarton's mother has a home within walking distance of where he lived, though that's not particularly helpful without a specific address."

"Anything we hear could aid us." He was certain the information about Edgarton's mother hadn't been discovered before. Leave it to Amelia to unearth such a personal detail. "I appreciate you telling me."

"I wish I had learned more."

"Amelia," he began sternly, or at least as much as his throat would allow, "I must ask that you don't pursue this any further. Edgarton could retaliate if he believes his family is being threatened." The thought chilled his blood.

Her gaze returned to his neck. "I understand. I will avoid doing anything that might gain his notice or cause you concern." She smiled as she smoothed his lapel, her touch doing much to calm him. "And may I ask that you do the same?"

He nearly smiled in return, only to realize she was serious. "I...I will try." That was all he could offer when it was his job to find the criminal.

"Hmm." Amelia reached for his hat and gloves while he donned his coat. "I was hoping for more."

More?

He didn't respond, not wanting to make promises he couldn't keep.

"Do you hurt everywhere?" she asked with a sympathetic look.

"A bit." In fact, his entire body ached.

She handed him a small bundle tied with string that sat on the nearby table. "Here's the peppermint and ginger tea blend you had earlier. It should help. I would recommend drinking it with a little honey, two to three times per day. Perhaps a hot bath would ease the other aches."

Henry hardly knew what to say, touched by her thoughtfulness. "How kind. Thank you very much." He held her gaze, wishing he didn't have to go. "I will alert you to any developments in the case."

"I appreciate that."

He reached for the door.

"Henry?" When he looked back, Amelia gave him a small smile. "Please take extra care. I...I would very much like to enjoy more of your company."

"I will." He smiled. "Have a pleasant evening."

Henry caught himself smiling as he walked along the dark street. Perhaps the day hadn't been a complete failure after all.

Eighteen

L ATE THE FOLLOWING MORNING Amelia donned her cloak, hat, and gloves, determined to enjoy the faint, undoubtedly temporary, sunshine under the guise of practicality. She needed to do a little shopping and hoped stepping out of the house would soothe the restlessness which had plagued her since Henry's visit.

His poor neck. She couldn't help but touch her own in sympathy and hoped the tea she'd asked her cook to prepare had helped him.

To think Edgarton had choked him with such force that it left those marks and made him hoarse horrified her. It was a terrible reminder of how precarious life was—a reminder she didn't need. That lesson had already been drilled home in a painful manner, twice, that made certain she'd never forget.

She'd done her best to hide her unease from Aunt Margaret, who'd stayed for dinner and seemed far more relaxed now that her worries were in another's hands. But Henry had obviously been in pain, based on the stiff way he'd moved. She supposed that wasn't uncommon in his occupation, but the memory of his injured neck was enough to make her shiver with worry.

What might Edgarton do next?

The question kept her from sleeping well, visions of Henry being hurt—or worse—plaguing her nightmares. He had tried to downplay the events, surely to protect her, but she had a vivid imagination which easily filled in the parts he hadn't told her.

"I shall return before luncheon," Amelia advised Fernsby, who watched her with a furrowed brow as she checked her reticule in the foyer.

"I would be happy to fetch whatever you need, madam. Yvette would, as well." The worry in his tone touched her even as it reminded her of the threat still in their lives.

What would it be like to have a normal, if boring, week again? How long had it been? "I am in need of some fresh air and exercise." Amelia smiled at the butler. "I shall request whichever constable is outside to accompany me." She had no intention of allowing Edgarton the chance to harm her, nor would she permit him to rule her life. Fear would not control her.

"If you're certain." Fernsby pressed his lips tight in obvious disapproval.

"I am."

He paused as he reached for the doorknob to glance back at her. "I do believe Constable Peters is our guard for the day."

Amelia huffed a breath of silent disappointment. He was the least favorite of those who watched the house. Exactly why, she couldn't say. He was friendly enough, but his company felt like wearing a hair shirt; uncomfortable and rather annoying.

Instead of expressing her dismay, she nodded. "How nice."

The look Fernsby gave her suggested she hadn't fooled him. "Between you and I, madam, I can't say I find his presence particularly comforting."

"Agreed." She tipped her head toward the door. "But he is an officer of the law, and my feelings do not change my plans."

With that, the butler opened the door and watched as she descended the steps, Constable Peters hurrying forward the moment he saw her.

"Good morning, Mrs. Greystone. A fine day, isn't it?" The constable asked as he glanced up at the sky. "Spring is finally in the air."

"Indeed." Reminding herself how much she appreciated having police protection given the potential danger, she smiled. "Such a fine morning that I am going out to do a bit of shopping."

The officer frowned. "Wouldn't it be best if you remained inside?" He glanced around as if trouble might leap from any corner. "We are yet to find the escaped prisoner."

"I am aware." She didn't tell him that Henry had stopped by or that she knew of his run-in with the fugitive. "But I must continue with my life."

"Then I would be pleased to accompany you, madam." He offered a stately bow with a hand flourish, which all seemed a bit much.

Irritated that such a small thing bothered her, Amelia nodded. "I appreciate that. Thank you. I will walk to my first stop." She gestured in the direction she intended to go.

"As you wish."

Only after they had taken several steps did she realize how awkward the outing would be. Having him walk beside her would make her feel compelled to converse, yet his presence behind her would make it obvious that he guarded her.

Which he was, of course, but she had to wonder what her neighbors thought. Never mind that a constable had been along the street for the past week, as well as several times in the previous months.

Perhaps once the danger was over and the police presence was gone, she should call on her neighbors to explain the situation—after all, they must be curious. Mr. and Mrs. Prescott especially, the couple who lived directly opposite her. She hadn't been overly friendly with any of them in the last few years, preferring to keep to herself. It might be time to change that.

Though she soon wished she'd hired a hansom cab because of Peters' silent presence at her side, she walked at a brisk pace to where the residential streets gave way to shops, and smothered the urge to make polite conversation. Thankfully the exercise and fresh air eased much of her angst.

But it wasn't enough to push the worry about Henry in danger from her thoughts, or the potential risk she faced either. She studied those she passed, determined to keep an eye out for Edgarton or anyone else who looked out of place. Relying solely on the constable to do so, on any constable, would surely be unwise.

The street grew busier once they reached the shops, forcing the constable to walk behind her so they didn't block the entire width of the pavement. Shoppers happily went about their business. Carriages, riders on horses, and carts piled high with goods drove past. The bustle was rather invigorating after so much quiet.

Her first stop was the chandlers to place an order. She used gas lamps throughout much of the house but there was nothing like hand-dipped beeswax candles, which she frequently used in her bedchamber, the drawing room, and the dining room, both for light and atmosphere as they burnt cleaner and longer. Paraffin candles would do for the rest of the house where necessary, and she arranged to have her order delivered the following day.

Amelia continued with her errands, enjoying the pleasant interactions with the shopkeepers and other customers. The bookshop came next, and she drew a relieved breath when Constable Peters stated he'd wait outside, leaving her free to peruse the shelves in peace.

Reading was one of her favorite pastimes and she enjoyed books on a variety of subjects. She selected a new mystery—though wondered why since she already had enough mystery in her life—along with another about traveling to India. The country and its people intrigued her. Since traveling alone didn't appeal to her, reading about other places would have to suffice.

As she waited for the shopkeeper to wrap the books, she glanced out the window and was surprised to see the constable, who had his back to her, speaking with someone. The man he conversed with didn't look like the friendly sort, nor did he seem to belong in the area with his rough clothing and grizzled face. Perhaps the constable had witnessed him doing something he didn't like? He was on duty for more than herself, after all.

Pushing the moment from her mind, she thanked the shopkeeper and departed.

"Where to next?" Peters asked with a bright smile, no sign of the other man in sight.

"Who was that you were speaking to?" She hoped she didn't sound too nosy, but her curiosity got the best of her.

"No one." The man shook his head. "Where are you going next?"

"There's a shop a bit farther down the street," she replied, displeased with his answer. Somehow she didn't think that was true, she decided as she glanced around. How could it be no one? She had definitely seen a man, and they had been conversing.

Prickles of tension sparked down her spine. Though the constable was with her, she continued to remain aware of her surroundings. Relying on others for her safety didn't sit well with her.

As a widow she always had to take care, and especially when an escaped prisoner—who had cause to be displeased with her—was on the loose. Yet she refused to hide at home and allow fear to rule her life. If she did so, she wouldn't have gone anywhere these last few months and that was no way to live.

Amelia led the way, noting traffic on the street had increased. The time for luncheon must be drawing near. She didn't particularly enjoy crowds, but then again, who liked being jostled while trying to make their way to a particular destination?

Halfway down the next street she glanced over her shoulder for Constable Peters—but he was no longer in sight. Startled, she paused to search for him. The crowd wasn't so thick that he could've lost her. After being bumped several times, she eased through the other shoppers to wait in front of the nearest shop to watch for him.

Several long minutes passed before she finally saw him approaching with his customary vague smile.

"I looked away for a moment, and you were gone," Peters said with a shrug.

Part of Amelia wanted to advise him to try harder. After all, his sole purpose during this outing was to watch over her. She refrained from saying anything and continued on her way, glancing back more often to make certain he followed.

"I will only be a few minutes," she advised as she reached for the shop door where she intended to purchase a new pair of gloves.

"Looks like you're about to lose this," he said, frowning as he pointed to a piece of paper sticking out from her reticule. "Careful, you nearly misplaced your list."

She hadn't brought a list, nor did she recognize the paper. With a frown, she pulled it free and opened it.

Stay away from Field.

You've been warned.

E

A shiver ran along her skin, knees suddenly weak. She looked around the bustling street, unable to believe that Edgarton or one of his associates could have been so close as to place the note in her reticule without her or the constable noticing.

"Something wrong?" An odd light gleamed in the constable's eyes as he watched her.

For a brief moment, she thought he smirked, but that couldn't be right. He didn't even know what the note said.

The question was, what did she tell him?

Clearly she'd been a fool to grasp for an hour or two of normalcy without anyone other than Henry at her side.

Nineteen

H ENRY, FLETCHER, AND STEPHENS returned to Whitechapel later that morning to continue the search for Edgarton. The faint sunshine gave Henry renewed hope they would soon catch him. At least, that was what he chose to believe. They were due for a break in the case, and there was no reason to think that couldn't happen soon.

Constable Peters hadn't accompanied them as he was watching over Amelia's house, though Henry worried how well he could offer her protection with his twisted ankle. Reynolds insisted that the constable would be able to fulfill his duties after talking with the man, and Henry was in no mood to argue with his superior.

His attempt to visit his parents about events at Scotland Yard the previous evening after leaving Amelia's had been unsuccessful. They'd been dining with friends, according to their butler who had answered the door, which meant Henry still had to manage the disquiet of the impending conversation. All the more reason to find Edgarton before the day's end.

They rode the omnibus again and arrived as close to Whitechapel as possible before walking the rest of the way. The faint hope Henry held slowly faded as they entered the neighborhood. The scenery was just as depressing as it had been the previous day, with run-down buildings and too many ragged, desperate-looking people along the street. Eyes were averted and a few people hurried away, no doubt concerned that they might become the target of a police officer's notice. Marcus had yet to make an appearance, but the lad had a knack for finding Henry. With luck, he'd do so again soon.

A constable had been sent to scour the streets near where Edgarton had lived in search of the man's mother, thanks to Amelia's tip. The officer was to locate Mrs. Edgarton's home, if possible, but not approach her.

Though it seemed unlikely they would discover anything, Henry knocked on the door of Betty Knox's rooms. It didn't come as a surprise when no one answered. After a few discreet inquiries, the old woman next door said she hadn't seen Betty or the man staying with her since the previous morning.

Henry paused as they exited the building, considering their options. "Let's try the same path Edgarton took yesterday. Maybe someone along the way saw something that could be helpful."

His voice was still sore and raspy, but the tea Amelia had provided helped. He'd had more of it before leaving his flat that morning and only wished he could bring it with him.

Inspector Duncan had been at the Yard when Henry had arrived to start his day that morning and gave a subtle nod as if to confirm their conversation. It was reassuring to know the man was doing what he could to help. Henry only wished he could be of more assistance with the plan.

He glanced at Fletcher, who walked by his side, with Stephens behind them. Perhaps he could do something, since the sergeant's uncle was among those Henry suspected. "How is your uncle liking the Yard thus far?"

"Well enough, I suppose. He's still adjusting." Fletcher's moustache twitched, making Henry think he had more to say. "He worked cases differently in the past and has been a bit frustrated with Director Reynolds."

"Oh?" Henry glanced back to make certain Constable Stephens followed closely. This was too dangerous of an area to lose him.

The younger man looked around as they walked, clearly distracted by the sights and sounds of the rookery—which was understandable. The constable hadn't been with the force long, and his current beat didn't include a neighborhood like this. It was difficult to remember they were near London when the rookery appeared so different than other parts surrounding the city.

"My uncle can be stubborn at times," Fletcher added.

Henry waited a moment, then added, "I noticed he's been spending time with Perdy."

Fletcher shook his head with a rueful expression. "I told him how incompetent Perdy is, especially of late, but I don't know that I convinced him. Can't imagine why he continues to remain so friendly with him."

Nor could Henry, but he kept the thought to himself. He didn't want to force Fletcher to defend his uncle and risk causing a rift in their friendship.

"Where did you say he served as a constable?" Henry asked casually, keeping his focus on their surroundings. They'd discussed it before, but people often shared a different version when retelling details.

"Norwich mostly, before moving to N Division in the city." His friend shrugged. "I saw him often growing up, but not as often in the last few years."

"People get busy," Henry suggested.

"Yes, well…there was a bit of a family disagreement at one point or another." Fletcher frowned. "I can't remember what the fuss was about. I should ask my father if he does."

Please do, Henry wanted to request. "Did Clarke always want to be an inspector?"

"He did. He thought it out of reach for a time, but something along the way changed." Fletcher glanced at Henry, his expression unreadable. "Sometimes it takes a bit of luck."

Henry nodded, even as he wondered whether the remark referred to his own quick rise through the ranks. But he wouldn't allow himself to worry over it when he'd worked hard to achieve what he had. And Fletcher knew that.

"Sir?"

Henry slowed his pace to look back at Stephens. The young constable's gaze held on an old man in a nearby doorway who gestured for them to come nearer. Bother—he'd been so absorbed with his conversation with Fletcher, he'd completely missed it. He needed to take better care. His throat should've been enough of a reminder of that fact.

"Yes?" Henry asked, approaching him.

"The man ye're lookin' fer…'e goes to St. Mary's reg'lar-like."

Henry and Fletcher shared a questioning look.

"The church on Whitechapel Road?" Fletcher asked, doubt coloring his tone.

The old man nodded, his gaze darting about nervously before he shifted his feet. "Ye might look there." With a dip of his head, he hurried in the opposite direction.

"Hard to believe an escaped convict would take time to visit the neighborhood church," Fletcher said as he watched the man go.

"It is," Henry agreed. "But who can say what's going through his mind? It's worth a look."

They continued in that direction, stopping to speak with several others without learning anything further.

Henry studied their surroundings before they entered the parish church which had been whitewashed, hence the name white chapel, but was devastated by a fire several years ago. It was soon rebuilt, including its distinctive spire, although Henry had always been disappointed that it was no longer white.

Unfortunately, there wasn't any sign of Edgarton at the church. The vicar was less than helpful, saying only that, "Everyone is welcome here." He would neither confirm nor deny whether the man had been there.

The remainder of the day passed slowly with no additional signs of Edgarton. They spoke with the local constable walking his beat, who said he hadn't seen him but would 'remain vigilant.'

But what comfort was that, if Edgarton had some of the police officers in his pocket?

By the time they returned to Scotland Yard at the day's end, Henry's feet ached and his spirits had lowered once again, especially after providing Reynolds with an update. The Director hadn't discovered anything further about the missing evidence either. No progress in any direction, in twenty-four hours.

Daylight faded to dusk and the air grew cold as Henry made his way to his parents' home, wishing he had better news to share. He hated disappointing them, had done his best to avoid doing so even as a child. But not today.

Would this be the moment when his father nodded, as if he'd expected something of the sort to happen all along?

The thought was illogical but still rattled around Henry's mind. If only he hadn't learned that he'd been adopted. If only he were a true Field and could lean on his ancestry for the honorable and admirable traits his father and grandfather had.

But ignoring the truth served no purpose. He would continue to strive to be the best detective he could be, given the attributes he had. Unfortunately, that didn't feel like enough.

His family home on Glentworth Street just off Marylebone Road, came into view in the dusky light. The peaceful street, with wrought-iron fences where he had played as a child, normally brought him a sense of homecoming.

Not this evening.

Henry reminded himself that he had done nothing wrong—other than allowing Edgarton to get the best of him, briefly. He was doing all he could to resolve the issues of both the stolen scarab and the escaped prisoner. He had operated by the book, and no one could accuse him of any crime. He held tight to those inadequate thoughts as he greeted Stubbs, their longtime butler.

"Good evening, Master Henry." The older servant took his things with a warm smile. "Mr. and Mrs. Field were quite disappointed to have missed you yesterday evening."

"I'm pleased I could return tonight." Henry smoothed a hand over his hair, nerves taking hold again. He felt much like a young lad who'd been in trouble at school and knew he would soon face disapproval and a lecture.

"They await you in the drawing room, sir."

"Thank you, Stubbs." He made his way there, the familiar path bringing comfort, as did the sight of his parents on the settee before the fire, his father with a book in hand and a drink at his elbow, and his mother doing needlework.

"Mother. Father." Henry smiled, even as he wished he'd come for the simple pleasure of a visit. Yet he knew the moment they saw his neck and heard his raspy voice, they would know otherwise.

His parents meant the world to him, and nothing could change that. He shouldn't worry that news of his recent problems would disappoint them...but he did.

"Henry." His mother's bright smile quickly faded as her gaze caught on his neck. She set aside her embroidery hoop and rose for a closer look. "What happened?" Her gaze raked the rest of him. "Are you all right?"

"I am," he said, managing a smile.

His father stood as well, watching as Henry took his mother's offered hands and kissed her cheek. It was too much to hope that his father's experience as a detective would mean he couldn't place exactly what had caused the marks.

Henry was grateful he didn't say it bluntly when it would only worry his mother. She did enough of that already.

He clasped his father's hand in his for a long moment, appreciating the steady, firm grip. "I trust you both are well?"

"We are—but do tell us what caused your injury." His mother's brown eyes held his, clearly trying to gauge how he was for herself, regardless of his answer.

Her burgundy gown with black trim showed her still slim figure to advantage. Her brown hair was drawn back into a loose chignon with only a few strands of gray. Time had been kind to her, something he appreciated, even though he didn't care to think of either of them growing older.

"Of course." He waited until they took their seats before doing the same.

"So what happened?" his father asked briefly. Thurmond Field was not one for idle conversation. He adjusted his gold-rimmed spectacles as he studied Henry, his movements stiff, revealing his agitation.

Better he tell them and be done with it.

He had worked out the best way to share the tale on his way over, but now that he was here, he couldn't quite remember. "As you know, we are still searching for Miles Edgarton, the escaped prisoner," he began, pausing to clear his throat. Bother—he should have brought some of Amelia's tea with him.

"He won't be able to hide forever," his father advised with a confident nod. "Mark my words."

"Yes, well, he didn't." Henry couldn't help but touch his neck. "Hide, that is."

"He jumped you?" The incredulity in his father's tone had Henry shifting in his chair, cheeks heating with discomfiture.

"Yes." The reasons why were on the tip of his tongue, but when it came down to it, there was no other way to describe it. He'd taken a misstep and nearly paid for it with his life. "Not one of my finer moments."

"Where?" The clipped tones meant the inspector had taken over his father.

"Whitechapel. I was given a tip that he was staying in a tenement there."

"You weren't searching for him by yourself, were you?" His mother's eyes darkened with worry.

"No, three others were with me."

"Fletcher?" His father lifted a brow. He held the sergeant in high regard.

"Yes. Well, first a constable and I chased the fugitive down three flights then Fletcher and I pursued him for several streets."

"With you in the lead," his father suggested with a faint smile.

Henry nodded. "I was close behind Edgarton until he rounded a corner and disappeared on a busy street. I came upon a narrow alley between two buildings. It looked like the perfect hiding place."

His father's mouth tightened. "And it was."

"Yes. I was half down it when I heard shouts from the street and I turned, thinking I'd missed him." He drew a breath as he met his father's gaze. "He was hiding in a doorway. He grabbed me from behind, but luckily, I escaped."

"Good heavens. Did he intend to kill you?" His mother's face, pale with shock, tightened his chest.

"Doubtful. More a harsh warning." Better that he didn't mention the knife.

"So you spoke with him?" his father asked quietly. "What did he say?"

"That I should leave well enough alone." He hesitated but wanted his father's thoughts on the next bit. "That he hadn't got where he was by himself. That I should look closer to home."

His father stilled, gaze shifting across the room, clearly considering what that meant. Yet how could he offer any helpful insights when Henry hadn't told them everything?

"There's more to the story." He braced himself, detesting that this part reflected poorly on the Field name. "Earlier that morning, we discovered something missing from the evidence room."

"What?" Thurmond's shaggy gray brows descended.

"The Egyptian scarab that was part of the case against Edgarton for selling illicit artifacts." Henry put out his hands, palms up, stomach twisting. "Gone."

"Wasn't that quite valuable?" his father asked.

"Very." He forced out the next bit. "My name was noted in the ledger for having taken it."

"But you didn't." His father's tone was flat.

"I did not." Henry enunciated the words carefully to make them clear, holding his gaze. "It was my name, but not in my hand."

His father jerked to his feet. "How could that be?"

Henry's heart lurched. Did his father believe him?

"How could anyone take it without another officer knowing?" His father waved a hand in the air. "It's impossible. We have procedures in place for that reason—no one can be in there alone."

He hadn't said anything Henry didn't already know, so he held his silence.

His father spun to glare at his son. "Who do you suspect?"

A mixture of surprise and relief struck Henry squarely in the chest. *Of course his father believed him.* Why had he doubted that for even a moment? "It is...too soon to say."

"Nonsense. You can tell me."

Henry hesitated. "Everyone."

For a long moment, his father showed no reaction. Then he slowly nodded. "As you should. In this case, all are guilty until proven innocent."

Henry nodded, pleased to know his father shared the same opinion. "What is also concerning is that Edgarton knew of the missing scarab."

"That suggests he was involved in taking it."

"Perhaps. But there is no sign of a break-in, so—"

"It was someone within. Whoever it is, along with Edgarton, is making a fool of Scotland Yard," his father interrupted, his brow furrowed. "That is the last thing the department needs after the bribery scandal."

"True enough."

His father shook his head. "Does Director Reynolds have any suspects?"

"Other than me, no." Henry couldn't claim that Reynolds thought him innocent. "Edgarton also said he didn't kill the prison guard who was murdered a week after helping him escape."

His mother glanced between them with concern. Though he didn't want to worry her and normally avoided talking about investigations in her presence, this situation wasn't one he wanted to hide when she might hear of it elsewhere.

His reputation...his very name mattered to him.

"Do you believe him?" his father asked as he returned to his seat, reaching out to place his hand over his wife's. The gesture was one of many intimacies Henry had witnessed over the years, which made it even more comforting. He appreciated knowing his parents had each other to lean on when needed.

Dare he hope he might someday have something similar for himself with Amelia?

The longing for exactly that surprised him with its strength.

"I do," Henry admitted. "It didn't make sense that Edgarton would return to kill the prison guard when he could've done that during his escape."

His father nodded pensively. "Unless he decided the guard was a liability for some reason, and his testimony would make things worse when Edgarton was caught."

"Possibly." But that didn't ring true as far as Henry was concerned. Though he couldn't name the reason, he tended to think Edgarton had told him the truth—that he hadn't killed Cobb. He'd certainly never strangled anyone before. Well, not until he'd nearly succeeded doing so to Henry.

"You're right. It seems odd that Edgarton would make a point of telling you he hadn't killed the guard if he had." His father dismissed the idea with a shake of his head. "Men like him rarely bother showing remorse."

Henry couldn't deny how good it felt to know his father agreed. "I wanted to advise you both of the situation as I tend to think you would have heard the news soon enough."

The trust in his father's expression meant everything. "We appreciate that."

"Your voice sounds terrible," his mother added, clearly ready to change the subject. "Your throat must be sore. Have you tried some tea with honey? Or perhaps some spearmint tea would ease the pain." Before he could answer, she rose to ring the bell. "Surely you can stay for dinner."

Henry smiled. "I wouldn't say no to that."

"You're not going to offer him tea now, are you?" his father asked with a frown. "A whiskey would serve him better at this time of day."

"Not with a sore throat. I believe we have some ginger wine, though," she said with a knowing smile. "I will ask the cook to prepare some spearmint tea for you to take home." She scowled as her gaze held on his throat. "But I don't know of anything to help with those marks."

"Mrs. Greystone provided some peppermint and ginger tea, and it has helped."

"Oh." His mother seemed uncertain what to think about that.

"The marks are already starting to fade, I promise you." Still, it was nice to have his mother fuss over him.

The support both his parents gave Henry steadied him more than he could say, and dinner certainly helped, as well. His landlady would have to find someone else to eat her unimpressive dishes.

"How *is* Mrs. Greystone?" his mother asked after they'd finished a delicious cod in lemon sauce with capers. "It must be terribly unsettling for her to know the man suspected of killing her husband has escaped."

"It is. A constable is watching her house until Edgarton is caught, but she seems to be handling the situation with her usual strength and grace." He continued to be amazed by Amelia's determination not to allow the missing prisoner to overtake her life—even though he wished she would stay in.

But then who would be the imprisoned one?

"We enjoyed meeting her." His mother tipped her head to the side as she held his gaze. "Is there a chance we will see her again?"

"Charlotte, now, do not pressure the boy," his father admonished with a smile that suggested he had been tempted to do the same.

It had been a long time since Henry had been called a boy, but somehow the moment comforted him.

"I'm not pressuring him." His mother lifted her chin, her expression one of barely believable innocence. "I am merely inquiring."

"I believe she would enjoy another visit," Henry said, certain it was true. "I forgot to ask how the pea fertilizer experiment is coming along."

"I should very much like to hear more about it if possible." His mother sent his father a pointed look. "And I don't think it causes any harm to let Henry know that we enjoyed Mrs. Greystone's company."

"She is an admirable woman," his father added with a nod. "Intelligent and independent with a good head on her shoulders."

There was no higher compliment from his father.

Henry was pleased that they liked Amelia, but he had no intention of sharing how much he liked her too. Not yet, when affairs remained unsettled between them. Once Edgarton was caught and faced trial, perhaps then their relationship could progress.

And that day couldn't come soon enough.

Twenty

A MELIA HAD SENT A message to Henry's lodging house the moment she had returned from her shopping expedition, describing the unwelcome note, and had been hopeful he would call that evening. She was anxious to show him the message and discuss her concerns about a certain young constable.

Contacting him at his home rather than Scotland Yard seemed wise, given the warning she'd received—and she'd advised Fernsby to ensure that regardless of which constable was on guard, he wasn't to be made aware that she'd reached out to Henry.

The evening had been a long one, with her spending far too much time looking out the window to see if someone other than the constable watched her house, wondering when Henry would come by. She couldn't deny her disappointment that he hadn't, or her worry about how his throat was.

But Henry would visit her as soon as he was able. She need only be patient.

After eating a light breakfast in the kitchen the following morning, as was her routine, Amelia paced the drawing room, realizing it would be impossible to settle into any of her projects until she spoke with Henry.

Her notes on the orchid collector article sat on her desk but held no appeal when she felt so uneasy. With a sigh, she decided she simply had to try to work since waiting was driving her mad, only to hear voices drifting up from the foyer.

She hurried to the doorway, careful not to let Fernsby nor their guest see her. The butler was a stickler about proper behavior, and he would not be pleased to find her eavesdropping.

Henry's deep tones echoed from below, and she drew a relieved breath even as happiness filled her. Was that how his mother felt each time he came by? Relief that he was well?

He would of course know what to do about the note, but her reaction to his arrival involved more than that. Each time Amelia saw him brought her joy, and she intended to hold on to that. She returned to the drawing room to await his appearance, a smile at the ready.

Within a few short moments, Henry stood in the doorway, his coat still on—making his shoulders look impossibly broad—and hat in hand. "Good morning, Amelia."

"Good morning." It was, now that he had arrived. "You sound slightly improved." His voice wasn't as raspy, and the marks on his neck had faded slightly, or at least changed color. "How are you feeling?"

"Better, courtesy of the tea you provided. Thank you again for it." He walked slowly forward, his brown eyes holding on her in that watchful way of his. The one that made her feel like she mattered and that he cared how she was faring. "I had dinner with my parents last evening and didn't receive your message until I returned home too late to venture out again."

Amelia nodded, pleased to think of him spending time with Mr. and Mrs. Field. His mother had mentioned how she wished they saw him more often, something she could relate to. "I knew you would stop by as soon as you were able." Aware he wouldn't have much time, she reached for the slip of paper on her desk and moved to hand it to him. "As I mentioned in my note, someone placed this in my reticule yesterday while I was out shopping."

He frowned as he read it. "A warning?"

"So it seems."

"Did you see who might have put it there?"

"No." She hesitated about how to phrase the next part. Normally, she wouldn't question a police constable, but she need only remember Perdy's actions on more than one occasion to know they weren't perfect. Not all were as honest and intelligent as Henry. "Constable Peters accompanied me. We walked from here to the shops and stopped at several."

"Walked?" His eyes narrowed. "I thought he had a sore ankle."

She blinked in surprise. "Sore ankle? He didn't mention it, nor did I notice him favoring one."

He looked back at the message. "Did he see anything suspicious?"

"Only the piece of paper sticking from my reticule. He pointed it out, saying he didn't want me to lose my list. But I didn't have one."

"Odd that he didn't see who put it there."

"Other shoppers separated us briefly—a minute, maybe three. Perhaps it happened then."

Henry's lips pressed tight, his disapproval apparent. "I have to wonder how good of a job he's doing if he allowed that to happen."

"I admit that crossed my mind as well." She shook her head. "Then again, I'm suspicious of nearly everyone these days."

"As you should be."

She wasn't sure whether or not to be pleased that he agreed so quickly. Staying on guard was exhausting. Did he feel it too? Was this what all who served in the police force suffered?

"Did you show it to him?" Henry asked quietly.

Amelia considered her answer, still uncertain if she'd done the right thing. "No. I did my best to hide my surprise at what it said and acted as if the paper didn't contain anything of consequence. Perhaps I should've told him."

"I understand why you didn't."

That was unsettling to hear. "There is something else. One other action of his that made me wonder—while I was in the bookshop, he remained outside and spoke with a roughly dressed man."

"Oh? Can you describe him?"

She had already given thought to the question and shared what she remembered. "I took note of his appearance as I thought it odd that Peters was speaking to him."

"Did he do so in a friendly manner, or perhaps to reprimand a wrongdoing?" Henry lifted a brow.

"Unfortunately I cannot say. The constable's back was to me, so I didn't see his expression. The other man stood fairly close and had an intense expression, which I suppose is why I thought they knew one another. It didn't seem like just a casual conversation between strangers to me. And he denied even speaking to anyone—but I definitely saw…"

Amelia bit her lip. It was unpleasant, to always be questioning oneself, always second guessing, suspicious of all around her.

"Interesting. The note is concerning for several reasons." He paused as if to gather his thoughts—or to decide what to tell her. "To begin with, we must now assume you are being watched."

She resented that conclusion, even if it was logical. A flash of anger had her saying what was on her mind before she could think twice. "Or perhaps—perhaps Constable Peters placed the note in my possession and went so far as to point it out when I didn't immediately notice it."

Amelia waited, closely watching Henry's expression to gauge his reaction. She expected shock or even dismay. Maybe displeasure or annoyance that she'd questioned the constable's morals and commitment to his job.

To her surprise, she saw none of those. If she had to guess, she'd say he held some of the same suspicions.

"What is your opinion?" she finally asked.

"I'm not certain what to think," he admitted. "Peters is relatively new and I don't know him well, and…I hate to say it, but there have been a few times when I've questioned his actions, as well."

She nodded, debating how much more to say. But they were in this together, she and Henry. He was the one she trusted. The only one. "I have no basis for what I'm about to say," she began cautiously.

"I am still interested in hearing your opinion." He offered an encouraging look.

How Amelia hoped that was true; that what she was about to tell Henry didn't give him a poor opinion of her. "I can't help but think back to the first time I encountered Constable Peters. When I was being held by Edgarton at Sable Importers."

"I remember," he ground out, suggesting it wasn't a pleasant memory.

A shiver ran along her skin at his reaction. Though she did her best to ignore it, she couldn't deny the warmth that filled her. "He acted overly eager to be the one to escort me. In fact, I was relieved you insisted on doing so." She waited, hoping Henry had noticed the same thing and that she hadn't imagined it. "It has crossed my mind more than once whether I would have made it home if he had escorted me."

Henry stilled, seeming surprised by her admission. "Yes, I noticed that as well. I thought myself the only one."

"He seems to practically stumble over himself to help with that disarming smile in place. Yet for some reason, it strikes me as...insincere."

He slowly nodded. "I have noticed that as well."

"Does he truly intend to be helpful...or is something else afoot?" Amelia bit her lip, still wondering if she had it all wrong. The constable might be innocent of any wrongdoing, and she was doing him a terrible disservice by mentioning her concerns. It was no crime to be forward, or enthusiastic. Speaking to a strange man wasn't a crime either, and neither was noticing a piece of paper. She might be completely overreacting.

But what if she wasn't?

"I don't know, but I will look into it." Henry slowly nodded. "It is also strange that he wasn't in pain as he was limping the day before. He twisted his ankle when we were pursuing Edgarton in Whitechapel—his chase was impeded due to the injury."

Amelia shook her head. "I didn't notice a limp. We walked side-by-side for part of the way."

"Interesting. At the very least, his behavior yesterday sounds suspicious and warrants questioning."

She grimaced. "I hope he doesn't resent me after those questions."

"I will leave you out of it," he said with a reassuring smile. "There is enough reason to consider his actions without sharing your doubts."

"Thank you. Or..." Amelia stared across the room as she considered their options. "Do we pretend nothing is amiss and merely keep a closer eye on him?"

Henry frowned. "I don't want him watching over your home if we can't trust him."

"Could he be switched to other duties without being told why?"

"Certainly. There's always work to be done." He hesitated. "I didn't intend to share this with you, but a...a problem has arisen at the Yard."

"What kind of problem?" From the shadow that crossed his face, she wasn't certain she wanted to know.

"Someone took evidence from a locked room at the Yard. Not just any evidence—the Egyptian scarab."

Shock seeped through Amelia like a tidal wave. "Oh, no. Do you think it was Edgarton?"

"Doubtful. There was no sign of a break-in." He held her gaze. "I'm sure I don't need to tell you that this is confidential."

"Of course." She reached to touch his arm in comfort. Henry hid his distress, but she knew him well enough to see it. "How upsetting, especially when it's evidence in one of your cases."

"It's definitely a problem. A big one."

"But if not Edgarton, then who?"

"I don't yet know, but I intend to find out." Henry's lips pressed together. "It's clear that the incidents are connected. I'm not certain who to trust at this point. I want you to be very careful from now on. It might not be enough for a constable to accompany you when we don't know who is involved in all this. Who we can trust."

She didn't care for the idea of that at all, though it had already occurred to her. "If I have to go out, one of my own servants will accompany me." How long would she need to worry about such things?

"Amelia, the handwriting of the message doesn't resemble Edgarton's from what I remember, but I could be wrong. It might truly have been from him." He held her gaze, worry in the brown depths. "You should never have got tangled in this, it's too dangerous. Perhaps it would be best if I kept my distance until all this is over."

Dismay speared through her. Her thoughts and emotions raced so quickly that it was impossible to put a name to them.

None were good. She drew a breath, but it didn't help ease her disappointment.

There was so much more Amelia wanted to say. How she'd worried when he hadn't come by the previous evening, even though she didn't have a right to. How she felt the safest when in his presence. That she would miss him if they didn't see one another for any length of time, let alone an extended period. How much their friendship had come to mean to her, a true pleasure in her quiet world that held so few.

Yet she also wanted to aid him in whatever way she could, no matter how small. She didn't want him distracted by worry about her.

"I would prefer you didn't do that." The words escaped before she could halt them. "However, if you think it would be for the best, then of course I will concur." Her heart pinched as she waited for his response, willing him to decide it wasn't necessary.

His slow smile crinkled his eyes in an appealing manner. "I prefer to avoid such a measure as I would have difficulty believing you were well without seeing so for myself."

That was a relief to hear. "I feel the same."

"If Edgarton didn't write the message, who did? Why would anyone care that we are friends? What harm could it cause?"

She gave a one-shouldered shrug. "I like to think we have become a good team over the last few months. Perhaps your recent successes with me as an unofficial assistant have gained their notice."

"Hmm. I don't like the idea that our association places you in danger."

Disappointed he hadn't agreed with her observation, she could only say, "I was already involved in the case against Edgarton. He started this some time ago." Just how long Matthew had been associated with him, she didn't know.

"True." He studied the message again. "As I said, the handwriting doesn't match what I remember. What do you think?"

"I thought the same, though I don't clearly remember the script on the list I found in Matthew's desk or the one at Locke's shop." They had concluded that Edgarton wrote them both.

"If it doesn't match those, it means Edgarton didn't write it." Henry seemed almost relieved by the thought. "I would like to take this to compare them so we know for sure."

"Of course."

"For now, I will keep my distance with the hope that it helps to keep you safe. If you have need of me, don't contact the Yard—send a message to my lodging house again."

"Very well." She hoped Henry didn't see how disappointed she was. It was only temporary, she reminded herself. Unfortunately, that didn't make her feel any better.

"It won't be for long."

"Right." Amelia took his reassurance to heart and hoped it would prove true.

Twenty-One

HENRY DIDN'T NEED TO compare the handwriting of the message he held with the letters still in the evidence room to know they weren't the same, but he would verify it anyway. He intended to pay close attention to every detail of this investigation to find the guilty party.

That Amelia had been drawn deeper into this dangerous case by the threatening message disturbed him deeply—a stark reminder that lives were at risk, including hers, not that he needed one. Regardless of who had sent the message, the danger was very real.

He returned to the Yard, waiting impatiently for Sergeant Miller to unlock the door of the evidence room, only to wonder as he waited if the letters would still be inside. The Director had said no other evidence was missing, but that was of little reassurance with the scarab still gone.

With Miller watching, Henry opened the drawer, relieved to find them right where he'd left them. It took little more than a brief study to compare them before confirming he was right. The handwriting had some similarities but was definitely different.

"Is that all?" the sergeant asked, lips pursed tight as he glared at Henry, who calmly returned the letters to the drawer.

"Yes, thank you." Though tempted to tell the man once again that he hadn't taken the damn scarab, Henry held back. It was only logical that Miller suspected everyone, including Henry, as he was doing the same. The man had his own reputation to protect, after all.

The truth would soon be clear, Henry reminded himself, even if his patience to solve it was wearing thin. He watched as the sergeant locked the room, though he now doubted whether such procedures served the purpose they'd intended.

Someone had got in. Someone had stolen. And that someone was among them.

Henry had provided the Director with daily updates since the scarab had gone missing. Though reluctant to tell Reynolds about the message Amelia had received when he didn't want her involved any more than necessary, neither did he want to hold back information. He wasn't going to be accused of hiding evidence.

"And Peters was guarding her when this happened?" The Director frowned as he studied the note.

"Yes, sir."

"But the message isn't truly from Edgarton."

"It doesn't match the handwriting of the other two samples we are certain are his."

Reynolds scratched his head. "Why would someone want us to think that Edgarton warned Mrs. Greystone to stay away from you?"

Henry hesitated before reluctantly answering, uncertain if he was right. "My only guess is that they meant for the message to distract us. To keep our attention solely on Edgarton rather than looking into who killed Cobb and took the scarab."

"You think one person did both?"

"Probably more than one, but they must be working together and of the same mind." He held Reynolds' gaze, deciding to speak bluntly. "And though it pains me to say this, sir, they are most likely a member of the department."

"Starting with Constable Peters." The Director tapped a finger on the note. "Seems like too much of a coincidence that he just happened to be separated from her when the message appeared."

"It certainly seems questionable in my mind. Of course, all of this is merely supposition until we have evidence to prove it." Henry wanted to ask if Reynolds had any leads on the scarab but held back. The Director would tell him if progress had been made.

"I thought we had the right group of men working here." The older man removed his spectacles and ran a weary hand over his face. "Disappointing to think we don't."

"Indeed it is."

"Let us proceed with caution. We need proof of guilt as we do with every criminal." Reynolds replaced his spectacles and steadily held Henry's gaze. "Keep the message between us. Let whoever it is think Mrs. Greystone didn't mention it. We shall give them enough rope to hang themselves. In the meantime, watch your back, Field."

"Yes, sir. Fletcher and I will return to Whitechapel again this morning. Finding Edgarton remains our top priority."

"Excellent." Reynolds gave a single nod. "He is the key to solving all of this."

While Henry agreed, he already knew catching Edgarton wasn't going to be easy. He returned to his desk and jotted some notes in the case file but didn't mention the message Amelia received.

"Shall we?" Fletcher asked as he reached his friend's desk.

"Yes." Henry closed the file and stood. Each time they went to Whitechapel, they gathered new information. He'd rather they found Edgarton, but he'd take anything they could get.

"Anyone else accompanying us?" the sergeant asked.

"Not today." Henry hoped the decision didn't place them in danger, but having another officer with them didn't make him feel any safer, and he had to believe Fletcher agreed.

Henry watched as his friend paused to glance around the Yard with a frown.

The sergeant shook his head. "Haven't seen my uncle the past day or so. Odd."

"He must be involved in a case," Henry suggested, and Fletcher nodded, yet his gaze lingered on his uncle's empty desk, making Henry wonder at his thoughts.

Inspector Whitlock walked in as they were walking out. "What do we have here?" His gaze shifted between them as he pulled a gold pocket watch to check the time. "You're just now starting the day?"

Though Henry knew the man was only trying to rile him, he wouldn't let him think he wouldn't give as good as he got. "New watch, Whitlock? Looks expensive."

Fletcher leaned forward for a closer look. "Hard to believe a man receiving an inspector's pay could afford that."

Whitlock quickly stuffed the watch back into his pocket as he glared. "My property is none of your business."

Fletcher raised a brow. "You're rather sensitive about it." He looked at Henry, a hint of suspicion gleaming in his eyes. "Makes you wonder why."

Whitlock muttered something under his breath and strode into the Yard.

Henry turned at the sound of a chuckle to see Sergeant Johnson watching them, a grin on his face.

"Well done." Johnson nodded. "He's the one who should mind his own business. That one's too quick to find fault with others."

Henry couldn't help but smile, appreciating the support from the dependable man. "We will return before the day's end."

"Going to Whitechapel again?" Johnson asked.

Though it was a logical guess, the question still made Henry uneasy, but he hadn't attempted to keep his plans for the day a secret. Johnson could have overheard it when Henry had asked Fletcher to accompany him earlier. "Yes."

"Be careful out there."

"We will," Fletcher replied as he opened the door, and Henry followed, realizing he was making too much of the moment. His suspicions were getting the best of him.

"How did he know where we were going?" Fletcher asked, starting down the street.

Henry nearly smiled. "I was wondering the same. He must've overheard us discussing it earlier."

"Between Edgarton and the missing evidence, I find myself looking at everyone with suspicion." The sergeant shook his head. "I'll be happy when we find them both."

Henry couldn't agree more and appreciated Fletcher's positivity. He only wished he felt more optimistic.

Their first stop in Whitechapel was at the lodging house where Edgarton had hidden, but once again, no one answered.

Fletcher tried the door, which was unlocked. With a questioning glance at Henry, he opened the door and looked inside, then opened it wide. The rooms stood empty, an undisturbed air about the place. It didn't look as if anyone had been there in the last couple of days.

"Do you want a closer look?" Fletcher asked.

"No. I want Edgarton." Frustrated, he reached to close the door and started down the stairs. "I don't think he'll return here any time soon. We need to search elsewhere."

"Any suggestions?" Fletcher asked as he followed.

"What would you do in his position?" Henry turned to look at his friend once they stepped outside. "You're a murderer, you're on the run. What do you do?"

"Turn myself in." Fletcher shook his head ruefully. "Too much pressure. Then again, I wouldn't have escaped in the first place."

"We must think like he does. You can't stay in one place too long. Not sure who to trust. You can't return home. Your businesses are closed." Henry turned to glance up at the dilapidated building. "You're forced to live in rooms hardly fit for humans and much different than those you're accustomed to."

Fletcher followed his gaze then nodded. "Dire situation. You'd be angry. Desperate. It would be important to keep it simple. Maybe return to what—and where—you know."

"Right. Which is why he's stayed in Whitechapel, where he was raised."

"Doesn't hurt that it's hard to find anyone on these unwelcoming streets. Does he have family around still? Friends? He'd need someone to rely on other than Betty Knox."

Henry scanned the street, trying to imagine what the man faced and where he'd go. "Edgarton is smart. Ambitious. Confident. He wouldn't be satisfied with merely surviving. He's determined to get his previous life back."

"He's not going to get it. Not with three counts of murder and a prison escape hanging over his head, among other charges."

Fletcher was right, but that didn't mean Edgarton wouldn't try. They'd chased down his numerous businesses and associates with limited success, but there had to be more of a network—more options for the man.

"Do you think he told the truth? That he didn't murder the prison guard?"

"He says he didn't." But someone had, and Edgarton knew who. They just had to find him and convince him to reveal what he knew. "Let's check St. Mary's again, where else?"

"Maybe he has a favorite pub nearby. The same one his father went to." The sergeant sent Henry a questioning look as if uncertain if he was right. "Tradition can be reassuring?"

"True. We know the street he grew up on, which isn't far. Let us see if anyone in the pubs there is willing to talk." It seemed unlikely, but Henry didn't have any better ideas.

Before they'd taken more than a few steps, the sharp shrill of a police whistle filled the air, followed by the rattle of a police clacker, the sounds signaling a police officer in the area needed assistance.

"Not sure I like the whistles, but you can hear them better than I expected," Fletcher murmured, glancing about to determine where the sound had come from. "What now?"

Police whistles had replaced the heavy, wooden clackers just the previous month, but some officers still carried both—change was not something those in the force particularly liked.

"We'd better have a look." Henry pointed in the direction where the alarm sounded again and took off at a run, Fletcher at his side.

Perhaps as he should have expected, the whistle led them to St. Mary's on Whitechapel Road.

Several people had gathered on the steps of the church, and one was pointing to the door. Before Henry reached it, a constable emerged from the church, appearing thoroughly shaken.

"Adams? It is Adams, isn't it? Did you sound the alarm?" Henry asked, recognizing the man as one of the local constables.

"Inspector Field, sir—Sergeant Fletcher." Adams appeared relieved to see them. "I did." He glanced around and stepped closer, lowering his voice. "There's a body, sir. In the church."

There was only one thing to do. "Show us." Henry and Fletcher followed the constable inside.

The dim interior had Henry hesitating as his eyes adjusted, the silence heavy and foreboding. Stained glass panels lit one wall, casting a golden glow through the space.

"Over here," the constable whispered, though the place appeared to be empty. He led them toward the pews and pointed to the floor.

Henry leaned closer to see a man sprawled between the wooden pews. The victim was on his back, the blood on the floor beside him reflecting a portion of the stained-glass panel in reverse.

Henry stared at the man in disbelief.

Edgarton.

Damn. Disappointment swept over him. The Director's words from earlier returned to haunt him: *He is the key to solving all of this.*

And now the key was gone.

"Is that—" Fletcher bit off the name to look at Henry, his expression incredulous as if certain he had to be wrong.

"Edgarton." Henry rubbed a hand over the back of his neck, thoughts reeling as he struggled to think what this meant to the investigation. "Miles Edgarton."

"Not—the escaped prisoner?" the constable asked, jaw dropping.

"Yes." Henry bent to check for a pulse but found none. Not a surprise based on the amount of blood pooled beneath him. "What happened?"

"I received word of two men arguing in the church and came to investigate." He gestured toward the body with a hand that trembled. "He—he's the only one I found."

"No one else was around?" Fletcher asked, his firm tone suggesting the constable needed to gather his wits and do his job.

Henry glanced around the dimly lit church for himself, desperate for an answer. Who had killed Edgarton and why?

Movement in the shadows between two columns in an alcove caught his eye. A face was briefly visible before it disappeared. "There!"

Fletcher rushed toward the spot and looked around, only to look back at Henry. "Where? There's no one back here."

Henry frowned, certain he'd seen someone...and he thought that person was Fletcher's uncle, though he'd only caught a glimpse.

Was he wrong?

Or was the very worst even possibly true?

Twenty-Two

"LIGHT—WE NEED MORE LIGHT to examine the body," Henry ordered. He couldn't shake the certainty that he'd seen someone in the shadows, and though the moment had passed in the blink of an eye, he'd swear it had been Clarke.

But Fletcher hadn't seen anyone. Would the sergeant lie to cover for his uncle? *No.* Henry refused to believe it.

Constable Adams returned with two lamps and the vicar, who had stepped out to meet with a parishioner. The man was horrified to learn someone had been killed in the church.

"Mr. Edgarton?" The vicar shook his head as he placed his palms together as if prepared to say a prayer for him. "That's terrible news."

Fletcher stared at him in surprise. "He was an escaped prisoner accused of killing three men, not to mention other crimes."

The vicar, a small man with a balding head and a kindly expression, pressed his lips tight. "Perhaps. However he was a loyal parishioner, donated to the church often, and helped the less fortunate. He never forgot where he came from."

Henry and Fletcher shared a disbelieving look, but neither said a word.

Drawing a breath to gather his wits and push away the shock, Henry bent down for a closer look at Edgarton's body with Fletcher holding the lanterns. The metallic scent of blood struck him as he bent even closer. The man's coat was unfastened, a two-inch slice near the middle of his jacket wet with blood. "He was stabbed in the chest."

Based on the location the blade might have found its way between his ribs and, if so, likely pierced his heart, though the surgeon would need to confirm that.

"Must've been a quick end based on the amount of blood," Fletcher murmured.

"See if anyone outside saw or heard anything," Henry ordered.

"Of course." Fletcher set down the lantern and started toward the door, only to pause as it flew open, revealing Constable Peters.

"I came when I heard the whistle," he said breathlessly, eyes bright with excitement as he took in the scene. "What happened?"

Henry watched him carefully as Fletcher explained the situation, wondering if what he'd said was true. His beat wasn't far, but Henry had difficulty believing he'd heard the alarm. And he remembered Amelia's—and his own—lack of trust in the man.

Fletcher continued out the door to question those nearby while Peters was sent in search of a wagon or cart to haul the body to St. Thomas' for examination.

Henry returned his attention to the scene and the waiting vicar. "What time did you leave the church this morning?"

"Oh, perhaps a half hour ago. I called on an ill parishioner who lives nearby."

"There was no one in the church when you left?"

"No." The man's gaze kept slipping to the shadowy figure lying in a pool of his own blood.

Henry pushed forward. "When did you last see Edgarton?"

The vicar sighed. "I suppose there's no harm in telling you now. He came by with a woman last Sunday not long after the service ended. I think he called her Betty. He left another donation."

Edgarton's charity was admirable, though the same couldn't be said for the rest of his life. While Henry appreciated that he helped those who lived in Whitechapel, the man hadn't come by the money honestly—it hadn't truly belonged to him. However, the vicar appeared willing to look the other way. Hopefully the funds had been put to good use.

Henry studied the body for a long moment. His coat and jacket were worn and dirty, spots on his once-white shirt suggesting he hadn't changed clothes for several days. No marks were on his face or hands, making it unlikely that any physical altercation took place before the stabbing.

Had he been familiar with who killed him? Had the knife come as a surprise? Edgarton's own victims had surely felt that way. Henry supposed there was an odd sort of justice in that.

"Did he often come to the church at this time of day?" Henry asked the vicar.

He shook his head. "I never knew when to expect him."

"Did you see anyone outside when you left?" Edgarton must have arrived soon after the vicar stepped out, and he hadn't been alone, that was for certain.

The vicar's eyes narrowed as he searched his memory. "Not really. There were people on the street, of course, but no one near the church door."

After advising the vicar not to speak of the murder in the coming days to allow the police time to investigate, Henry continued with his survey of the scene.

He checked Edgarton's pockets, finding a dirty handkerchief and a few coins in one before moving to the next one, the scent of blood nearly overwhelming. The feel of a bulky object with hard edges had him reaching into the pocket gingerly. The cool metal beneath his fingertips gave him pause. He briefly closed his eyes, already knowing what the item was. What else could it be?

The golden scarab.

Damn. Henry pulled it out, taking care not to damage the artifact. Whoever had placed it in that pocket—and not for a moment did he believe it was Edgarton—wanted it to be found. Probably to imply that Edgarton had taken it. Perhaps to end the pressure they were under as the search for it continued.

Though pleased to have it back, especially when his name was associated with the missing evidence, its presence on Edgarton's person created more questions than answers, and possibly more problems for Henry. Yet what could he do but wrap it in his own handkerchief and gingerly place it in his pocket.

Next he carefully combed over the floor and pews for clues, careful to stay out of the blood, but didn't find anything else of interest.

Peters returned, and the body was soon carried out to the wagon he'd procured with a blanket draped over it.

With a heavy sigh, Henry joined Fletcher outside. "Anything?"

The sergeant held up his notebook and pencil. "A few names of those who were nearby, but no one noticed anything unusual until the constable sounded the alarm." He showed Henry the brief list. No help there.

"Whoever killed him could've come in through one of the other doors," Henry surmised as he surveyed the bustling street and numerous people passing by. "I suppose as busy as this area is, anyone acting suspiciously wouldn't necessarily have drawn notice."

"One person did say he thought he saw a policeman who wasn't in uniform." Fletcher shrugged. "Not particularly reliable or detailed, and he already seemed the worse for drink, despite the early hour."

The information piqued Henry's interest, given that he thought he'd glimpsed Clarke. "Did you get a description?"

"Yes. Average height and weight. Dark hair. Not much facial hair. No other identifying features—no helpful scars or convenient spectacles. Unfortunately, that fits more than half of the department, including you."

Henry sighed, setting aside his disappointment. "We will see if Mr. Taylor can offer any clues after he examines the body. For now, let's return to the Yard and advise Director Reynolds of the news." He didn't mention that he was anxious to discover where Clarke had been at the time of the murder. "You're not going to believe what was in Edgarton's pocket."

"The scarab?" Fletcher asked, his brow lifted.

Henry stilled. How on earth had he guessed? "Yes." Unease ran along his spine, and he dearly wished someone had witnessed him finding it.

"You're joking." Fletcher's look of disbelief might've been amusing under other circumstances. "Truly?"

At Henry's nod, Fletcher's moustache twitched. "Damn. So Edgarton was the one who took it."

"I don't think so," Henry countered. "Remember, there was no sign of a break-in at the Yard. How could he have?"

"Right. So whoever killed him...put it in his pocket?"

"That appears to be the case."

"Double damn."

Henry lifted a brow. "I thought you'd sworn off swearing." After all, the sergeant had promised his wife he'd quit a few months ago. Henry had yet to meet her but looked forward to it.

"Impossible when you have this job. I still try not to swear in front of the missus, though."

Henry nodded, the lighter moment a reminder of why he liked Fletcher. The sergeant made him smile. He only hoped his uncle wasn't involved in the recent events—and that Fletcher wasn't either.

They returned heavy-hearted to the Yard and Henry went directly to Reynolds' office to provide an update.

The Director was less than pleased to hear of Edgarton's murder. "Now we have yet another case on our hands."

"There is one more thing you should know." Henry couldn't deny a feeling of relief as he placed the scarab on his superior's desk and unwrapped it. The missing evidence had bothered him even more than he realized. Yet a small seed of worry remained at the fact that no one had seen him find it. "*This* was in Edgarton's pocket."

The Director stared at it with a scowl. "I'm not certain whether to be pleased or more frustrated."

"I admit to feeling the same." Henry braced himself for the inevitable next question, wishing he had a better answer.

"And who else was there when you found it?" The Director's gaze held on Henry.

"No one. Fletcher was outside, looking for witnesses. The vicar had stepped away. Peters had arrived suddenly, but by then had left to find a cart to haul away the body. There was no one else in the church."

The scowl deepened as Reynolds stared at the scarab. "That's unfortunate."

It was natural that his superior wanted corroboration—evidence. They both wanted to clear his name. "Perhaps not ideal, but that doesn't change the truth. I didn't take the scarab, so I couldn't have placed it on Edgarton's person."

"Right." The Director held his gaze for a long moment before slowly nodding. "Do you have any suspects for the murder of our prime suspect?"

"Not yet. There's little to go on at this point, though perhaps Mr. Taylor will offer some clues."

"How can there be so many people in Whitechapel, yet no one saw anything?"

"Not a complete surprise when the police are not trusted there." Henry glanced around the numerous desks in the office then back at Reynolds. "There was one possible witness who claimed to see a police officer out of uniform. Said he had dark hair, average height and weight."

"Not particularly helpful."

"Agreed. Have you seen Clarke this afternoon?"

"No, why?" Reynolds frowned.

"I thought I saw him in Whitechapel." Henry shook his head. "Thought maybe he was who the witness saw since I thought I saw him too."

"Doubtful. He's working a theft case on Arlington Street."

That didn't mean he hadn't been in Whitechapel, though Henry had to admit it was unlikely—the two places were at least an hour's walk apart, perhaps an hour and a half.

Somehow he needed to find out exactly where the other inspector had been that morning—perhaps all the inspectors.

The threads of several mysteries appeared to be unraveling rather than falling into place.

Twenty-Three

THE FAINT SOUND OF voices in the foyer caused Amelia to glance toward the clock on the mantel to see it was nearly six o'clock. She'd spent the last hour reading the new book she'd purchased, enjoying the sensation of losing herself within the pages of someone else's world. As always, it provided the perfect escape.

Based on the hour, a new constable had arrived and was advising Fernsby of his presence. The thought had her setting aside her book to cross to the window, pausing before she looked out to pet Master Leopold who napped in his favorite chair nearby.

As always, a wave of relief washed over her as she confirmed that no one was watching the house. How ridiculous to worry when a constable would discourage any strangers who attempted to do so.

She turned away from the window to find Henry in the doorway, a cautious smile on his face. A jolt of pleasure spread through her, warming her from the inside out. "Henry. What a pleasant surprise."

"Amelia." He dipped his head as he continued in, his eyes searching her face, making her wonder what he saw—or what he hoped to.

The cat meowed as it sat up and stretched before hopping down to stroll toward Henry's legs.

"Hello, Master Leopold." He scratched the cat behind its ears before looking back at Amelia. "How was your day?"

Once again, shadows lingered in his eyes. *Clearly something had happened.*

The thought saddened her, making Amelia wonder once again how he stood it. The ups and downs—mainly the downs—of his job must cause emotional distress every day. He still wore his coat, implying he wouldn't remain long. That was disappointing.

Preparing herself, Amelia refused to allow the possibility of bad news to steal her happiness at his visit. A few minutes of enjoyable conversation were first in order, and it would do him good as well.

"The day has been a good one. Productive for the most part." She gestured toward her desk. "I worked more on my magazine article, and the pea pod experiment is coming along nicely."

He smiled at the mention of the fertilizer testing, just as she'd hoped. "I am pleased to hear that, and my mother will be as well."

"Do you have time for a drink or does duty call?"

He smiled, clearly tempted. She liked that, too. How lovely to think he might enjoy their time together as much as she did.

"I have time if it doesn't interfere with your evening."

She nearly laughed. Her evenings were very quiet. Perhaps too quiet. "Not at all. I would enjoy it, too." Ignoring the heat in her cheeks at the admission, she went to the sideboard to pour their usual drinks. It was beginning to be a routine of theirs; one she treasured.

After handing him a whiskey and settling before the fire with her sherry, she cleared her throat, watching as Leopold circled before determining the ideal place to rest was on the rug at their feet. "I had a wonderful letter from Maeve's aunt today."

"Oh? How is she?" The light of interest in his eyes warmed her even more than the fire.

The ravenkeeper's daughter had made her way into both their hearts. Her life wouldn't be easy, being deaf and mute and with both her parents gone, but she had a fierce spirit that couldn't be denied, even after witnessing her father's murder.

"She's doing very well. It took some time to adjust to the school she's attending, but her teachers have nothing but praise to say about her and how quickly she's learning. She has made several friends, which I am pleased to hear."

"That is excellent news. Is there any chance we will see her this summer?" He took a sip of his drink and some of the stiffness in his shoulders eased as he relaxed into the chair.

Henry's life focused too much on his job. If she could distract him, even for a quarter of an hour while they exchanged pieces of their day, she would do so. Whatever news he had could clearly wait.

"Her aunt didn't mention a visit, but I will inquire when I reply." A tingle of nerves ran along Amelia's skin. "I also received a letter from my parents. They are coming for a visit next week."

"You must be looking forward to that. It's been some time since they've been to see you, has it not?"

"Yes. It's difficult for Father to leave the apothecary for long, but he has a promising new assistant to take his place for a few days." Dare she ask what had come to mind the moment she'd read about their upcoming visit, or was it too forward? "If possible, I should like you to meet them. May I invite you to dinner while they're here?"

She had mentioned Henry in her letters and spoken of him when she'd visited her parents at Christmas. Her mother had seemed to sense her growing feelings but had also expressed concern about the danger of Henry's job as an inspector.

Amelia appreciated that worry. She'd already lost her daughter and husband; losing another person in her life would be devastating, especially when she still felt weighted by grief. But neither could she deny how much she enjoyed Henry's company. How every day lightened when he was within it.

It had been easy to call what she felt for the handsome inspector mere friendship for a time, but her feelings were moving beyond that at a quick pace.

Perhaps quicker than she was comfortable with.

Henry's brows rose as if he were surprised by her request, but she hoped it was a pleasant sort of surprise, a hope seemingly confirmed as he said, "I should very much like to meet them. I remain at your disposal."

The light of interest in his expression had her smiling, already imagining how well he and her father would get on. They both had a curiosity and logic to their thoughts, something she appreciated. "Good. I expect to know their schedule soon and will keep you advised."

She took a sip of sherry and decided she was ready to hear whatever news he had to share. "Based on your expression upon arriving, I assume something...unfortunate occurred today?"

He sighed. "You could say that." He held her gaze for a long moment. "Edgarton has been found dead."

Amelia drew a quick breath of surprise. Relief flooded her, followed quickly by concern. Somehow, it seemed doubtful his death had resolved the situation. "How? Murdered?" Otherwise, Henry wouldn't be so concerned.

He nodded then took another sip of his whiskey. Clearly, he was still processing the news and what it meant.

"Where was he...found?" She preferred to know as many details as possible. As many as Henry could tell her.

"At St. Mary's in Whitechapel."

She frowned as she considered the information. "An odd place for a criminal to go. And he was killed there?" She pressed a hand to her chest at the terrible thought.

"Yes. Stabbed."

The single word brought to mind memories of the man she'd found stabbed at Edgarton's bidding. A man she and her husband had known. The pool of red beneath him. The helplessness which had swept over her as she'd tried to staunch the bleeding.

Amelia closed her eyes to shut out the memory but with little success.

Henry's hand on her arm halted the cascade of panic and she opened her eyes to meet his.

"My apologies. I didn't mean to upset you."

"You didn't. Edgarton did." She shook her head. "Memories of Mr. Locke's passing are still difficult."

"Of course, they are. I perhaps shouldn't have shared that detail, but I thought you'd want to know."

"I do." She placed her hand on top of his without thinking, needing the connection. "I would rather hear such things from you than from the newspaper or the like."

Henry studied her face, then withdrew his hand and sat back in the chair. "I don't care to see you upset."

"I appreciate that." Life clearly had other plans. She'd spent much of the past few years feeling exactly that. But she was stronger than she'd realized, and the thought had her lifting her chin. "I truly would prefer you were always honest with me."

He slowly nodded. "I would like the same."

She smiled at their agreement on what seemed like a fundamental part of a relationship. She need only think of how she and Matthew had lost trust as they'd grown apart to know how important it was to any bond.

"Amelia," he began only to frown. "I wanted Edgarton tried and convicted for your late husband's death. There is no doubt in my mind that he did it. I hate that we weren't able to see justice through to the end for both your sakes."

"As do I. But it is enough to know Edgarton was arrested, even if he escaped, and is now gone. And I suppose one could say he paid the ultimate price for his crimes, even if it wasn't at the hand of the law." How unfortunate she would never know further details about what happened to Matthew...but Amelia was no longer certain learning more would bring her peace. Everything she had learned so far had brought her naught but turmoil. "Do you have any idea who killed him? I can imagine there were many who wished him dead, from disgruntled employees to other criminals and those he'd crossed."

"No distinct leads yet." Henry tapped a finger on the arm of the chair, suggesting he considered various ideas in answer to the question much like she did.

"How does this affect the case of the murdered prison guard?" Amelia recalled how Edgarton had been the most likely suspect in that investigation, though Henry had previously mentioned that he had doubts about his guilt.

"It always complicates matters when a possible suspect in a case is murdered."

"Much like what happened with Mr. Locke." Locke had been suspected of killing a fellow import-export shop owner until his own death. Amelia bit her lip. So many deaths...

"Right. Another body is a clue of sorts but not preferrable to other ones," Henry said wryly.

"I'm sure you would rather have a simple theft to solve instead of all these recent murders."

"I have a few of those, too, but haven't been able to spend much time on them." Henry shrugged as a smile played at the corner of his mouth.

Amelia had to bite her lip to keep from asking for details. How ridiculous that she found such enjoyment in hearing about his cases. They were like puzzles with high stakes. But those involving murder, especially of someone connected to her, were unsettling...yet all the more important to solve.

"Does Edgarton's death mean it will no longer be necessary for a constable to watch over things here?" She hoped that was the case.

"More than likely, yes, but I need to confirm that with the Director before I dismiss them. Logic suggests that your testimony against Edgarton shouldn't matter to anyone other than him."

Amelia allowed a long exhale to relieve the tension in her body. "While I am sorry his death complicates your job, I won't miss worrying about whether he might appear on my doorstep."

"Nor will I." He finished his drink and shifted to the edge of his chair. "I should be going."

"Of course." She hoped her expression didn't reveal her disappointment. Though tempted to ask him to stay for dinner, she had the feeling he'd decline the invitation. Mayhaps it was better to wait to do so next week, when her parents were here.

She rose with a quiet sigh, the moment a reminder of her loneliness. There was a difference between being alone and feeling lonely. That wasn't something she'd fully realized until the last few months. "I will send word when I know more about my parents' schedule."

"I look forward to meeting them." Henry turned to go only to turn back. "Amelia, the message you were given while shopping didn't match Edgarton's handwriting."

She'd nearly forgotten about that. "Yes, I didn't think it looked the same from what I remembered."

And yet his worried expression remained. "That means there may be someone else who doesn't want you involved in the investigation."

Amelia shook her head, perplexed by the idea. "I can't imagine who that could be or why."

"Nor can I." Henry bent to scratch the cat again and was rewarded with another satisfied purr. "Regardless of whether a constable remains, I would ask you to take care and remain on the lookout for any unusual people in the area."

"I will." That seemed to be a habit she wouldn't break. "You should take care as well, Henry." She held his gaze once he straightened, hoping he would take her words to heart.

His brown eyes heated, her chest doing the same in response. "Thank you. For thinking of me." He looked away, seeming to hesitate whether to say more.

Say it, she wanted to plead as anticipation filled her.

He reached to take her hand and clasped it gently between both of his. "I think of you often, Amelia. I have come to treasure our friendship."

Her heart fluttered as a shiver ran along her skin. She wasn't certain what to say in response. "As have I." She moved her thumb back and forth along his hand, a small gesture of affection. Whether she—or he—was ready for more remained to be seen.

He smiled and released her. "I'm pleased to hear it. I will be in touch as the investigation evolves. Good evening, Amelia."

Amelia watched him go, pressing a hand to her pounding heart. "Be well, Henry," she whispered.

"Meow." Master Leopold rubbed against her skirts as if in solidarity.

She bent to pick him up. "Thank you for understanding," she whispered against his fur, emotions mingling and warring within her: fading fear as the danger seemed to retreat, shock and revulsion at Edgarton's death...and emotions she would not name whenever Henry smiled at her.

Relationships were complicated, involving highs and lows. She knew very well how much some moments could hurt, but others brought deep joy, and that was what she would focus on for now. *Joy.* "One day at a time, right, Leopold?"

The cat purred once again as if in agreement.

Twenty-Four

"**H**EARD YOU FOUND THE escaped prisoner, Field." Perdy chuckled and glanced at the few others already at the Yard as Henry walked to his desk the next morning. "Too bad he was already dead."

Henry resisted the urge to turn on his heel and depart. Instead, he pulled out his chair and sat. The other inspector would only hold his comments until the next time they met.

If Henry didn't know better, he'd think Perdy had arrived early so that he could jab at Henry about Edgarton's death. He was hardly one for early mornings.

Whitlock strolled forward to join Perdy, sharing a look of amusement with him. "At least he won't be murdering anyone else. But now you have to find who killed him."

"Did he have the missing evidence stashed in his pocket?" Clarke asked from his desk as he opened a folder. "That would've been convenient."

The three men chuckled darkly.

Henry braced himself for further derision at what he was about to say, but all he could do was tell the truth. After all, Reynolds hadn't said to keep that part to himself. "As a matter of fact, he did have the scarab." He leveled a steely glare at

Clarke. "Interesting that you knew he not only had it, but that it was in his pocket."

Clarke's face turned ruddy even as his eyes narrowed. "What are you implying?"

"I'm merely making an observation." And if it put the man on notice that Henry was watching him, all the better. "I'm sure the three of you will rest easier knowing he's dead and the missing evidence recovered."

"Indeed, we will." Perdy nodded with a smirk, tucking his thumbs in his pockets. "Now the question is, who killed the escaped prisoner. Got any leads?"

"Not yet." Henry leaned back in his chair, forcing himself to relax. Allowing them to get under his skin would only encourage them. That was something he refused to do. "Perhaps one of you has an idea?"

He watched Perdy closely. Not for a moment had he forgotten the unsolved Douglas Grant case, a murder victim who had worked for Edgarton and was found dead with a single bullet to his temple. Several months later, Matthew Greystone had been killed in a similar manner.

Perdy had been assigned to the case but from what Henry could tell, had done little to solve it. If he had, Edgarton might have been caught and convicted a year ago...and they wouldn't be in this mess.

"We'll leave it to you since you're the expert in finding dead bodies." Whitlock waved a hand in Henry's direction. "Clearly, we're not needed on this one."

Henry shifted his gaze to Clarke, still wondering if he'd lurked in the shadows at St. Mary's despite Fletcher insisting he'd seen no one. Had Henry's imagination placed the man there? Had it been some trick of the light?

Clarke looked away when Henry continued to stare. The other inspector glanced at those standing nearby, almost appearing uncomfortable.

The silence drew long, filling the room.

At last Henry asked quietly, "What of you, Clarke? Surely you have an opinion on who killed Edgarton." He slowly moved his focus to each of the other men. "One of you *must* have a theory."

At that moment Duncan stepped into the room and glared at all of them, including Henry. "If you need help with the case, Field, just say so. No need to play games."

Henry drew a quick breath, reminding himself Duncan was on his side. At least, he hoped that was still true. The man could have a second career as an actor, so believable was his performance. "I would take any *constructive* suggestions. We all want the same thing, don't we? Justice? The sooner we solve both the prison guard's murder and Edgarton's, the better."

"The prison guard?" Perdy frowned. "That was Edgarton. Who else could it have been?"

It didn't surprise Henry that Perdy reached for the easiest answer, but that didn't make it right.

"If Edgarton wanted to kill the prison guard, why would he have waited a week to do so?" Henry asked quietly, trying not to stare at any one man too long. "Even if the guard confessed to aiding him, it wouldn't change the murder charges—and therefore wouldn't matter." He paused for a beat. "The question is, who didn't want Cobb to talk? To admit to taking a bribe?"

"What is that supposed to mean?" Whitlock's eyes narrowed. "Surely you're not accusing one of our own."

Henry didn't miss the warning look Duncan sent him, so he gave a casual shrug. "I am not accusing anyone. I'm merely sharing the questions running through my mind about the case."

"Keep 'em to yourself." Perdy shook his head ill-temperedly as he turned away. "We have investigations of our own to worry about."

"You're the one who raised the subject," Henry reminded him, returning his attention to the files on his desk, hoping his frustration didn't show.

The three men went on about their business, though Henry continued to feel the occasional weight of their stares. Undoubtedly, one or more thought Henry had taken the scarab for his own gain and had only returned it because he was being looked at too closely.

But no one else in the department seemed to believe that, including Fletcher, Duncan, Johnson, and Reynolds. That had to be some comfort.

As much as he didn't like Perdy, Henry wasn't sure the other inspector had the ambition to accept bribes from a man like Edgarton or the grit to kill him if the situation grew out of hand.

But Whitlock or Clarke might.

While Henry hesitated to rely solely on a hunch, that was all he had at the moment, and time was of the essence.

Had Duncan discovered anything useful? He certainly hoped so, and wanted to ask if he could determine Clarke's whereabouts at the time Edgarton had been stabbed.

One thing was clear now Edgarton had died—Henry needed a new plan. He had to approach both Cobb and Edgarton's investigations from a different angle. Murder was often personal, and that seemed accurate in both cases. The victims had more than likely been familiar with their killers. And the murderer of the two men might have been one and the same.

So who benefited from silencing both Cobb and Edgarton?

Excellent question, but impossible to answer at this point. He needed to determine who knew both victims, and more importantly, *how* they had come to know them. Looking more deeply into the men's lives, especially Edgarton's, might reveal a vital clue. He'd make another attempt to find Betty Knox, the woman Edgarton had been living with in Whitechapel, to see what she knew. With Edgarton dead, she might be scared and willing to talk.

That was, if they could find her.

After a half hour of updating his notes on a few cases and leaving orders for a constable who worked on another of his investigations, Henry went to speak with Director Reynolds, only to find his door closed.

It was a rare occurrence and raised Henry's curiosity about who was with the Director.

Not your problem, Henry reminded himself as he turned away from the door. There was enough mistrust and distrust in this building already.

He'd taken a step back toward his desk when Reynold's door clicked open, and Whitlock emerged. The other inspector glared at Henry as he passed, his face flushed.

"Field?" Reynolds called.

Henry pulled his focus to the Director and stepped into the doorway, wishing he knew what had been said. "I wanted to update you on what we know so far on Edgarton, sir."

"Good." Reynolds waved him in.

Since Henry didn't have much, the conversation didn't take long. There weren't many leads to pursue. "I'm going to attempt to find Betty Knox again—and it might be worth having another conversation with the men connected to Edgarton's lottery scheme who were arrested. There's always the chance I will find Cobb's killer as I pursue Edgarton's murder investigation."

"Someone has to know something," Reynolds said as he removed his spectacles to polish them on a handkerchief. "Keep asking until you get an answer."

"Yes, sir." The weight on Henry's shoulders increased. The order wasn't helpful.

"Thought I'd brighten up your morning with another problem." Reynolds replaced his spectacles and reached for a newspaper on his desk to hand to Henry.

Rookery Killer Strikes Whitechapel. Henry frowned as he skimmed the story that described Edgarton, his childhood ties to Whitechapel, mysterious and admirable generous donations to St. Mary's, and his scandalous murder within the church.

Oh, excellent. "Why would the press choose to show Edgarton in such a favorable light when he'd been arrested for the murder of several people?"

"Exactly what I'm wondering." The Director scowled. "And details about the murder scene that very few know are described in the article. What is going on, Field?"

Henry continued reading, only to shake his head. "I...I don't know. Perhaps it would be worthwhile to have a word with the reporter to see if he knows something we don't."

"It's a sad state of affairs when Fleet Street knows more than we do," the Director grumbled. "Keep me apprised of what you learn."

"Of course, sir." Henry didn't care for the poor light the article cast upon the police. Clearly, neither did the Director.

He returned to his desk, pleased to see Fletcher had arrived, still wishing he knew what had been said between Whitlock and Reynolds.

Before Henry could approach him, the sergeant walked across the room to speak with his uncle. The conversation was too quiet to overhear, but based on the men's demeanor, whatever they discussed was serious and involved.

Henry waited at his desk until the two finished. Clarke rose and placed an arm over Fletcher's shoulders, a reminder of their close connection.

Family. And what wouldn't Henry do for his own family?

Discomfort twisted his gut. Was Henry wrong about the new inspector? If Fletcher didn't have the same doubts, then Henry had to wonder if he was making something out of nothing. What would Fletcher's reaction have been if he'd witnessed Clarke's earlier hostility toward Henry? Henry was almost glad the sergeant hadn't.

All he could do was continue to press for answers until one arose.

That didn't alleviate the uneasy feeling when Fletcher approached him with a grin on his face, a clear result of his conversation with his uncle. "Do you have need of me, sir?"

"I do." Henry stood and reached for his coat and hat. "We have a few stops to make."

They walked out of the Yard, and Henry couldn't help but glance at Fletcher, wondering at his thoughts. "Good conversation with your uncle?"

"Yes. I've missed his company over the last few years. He is a good man."

Is he? Henry shrugged away the question. He didn't want to ruin the friendship he and Fletcher had by voicing his concerns. Not until he had evidence that proved Clarke was involved. He only hoped the man was innocent; he could imagine how upsetting anything else would be for Fletcher.

"Where to first?" Fletcher asked.

"Fleet Street to speak with a reporter, then back to Holloway Prison."

"I saw the article this morning about the Rookery Killer. Is that why we're going to Fleet Street?" At Henry's nod, the sergeant shook his head. "Where do they get their information?"

"I'd like to know that as well."

Fleet Street was a short distance away, and they quickly arrived at the offices of *The Standard*, where chaos reigned. The office was packed with numerous rows of desks piled with papers, and reporters strode about with frazzled expressions. The atmosphere was even faster-paced than that of the police station, which Henry found puzzling. How could writing news stories possibly be more intense than solving crimes?

"Howard Stratton, please," Henry requested at the first desk.

"Right. Allow me to see if Mr. Stratton is available." The young man at the desk sent a disdainful look in Fletcher's direction, seeming to take issue with his uniform.

Henry could plainly see Mr. Stratton, the reporter he'd spoken to many times, sitting at his desk scribbling on a piece of paper but Henry nodded even as he heaved an impatient sigh.

"If he's available?" Fletcher asked as the young man walked away. "We can see that he is."

"Have no worries. He will speak with us if I have anything to say about it," Henry replied, his gaze holding on the man in question.

The reporter glanced their way, lips tightening as he undoubtedly recognized Henry. They'd had several conversations in the past, and not especially friendly ones. Too often the press and the police were so often on opposite sides of issues.

Henry didn't mind the press's stated pursuit of the truth as he had the same objective, but he did not appreciate the sensationalism many of their articles contained in their quest to sell more papers.

"Inspector Field." Mr. Stratton nodded as he approached. "What an...unpleasant surprise."

Henry forced a polite smile. "Stratton. We have a few questions for you about an article you wrote."

"Oh? I'm glad you enjoyed it. Which one?" The man, who appeared a bit younger than Henry and was a head shorter, lifted a brow as if he couldn't begin to guess.

"The rookery killer," Fletcher ground out.

"Ah, yes. Terrible situation, isn't it? To have a killer on the loose in Whitechapel. Some believed the victim was a Robin Hood of sorts, giving back to the streets he grew up on. Commendable, in his way."

"The 'victim' was an escaped prisoner with more charges against him than I have fingers, as you well know," Henry countered. "What purpose is there behind not only idolizing Edgarton but claiming a killer is on the loose in Whitechapel?"

"I merely report the facts as they are given to me."

"Who gave them to you?" Henry pressed.

Stratton's smile suggested he had no intention of sharing that. "Oh, I couldn't say. Confidential information, you know."

"Was the vicar at St. Mary's one of your sources?" Henry pressed. He was the only one other than the killer and the police officers to have seen Edgarton's body before they'd hauled it away. It had to be him.

"The vicar? No, but I shall make a note to have a word with him." Stratton's flippant attitude grated as he grinned. "Thank you for the tip."

"Then who?" Henry took a step closer, not opposed to using his larger size to intimidate the man. He wanted to make it clear this was a serious matter, and he expected an answer. A truthful one.

"I'm pleased to think the story was accurate enough to warrant a visit from Scotland Yard. One would almost think I had some sort of *inside* information." The knowing gleam in the reporter's eyes made it clear he was enjoying the conversation.

"Inside?" Fletcher repeated with a concerned look at Henry. "And what is that supposed to mean?"

"I didn't *say* I did," Stratton quickly denied. "I'm not saying I didn't. Now, if you gentlemen will excuse me, I must return to work. Another important story awaits my attention. In fact, I look forward to hearing what you think about it. You may visit to congratulate me tomorrow, when it's printed." With a smirk, the reporter turned to go.

"Stratton." Henry waited until the man looked back. "I'd be careful whom I asked questions of if I were you. Watch yourself."

"I didn't know you cared for my well-being, Inspector Field. I'm touched." With a nod, the reporter returned to his desk.

"He's a piece, that one," Fletcher muttered. "Who would have given him such a detailed description of the crime scene?"

"And why?" Henry added under his breath. That question pointed to a dark motive; one that he was determined to uncover.

Twenty-Five

HENRY AND FLETCHER WERE fortunate enough to have timed their visit to Holloway Prison during the hour allotted for exercise for the male inmates. In the large yard male prisoners, some awaiting trial and others already sentenced, walked about for a brief period each day.

Not everyone wore prison garb. A few were clearly well-to-do based on their attire and could pay extra for better accommodations, food, and a creature comfort or two, as well. Luckily, this wasn't a trial day, making for a calmer atmosphere. A guard directed them to where the prisoner with whom Henry wanted to speak stood.

Samuel Richards. His involvement in a crooked lottery scheme, another of Edgarton's illegal businesses, had led to his arrest—and while they were questioning him, Amelia had happened to come by the police station and recognize him as the same man who had stabbed and killed Locke, the import-export shop owner.

Richards had agreed to testify against Edgarton in exchange for a lesser sentence. Henry hoped there was more Richards hadn't told them but would if pressed, especially since Edgarton was now dead and Richards' hope for a reduced sentence was in jeopardy.

Henry's gaze swept across the lifeless yard. The female prisoners were somewhere else, working away—in solitude, key to their rehabilitation according to the great political minds of the day. It was an odd notion, but such matters were beyond his control. Men of all types walked around the yard, and a variety of accents could be heard. Henry picked out French, Spanish, something that sounded like Yiddish—all languages he heard frequently on the London streets. Pickpockets, costermongers, and sailors were among them, a few that Henry recognized as he'd arrested them himself.

Richards looked none too happy to see them, eyes narrowed and flashing with displeasure at their approach, especially as other prisoners watched with interest.

"Enjoying the fresh air?" Henry sent a doubtful look around the yard. The prison was situated near several factories, and the sky over it often appeared dark and foreboding, bad weather paired with heavy smoke. This March day was no exception.

"Not hardly." The man's lips tightened. "What do the two of ye want?"

"Information," Fletcher replied curtly.

"I already told ye what I know. Leave off."

Henry glanced at his sergeant. "There is still the matter of the missing man who complained about the numbers behind the lottery scheme, isn't there? We have yet to name a suspect for his assumed murder."

"Mr. Spencer, the accountant with an affinity for details who disappeared without a trace," Fletcher added nonchalantly.

"Weren't we told that Richards was the one he mentioned the problem to?"

"You know, I believe we were. And soon after, Mr. Spencer disappeared." Henry turned back to face the prisoner. "The scar beneath your eye is apparently memorable."

"I don't know what ye're talking about." The man shuffled his feet, clearly not liking the conversation but unable to walk away when he had nowhere to go.

"Sure you do," Henry prompted, trying to keep his voice level. "Mr. Spencer was the reason you were forced to close the lottery office and stay out of sight for a time, remember?"

"Doesn't sound familiar." Richards stared across the yard, obviously wishing he were somewhere else.

He wasn't the only one.

"If you'd rather not be investigated for his death, then let's talk about Edgarton," Henry suggested. In truth, it would be nearly impossible to charge anyone for Spencer's assumed murder with little evidence and no body.

"What about him?" Wariness tightened the prisoner's expression.

"He's dead." Henry watched the other man closely for a reaction, noting the shock that briefly crossed his face.

"Not a surprise, I suppose," Richards said at last, trying to sound casual. "He made more than a few enemies."

"Care to share a name or two with us?" Henry asked.

"No. Don't know anything about it."

"Who other than you worked closely with Edgarton? Who was second in command?"

Richards considered the question for a long moment. "Belcher, but from what I heard, he already left London. No harm in naming him when he's long gone."

Belcher. "What's his full name?"

"Robert Belcher. Lived in Whitechapel. Best of luck finding him."

The name wasn't familiar to Henry, though he would certainly look into him. A name—but it wasn't enough. "Who else? Edgarton had a large network. Who wanted him dead? The bribe he gave to the prison guard wasn't the only one he handed out."

Richards scoffed. "Ye're right about that." He studied Henry. "He had 'is finger pressed on a few of ye in addition to the guards."

Henry stilled, as did Fletcher. This was what they needed to know, even if he didn't want to hear it. Not when it confirmed he'd been right to be suspicious of his fellow officers. "Who?"

Richards shook his head as he glanced around. "I'd be a fool to say anything when I'm penned in 'ere. Too easy fer one of yer kind to 'ave me silenced, permanent-like."

"Not if we arrest them first." Even as he spoke, Henry wasn't sure he could promise anything of the sort. He'd suspected at least one other guard beyond Cobb was involved in allowing Edgarton to escape, but who else? And who within the department?

Startling at shadows, suspecting the loyal, where did it end?

"It's bad enough that everyone sees ye talkin' to me now." Richards shook his head again as he glanced around the exercise yard. "Anything 'appens, they'd know it was me who sold 'em out."

"We need a name," Henry insisted, though he doubted it would do any good.

"Look around yer police station and see who isn't doin' what they're supposed to be." Richards smirked. "Shouldn't be so hard."

The urge to shake the man until he gave them more took Henry by surprise. He clenched his fist to hold back the impulse, reminding himself that such behavior wouldn't give them what they needed.

"Let us know if you change your mind." Henry hesitated, uncertain he had the authority to offer anything more, but decided he had to try. "I would do what I could to gain your release."

The eye roll suggested he was clearly unimpressed. "Don't count on it. Being 'ere is better than bein' dead."

Henry bit back his disappointment as he bid him goodbye and led the way out, aware of the unfriendly gazes of other prisoners following them. Several minutes passed before the doors were unlocked and they were allowed to exit the prison.

"He can't be telling the truth," Fletcher said in an undertone the moment they reached the street.

"I think he is." That didn't mean Henry liked it.

"But there's no one at the Yard, other than Perdy, who could be a traitor and involved in taking bribes."

Henry held back a response since he disagreed. Instead he waited to see if Fletcher more carefully considered the facts and realized the truth.

Several minutes passed as they walked at a fast clip before the sergeant muttered an oath. "Damn. If you take in the missing evidence, Cobb's murder followed by Edgarton's, as well as what Richards said...it makes you wonder."

"Yes, it does." Would Fletcher also see the timing of it all? That a series of unfortunate events had escalated within Scotland Yard soon after his uncle's arrival?

"But who?" Fletcher asked. Again Henry didn't answer because, in truth, he didn't know. "I *want* it to be Perdy," Fletcher added. "It would be a pleasure to take him down."

Henry had to smile as he glanced at his friend. "I confess to having thought the same. But we can't allow our own opinions to sway us."

"Yes, but sometimes you have to go with your gut, eh?"

"Not if personal feelings cloud it. Besides, hunches don't convict criminals. Evidence does."

Fletcher groaned, as if he didn't like the reminder. "True enough. Too bad we don't have more of it at the moment."

Henry sighed at that inarguable remark. Though he'd already decided it would be worthwhile interviewing the supposed witness in Cobb's building, he had few other ideas. "Let us find something to eat and discuss our hunches. Maybe they can lead us to evidence."

First to evidence, and then hopefully to an arrest that would ensure Amelia was safe.

Twenty-Six

AMELIA SIGHED WITH SATISFACTION as she completed the final draft of the orchid article. *There.* She'd interviewed another collector and polished her story until it shone. Now she intended to deliver it to the editor herself.

Excitement filled her at the thought of leaving the house without the threat of Edgarton finding her or needing a constable to accompany her. She had yet to stop looking out the window at the street below, but hoped that day would soon come.

Her parents would arrive for a visit the following afternoon and she looked forward to seeing them, along with introducing them to Henry, who was to join them for dinner that same evening.

Life was finally returning to normal, and she intended to enjoy every moment.

A hansom cab took her to the offices of *London Life* on the Strand. As she looked up at the stone façade with its ornate cornices and arched windows, she had to pinch herself once again that she was lucky enough to be a small part of the publication. Would a new assignment be waiting for her? She certainly hoped so.

Amelia didn't have to wait long in the small reception area with its dark wood paneling where several magazine covers were displayed before she was escorted to the second floor. Long wooden desks held stacks of papers and ink wells. Numerous staff members filled the space. Her editor's office stood against one wall where he oversaw the periodical's publication.

"Mrs. Greystone." Paul Stearn stood as she was shown into his office, a welcoming smile on his face. "Always a pleasure."

"Mr. Stearn." She smiled in return. "I hope the day finds you well."

"It does." The older man was tall, thin, and—as always—well-dressed in a black woolen suit. His dark hair was peppered with white and combed neatly to one side. A closely trimmed beard held less white, making her think he might be younger than she realized, especially when his energy seemed never-ending.

He had been nothing but encouraging since she'd started as a special correspondent covering the unique and unusual for *London Life* just over six months ago. His edits were light-handed, and she'd already learned much about writing from him, including how to make the reader feel like they were learning about a subject right along with her.

"Assume they are unfamiliar with the subject matter and share what intrigues you because it will more than likely interest them, too," he'd told her.

She'd taken that advice to heart and had received several compliments on her efforts from Mr. Stearn as well as fellow correspondents who also worked for the periodical.

He lifted a brow. "Does your arrival mean your latest article is complete?" His hopeful look made her grin.

"It does." She withdrew the folded sheets from her reticule and handed them to him, nerves tingling. "I hope you find it satisfactory."

"I know I will, as I have all your previous stories." He dipped his head in a bow. "We are lucky to have you as part of our staff."

Pride filled Amelia and helped chase away the nerves. Despite having written well over half a dozen articles, she still felt anxious each time she turned one in, so she appreciated his praise. That alone was enough reason to continue her position, along with the money it provided.

Amelia liked to think she was paying her own way in life and not simply relying on the funds Matthew had left her. That independence was important, becoming even more so now that she wasn't certain if Matthew had earned what he'd left her honorably. "You are too kind."

The sense of purpose the writing position provided was also welcome, and something she continued to yearn for. Serving as a correspondent allowed her to indulge her curious nature, learning about everything from the ravenkeeper at the Tower of London to the oldest clockmaker in the city.

"I only speak the truth. I am anxious to read it." He placed the pages, which she had carefully copied into a final form after much editing, in the center of his desk as if to give them precedence. She suspected he'd read it the moment she departed. "If you have a moment, I would like to tell you about a special request I received from an admirer of your reports."

"Oh?" An admirer? The thought thrilled her. Amelia had received a few notes from readers who enjoyed her articles, but she wouldn't have called them admirers. "I should very much like to hear about it." Whatever it was, the idea must hold merit if Mr. Stearn was taking the time to share it with her.

The man gestured to the chair before his desk, and they both sat. Then he retrieved a paper from a drawer, only to frown as he reviewed the contents, seeming to gather his thoughts, the delay further rousing her curiosity.

"The subject is...unique, something we haven't yet delved into," he began as he tapped a finger on the sheet. "Though many have heard of it, few are well versed on the topic, which means it would make an interesting piece."

"Now you simply must tell me about it," Amelia said, wanting to relieve the sudden tension in the air. "Who was it that wrote to you?"

"A Mrs. Mary Nettle. She writes that both she and her husband are avid readers of the magazine, particularly your stories."

Pleasure fluttered through her, and she couldn't help but press a hand to her heart. "How nice to hear that someone enjoys my perspective."

Mr. Stearn smiled warmly. "Madam, there are many who do. We frequently receive comments on your articles."

Amelia's confidence soared at the news.

"However, this is a unique request, and I confess I am not certain how to...discuss it with you." He frowned as he looked at the letter then met her gaze. "It involves divination."

"Divination," Amelia repeated as she considered what little she knew about the term. "Of what sort?"

"Mrs. Nettle claims to be able to channel spirits who provide information about those who have passed." He studied her as if waiting for her reaction.

Amelia considered for a moment, drawing on the scant information she could recall on such a subject. She had almost certainly read...yes, she had read an article explaining how the practice of contacting the deceased through seances or other supernatural means had gained in popularity in recent years.

Death fascinated people, she could understand that, and one could tour notorious crime scenes or attend a play that dramatized the story of infamous murders. It was natural that numerous people attempted to contact their loved ones who had passed before them. Though fraudulent mediums were frequently uncovered, it hadn't slowed the interest in such things.

Amelia clutched her reticule, stomach tightening with unease at the thought of exploring the topic. As much as she longed to have one more conversation with Lily or Matthew, she didn't truly believe it was possible.

At least, not in the sense that made it tempting enough to try.

The very idea of hearing from them made her uncomfortable. Life was difficult enough without them, but if she were to learn they were unhappy in the afterlife, what then?

How could she bear it?

"What is the exact nature of her...request?" she asked, suddenly breathless.

"An interview that shares how her ability works." Mr. Stearn adjusted his position in his chair, almost seeming to regret raising the topic. "She is rather well known for having helped to find missing persons."

"Interesting." And it was, except for the fact that Amelia had experienced so much loss of her own. She remembered seeing something about divination in one of the newspapers only last week, but she hadn't read the accounts as little about it appealed to her.

From a long way off, her editor continued. "She says the spirits often share clues pertaining to the whereabouts of the person, and she jots them down. Her notes and drawings don't make sense at first, but eventually, they come together to create a description that leads to the location of a body."

"Body?" Amelia hesitated as she considered that vital detail. "She...she only locates missing people who are deceased?"

"Yes." Mr. Stearn offered a wry look with a shrug. "An unusual ability, though I suppose that if successful, it might offer closure for a desperate family."

She nodded, still uncertain if she was prepared to learn more about the process. While she hated to think she didn't have the courage to investigate the topic, that might be the truth. She was already missing the orchids.

"Is interviewing her something you'd be willing to consider?" Mr. Stearns' kindly expression suggested she hadn't hidden her hesitation. He knew about the losses she'd endured and surely realized such an interview wouldn't be easy for her.

She took a moment to think it over, trying to set aside her emotions. The subject was certainly intriguing to many. She'd never spoken to a medium of any sort. Was she willing to?

What if Matthew or Lily reached through? Mrs. Nettle's talent didn't seem to have anything to do with Amelia's fears but even so, she couldn't help but worry about that possibility.

"I...I am sorry, but I think it would be best if another correspondent covered this particular story," she said after a long moment, certainty settling in her chest. "After losing both my daughter and my husband, I...I don't believe I would be objective enough to provide an unbiased report."

"I understand completely." Mr. Stearn nodded sympathetically. "I wouldn't have asked if Mrs. Nettle hadn't mentioned you by name. I will advise her that your schedule won't permit it and suggest another correspondent in your stead."

Relief shot through her. Clearly she'd made the right decision based on that feeling alone. "Thank you. I appreciate it." She rose, unable to hold back the sudden need to escape. "I should be going," she added at the editor's look of surprise.

"Oh. Certainly." He stood as well. "I will look over the other potential interviews, find a more suitable one, and be in touch."

"Thank you."

He started around the corner of his desk, and she walked toward the door, ready to put the request behind her.

"Do let me know if there is a topic you think our readers would enjoy," the editor said, sending her a concerned look as he held the door.

"I will." She forced a smile. "Thank you, Mr. Stearn."

"Good day, Mrs. Greystone."

It took all her will not to rush out of the building. The panic gripping her was impossible to understand, it made no sense. She'd turned down the offer, and Mr. Stearn accepted her answer. The matter was over and done.

Amelia placed the blame for her reeling emotions on recent events. She'd been living with danger of one sort or another hanging over her head for months. The interview might have been one she would enjoy conducting—if her husband and daughter still lived.

But if they were living, she would not have felt unfulfilled, without purpose. She would never have gone to the magazine, never started writing. She...she would have had a child, and a husband to care for, to devote herself to.

Stars spun in the corners of Amelia's eyes at the reminder of how much her life had changed so quickly.

She stepped onto the pavement and paused to draw a slow breath, forcing her attention to the people walking past—an older woman with bright pink feathers in her hat. A young man who walked with a rolling gait and a crooked grin. The cart driver who drove by, his cap pulled low and collar turned up.

The normalcy of the moment helped to ease her distress. There was no need for concern, she reminded herself. No need to feel unsettled. And most certainly, there was no need for the guilt that weighed on her.

A lump formed in her throat, bringing tears to her eyes. Had she done the right thing by refusing? Should she try to reach Lily and Matthew by whatever means necessary? The idea had crossed Amelia's mind before, but she'd never acted on it.

She certainly had unanswered questions, especially concerning Matthew. Yet a voice inside suggested she wouldn't gain satisfactory answers for his behavior or for what had happened to him through a medium.

And sweet Lily.

Was her daughter well? Did she even remember her mother?

With a steadying breath, Amelia waved to catch a hansom cab driver's attention, relieved to find one so quickly. She must return home before her emotions got the better of her.

After giving the cabbie her address, she quickly stepped inside. The terrible ache in her chest was one she hadn't felt for some time.

Thank goodness she'd declined the interview. How much more upsetting would it have been if she'd even considered going through with it?

By the time she arrived home, Amelia had her emotions better under control. Still, she retreated to her bedchamber, pausing by her daughter's door to press a hand on it...and wished for things that could never be.

Twenty-Seven

*S*COTLAND *Y*ARD *F*UMBLES *R*OOKERY *Killer Investiga-tion!*

Henry stared at the headline in disbelief, then shoved back in frustration from the table in the empty dining room at his lodging house. He'd made a point to read the paper this morning after the reporter's cryptic comment the previous day, and quickly realized the story was worse than the first one about a supposed rookery killer which had painted Edgarton in such a positive manner. When Henry's eye caught on his own name amidst the printed words, anger took hold.

An escaped prisoner, missing evidence mysteriously returned, and two murders. Where might the rookery killer strike next while the police force's blunders mount? Perhaps Inspector Field, who supposedly leads the investigation, isn't cut from the same cloth as his well-respected father and grandfather, who both served and protected our city with honor. The current Field's quick rise through the ranks seems to be undeserved and begs one to question the leadership of Scotland Yard.

"Damn." He held back the urge to crush the paper into a ball and burn it. That wouldn't erase the story. The newspaper had already been distributed, the damage was done.

He ran a hand over his face, a terrible sinking sensation in the pit of his stomach at the thought of anyone reading it. Or Director Reynolds. Henry sighed. The Home Secretary would be displeased as well, and would more than likely demand action be taken.

Was this the moment Henry lost the chance to continue as a detective, a career he'd wanted since his youth and worked hard to excel at?

Not if he had anything to say about it.

He jerked to his feet, startling his landlady as she entered with a tray in hand.

"Good morning, Inspector." She watched him warily.

"I'm sorry, Mrs. Douglas, but I just remembered I have an appointment."

"At this hour?" she asked. "Don't you want your breakfast?"

The steaming bowl of grey lumpy porridge on the tray held no appeal. "I don't have time. Sorry," he murmured again and took his leave, newspaper in hand.

The same reporter who'd penned the rookery killer article had written this one. Who was feeding him this information, and why? That was what Henry needed to determine. Having a goal would feel better than swirling in his helpless anger.

He returned to his room, donning his jacket and grabbing his hat only to pause, his steps faltering. His parents—certainly his father—would read the news sheet within the hour, as was his standard practice. And more than likely, Amelia as well. What would they think? His chest ached at the thought. While he'd told them about recent events, including the missing evidence, having his investigative skills compared unfavorably to his father and grandfather on the front page of a popular news sheet was another matter entirely.

A nightmare come to life.

Then there was Fletcher, Duncan, all the others at the Yard. Anyone who hadn't read it would soon hear of it. The thought of enduring the stares and whispers, jubilant or suspicious, tightened the knot in his stomach.

Henry shoved aside his worry and reminded himself to focus on what was within his control as he walked to the Yard. He wouldn't remain there long but wanted to show he wasn't guilty of any wrongdoing, and would continue to do all within his power to solve the cases. Unfortunately, that didn't feel like enough; especially now that his skills, or lack thereof, were being publicly questioned.

The brisk air did little to ease his upset. He paused before the door of the Yard and drew a calming breath. He needed to release some of his frustration or risk saying something he shouldn't to the first person who mentioned the article.

Uncertain whether he'd succeeded, Henry opened the door and walked in, bracing himself.

"Morning, Field." Sergeant Johnson sat at his usual post at the front desk. He gave his customary nod and returned to his work.

"Morning." Though relieved not to be immediately confronted, Henry continued past, knowing he couldn't expect that with the other inspectors. He walked directly toward the Director's office. There was no doubt he'd already seen the news story.

He nodded at the few other inspectors who were at their desks, annoyed to see Perdy among them, and knocked on Reynolds' open door. "Sir?"

Reynolds looked up, his gaze holding on Henry long enough for nerves to take a firm hold. "Hell of a story in the paper this morning, eh, Field?"

"Yes." Henry lifted the newspaper he still held. "When I spoke with Stratton yesterday, he hinted more was coming but wouldn't say what it contained."

The Director's eyes flashed with anger. "The events of the last two weeks have become a disaster, and thanks to that damned reporter, the public will now be up in arms." He shook his head. "What a circus. This isn't going to help people trust us, and I personally don't appreciate having my leadership skills questioned."

Henry held his silence; agreeing seemed pointless.

"I expect the Home Secretary will request an explanation." Reynolds' gaze shifted to the office behind Henry. "Apparently, one of our own decided to share the details about the cases with Stratton."

"It's disappointing to think so—but not as unsettling as knowing one of us has chosen to break the oath of office and allegiance to the Crown that he took." And threaten Henry's future with the department. While he was accustomed to the jabs and snide comments about his quick rise in the force, the remarks in the story held a sinister edge.

"I have yet to decide if whoever it is dislikes you so much that they made you their target or whether you were simply a convenient scapegoat." The Director scowled. "Who could it be?"

Henry couldn't offer his suspicions when he had no proof. Did Reynolds have a guess as to who was involved?

"We need answers, Field." The Director pressed a finger to his temple. "If we don't have something soon, I'll be forced to remove you from the case and assign someone else."

Henry stilled. He'd feared something of the sort, but the idea didn't sit well with him. "I would prefer to continue to take an active role in the investigation." He held the Director's gaze. "No one is more invested in the case and clearing my name and that of the Yard than me."

"True. However, the issue might be out of my hands. We'll see what the Home Secretary says. Meanwhile, do what you can to determine who is behind this."

"Yes, sir." Henry took his leave, wishing Reynolds would've confirmed that he believed Henry was innocent. The Director had been maddeningly silent on that topic. A show of support, however small, would be welcome.

Henry returned to the office and approached his desk, stomach churning at the sight of the newspaper placed squarely in the center of it. Someone wanted to make sure he hadn't missed the article. He set his own rumpled copy on top of it and glanced around to see who watched.

Perdy, Clarke, and Whitlock were all seated at their desks, each one offering some version of a knowing smile or look. Others were there as well, including Constable Stephens and Constable Dannon, though they paid him no attention as they wrote reports.

He had to think one of the three inspectors who appeared so amused had put the paper there, though their presence didn't prove anything other than that they were enjoying the situation.

"Entertaining reading," Henry announced to the room at large as he tapped one finger on the paper. He was innocent; he refused to act guilty in any manner.

"Informative is a more apt description," Perdy said as he leaned back in his chair, a heated glint entering his eyes. "It's a shame to see the force shown in such a poor light."

"And here I thought I was joining London's finest," Clarke added as he gestured with a pencil nub. "A true shame."

Henry looked to Whitlock, certain the other man had something to say as well. To his surprise, other than glaring at him, the inspector returned to his work without a word.

"Can't believe you're still here, Field." Perdy kept his voice low, a glance toward the Director's open office door revealing the reason why. "Thought you'd have been dismissed by now."

"On what grounds? I'm not guilty of anything, and I intend to discover who is behind the recent events." Henry held each man's gaze. "I'd think you would want to know who it is as much as I do."

"Seems clear enough to me who the problem is." Perdy's lip curled as he glared at Henry.

"I have done nothing wrong," Henry stated in a firm voice, ignoring a pang of doubt. That might be true, but neither had he taken the *right* action since he had little to show for his efforts—as of yet. "And soon you'll be forced to admit that."

After one last look at Perdy, Henry returned his attention to his work and went through several files, updating his notes. It was more of an act than productive work when his thoughts were spinning, making it impossible to concentrate.

Someone here, someone watching him, had betrayed them...but who?

Fletcher entered from the rear of the office, which meant he'd either been in the evidence room or speaking with the Director. He nodded at Henry but continued toward his uncle, leaning close to talk to him in a low voice for several minutes.

Henry checked his watch and decided the reporter should be at his desk by now. Another conversation with the man was in order, though he doubted much would come of it based on their previous discussions. It was nearly impossible to force anyone from Fleet Street to reveal their sources.

He closed the file he'd been reviewing and headed out. Action had to feel better than staring at case files, wondering what else he could do to shake loose a clue.

Only the reminder that he was to join Amelia for dinner to be introduced to her parents helped to ease his current upset. He was grateful to have it to look forward to, considering how poorly the day was going.

"Field!"

He turned to see Fletcher hurrying toward him.

"You don't intend to confront the idiot without me, do you?"

The sergeant's fierce glower was nearly enough to make Henry smile. "To whom are you referring?" he couldn't help but tease.

"Stratton, of course. Blast him. What kind of reporter writes such rubbish?"

Henry continued forward with the sergeant, uncertain if he should say what was on his mind, yet he couldn't help himself. "Your uncle seemed to think it interesting."

"He doesn't know you like I do. Don't you worry." Fletcher nodded. "He'll come around soon enough. Anyone with a brain is aware of your record, especially these last few months." His friend held his gaze. "Saved the Queen, didn't you?"

"*We* did," Henry corrected, something he'd done countless times whenever Fletcher raised the subject. "Couldn't have done it without you."

"Humph. I was just along for the ride." Still, Fletcher tugged on the bottom of his navy jacket proudly at the reminder. "We solved the last few cases, and we'll solve this one, too."

Henry wished he had half of Fletcher's confidence.

Unfortunately the stop at Fleet Street was pointless. Mr. Stratton merely smirked, refusing to reveal any names, and his editor sided with the reporter, stating they had only written about what they'd been told by a 'reliable source.'

"Seems as if you wouldn't be so upset if there was nothing to the claims against you," Stratton was so bold as to suggest.

"Why you—" Fletcher growled as he started forward.

Henry halted the sergeant with a hand on his arm. A physical altercation of any sort would only reflect poorly on them—and the uniform his friend so proudly wore. "We will soon discover who provided those details to you." Henry smiled with a confidence he didn't feel. "When the full truth comes to light, you'll actually have a story worth writing."

Stratton's eyes narrowed, but Henry was certain a glint of interest shone in them.

"Let's go, Fletcher." Henry departed with the angry sergeant in tow.

"Blast him." The sergeant pounded his fist into his hand once they exited the building. "We should haul him to a dark alley and force him to tell us the truth."

"Tempting, isn't it?" The confrontation had worsened Henry's mood. "But we have more important matters to attend to."

Fletcher was silent for several minutes as they walked, seeming to need time to calm down. "Where are we headed next?"

"St. Thomas'. Mr. Taylor should have results on Edgarton by now."

The walk didn't take long. Fletcher hesitated when they reached the door. "If you don't mind, I'll wait here." He wrinkled his nose. "The smell in there is enough to turn my stomach. I'd rather not endure it—unless you have need of me."

Henry nodded. He couldn't blame the man. "I'll return directly." Remembering to breathe through his mouth rather than his nose, he opened the door and made his way to Mr. Taylor's examination room. Even so, the mixture of chemicals and decomposing bodies was, as always, inescapable and unpleasant.

Arthur Taylor stood over a body laid out on the cold slab before him, wearing a leather apron with his sleeves rolled up and a scalpel in hand. No assistant stood at his side, an unusual occurrence.

The surgeon and Henry had formed a friendship of sorts over the last few months, one Henry appreciated since he had so few.

"Morning, Henry." Arthur nodded as he caught sight of Henry in the doorway. "I'm sorry to say I'm a little behind, but I see you've been busy again." He gestured to the body.

It took Henry a moment to recognize the corpse with its chest pried open as Edgarton. Death was humbling, even to the wealthy criminal who'd risen far above Whitechapel. "I can't take the credit," Henry countered. "Though I seem to have been involved in far too many of late."

Arthur sent him a sympathetic look. "I saw the news sheet this morning."

Henry scowled in response. "Unfortunate."

"If it is of any comfort, I believe in you."

The knot in his stomach loosened slightly at the words of support. "Thank you. I appreciate that." It didn't matter that they were speaking back and forth over the body of a criminal. Henry was grateful for his support all the same.

"From what I read, Stratton tends to exaggerate any information he receives then adds his own dramatic twist." Arthur gestured with the scalpel still in hand. "The truth doesn't sell newspapers."

"Thanks for the reminder." It was of little comfort. Henry hated to think he'd brought any shame to the Field name, or the force. Nor could he get the worry of his parents seeing the article from his mind.

"As for your victim," Arthur began, all businesslike, "we have a stab wound made by a five-inch blade. The killer twisted the knife to ensure maximum damage. The victim has little to no signs of struggle, as I'm sure you noted, making one think the knife came as a surprise."

Who had Edgarton been speaking with? Who had the gall to kill him in a church? The murderer must have considered

Edgarton either a threat or a liability. Could it truly have been a member of the police?

"The last meal appears to have been a simple one," Arthur continued. "A pint and a meat pie would be my guess."

"From what we know, he was hiding in Whitechapel, so he could have eaten that anywhere."

Arthur nodded. "Wish I could tell you more."

"Every piece of information helps."

"I'm nearly finished and will send over the formal report this afternoon."

"Thanks, Arthur." Nodding his gratitude, Henry returned outside to where Fletcher waited.

The sergeant leaned close to Henry when he joined him and sniffed carefully. "That odor sticks to everything. Nasty."

Henry had to agree. "I don't know how the surgeon stands it."

"Is he married?" Fletcher asked as they walked down the street.

"He is." The question reminded him to ask after Mrs. Taylor next time. Blast. "Though given how much time he spends working, I'm not sure how that's possible."

"Not to mention the terrible stench." Fletcher gave a mock shudder.

"Let's return to Whitechapel and see if we can find any of Edgarton's men or the woman he was staying with."

They'd found where Belcher, the man Richards had mentioned who also worked for Edgarton, had been staying—but as Richards had suspected, the rooms were empty. A neighbor told them Belcher had left several days before but didn't know why or where he'd gone.

Another dead end—though hopefully, not as dead as Edgarton.

"As many men as Edgarton employed, they're sure hard to find," Fletcher said. "A few of them still must be around, but this Betty Knox could prove helpful, too."

They were walking past the Yard when Constable Stephens came running out, nearly bumping into them.

"What's your hurry, Stephens?" Fletcher asked the younger man.

The constable looked between them, eyes wide. "I'm—I'm in search of the two of you." His gaze shifted to hold on Henry. "There's been another murder in Whitechapel. A woman. The rookery killer has struck again."

Surprise stiffened Henry, followed quickly by dismay and dread.

How was that possible? And *who* was the rookery killer?

He had to determine that—before he lost his job, and another person lost their life.

Twenty-Eight

A VEIL OF SADNESS still clung to Amelia as she awoke that morning. Determined to remove it, she rose and went about her routine, deciding she would do some thinking of her own to come up with a topic for an article to propose to Mr. Richards. That would surely make up for her reticence the previous day.

Luckily she had her parents' upcoming visit to look forward to, along with the dinner with Henry. She hoped her parents liked him as much as she did. The household bustled with activity in preparation for their visit, the guestroom prepared by Yvette, Cook preparing a giddy variety of sweet treats, Mrs. Fernsby carefully reviewing the linen cupboard. It made the house feel busy, joyful. But it wasn't enough to dispel the lingering disquiet.

The morning passed far too slowly for Amelia, and ideas were even slower. Just before luncheon, she picked up the newspaper with the hope it might generate a spark, only to gasp in alarm at one of the headlines.

At first she skimmed the story, but the sight of Henry's name had her reading more closely.

"Good heavens!" She read it a second time, anger stirring on his behalf. "Unbelievable."

"Is all well, Mrs. Greystone?" Mrs. Fernsby paused on her way past the drawing room with a concerned look on her face and a feather duster in hand.

"It is not—this story is outrageous." Amelia held up the paper. "This reporter suggests that Scotland Yard is bumbling the rookery killer investigation and Inspector Field is partly to blame."

"Inspector Field?" Fernsby joined his wife, brow furrowed. "Why on earth would they make such a claim?"

"I have no idea." Amelia shook her head, rereading the paragraph that mentioned Henry. "The reporter seems eager to show him in a poor light."

"Perhaps he has an axe to grind with Inspector Field," Mrs. Fernsby suggested. "Reporters tend to think they can write their personal opinions rather than facts, don't they?"

"It makes me so angry." Amelia could only imagine how the article made Henry feel. He took his position and his duties seriously, something made evident by the long hours he kept and his dogged determination to find the truth as he solved each case. "I'd like to have a word with the reporter."

After Matthew's death, Henry had stopped by frequently both to provide updates and to inquire after her welfare. Even after the case had gone cold, he'd continued to do so. She doubted other inspectors would've bothered to make the same effort.

Mrs. Fernsby shook her head. "The reporter should have been here when young Maeve was staying with us after the ravenkeeper's death. The Inspector spent several nights watching over all of us—and that was only the beginning."

"Precisely," Amelia agreed. "And his efforts to find who had killed the mudlarks, even when the police refused to open an investigation, were more than admirable."

"Those efforts got him stabbed!" The housekeeper shook the feather duster, clearly annoyed. "How can anyone think he isn't doing his job?"

Amelia would never forget the sight of a disheveled and bloody Henry sitting in her kitchen when he'd come to warn her that she, too, was in danger. He'd gone above and beyond his duty during that investigation.

"News sheets print stories they think will rouse public opinion," Fernsby advised quietly. "This one sounds as if it will do exactly that, all to sell more papers."

"True." That was another reason she appreciated Mr. Stearn and his careful selection of topics for the periodical. He never suggested they write anything but the truth, and certainly not at the expense of a person or business. "It's unfair that there's no mention of Inspector Field halting the attempt to assassinate the Queen. He's a hero."

"Humph." Mrs. Fernsby's disgruntled expression matched how Amelia felt. "That comes as no surprise."

"The reporter didn't say anything about the success of any of his previous cases," Amelia murmured. "I have half a mind to go see the man myself to share my poor opinion of his story."

"I would be pleased to accompany you if you wish, madam," Mrs. Fernsby offered boldly, much to Amelia's surprise. "I'd like to share my opinion with him, as well."

The housekeeper rarely stepped out, preferring to attend to her duties in the house and sending the maid on errands when necessary. But she was a formidable woman with high standards that she expected everyone to adhere to. The reporter would have his hands full if Mrs. Fernsby chose to give him a piece of her mind.

Amelia sighed, knowing it wouldn't help. "I suppose doing so would only stir the reporter's interest, when that is the last thing Inspector Field would want." How frustrated he must be. "Still, there must be something I can do to aid him."

In truth, the urge to do so weighed on her, especially since the current case still indirectly involved Matthew's murder. Now that Edgarton was dead, what harm could there be in looking into his life a bit more?

Besides, as Henry's unofficial assistant, she'd helped in small ways in the last few cases. Clearly, the time had come to do so again as Edgarton was no longer a threat.

Amelia briefly closed her eyes, willing to admit she needed this endeavor to help drag her from the despair that had overtaken her the previous day. She couldn't allow herself to wallow in grief and guilt for refusing to speak with the woman involved in divination.

She hadn't been able to bring herself to share what had distressed her with Mr. and Mrs. Fernsby. It would be best to put the situation behind her, and finding a way to aid Henry would certainly help do that.

"Fernsby, please send for a hansom cab. I have an errand to see to." At the lift of his brow, she shook her head with a wry smile. "No, I don't intend to speak with the reporter. Not yet, at any rate." She looked at the housekeeper. "And if I do, I will certainly bring you to assist me."

"I hope you do, madam," Mrs. Fernsby said with a single, decisive nod. "Inspector Field is an honorable man, and the police are lucky to have him."

"I couldn't agree more." Amelia was grateful for his friendship and could think of no better way to show him than to help put this case behind him.

Behind them *both*.

An hour later, Amelia was riding in a hansom cab with Yvette at her side to the street where Miles Edgarton had lived. Though her errand was likely to be a wild goose chase rather than a successful inquiry, she had to try. It had taken no more than another glance at the newspaper headline for her determination to strengthen.

In truth, she'd pondered the possibility since her conversation with Mr. Powell at his museum when he'd mentioned Edgarton's mother. With Edgarton's address in hand, which the newspaper had reported along with the man's death, she should be able to locate his mother's house. A few inquiries of Edgarton's neighbors would hopefully lead her to where Mrs. Edgarton lived since they had lived near one another.

During one of his previous visits, Henry had said they'd already spoken to her and that she hadn't been helpful and acted distrustful of the police. That wasn't a surprise. But what harm could come from Amelia calling on her to see if she had any ideas about who might have killed her son—if she could determine where the woman lived? Perhaps Mrs. Edgarton would feel more inclined to speak candidly with another woman than she had with the police.

Especially when both of them knew what it was like to lose a child...

"It might take a few attempts to learn where Mrs. Edgarton resides," she warned the maid.

"Hopefully one of the neighbors can point us in the right direction," Yvette said bracingly.

Though tempted to go without anyone accompanying her, Amelia didn't want to take any unnecessary risks. Mrs. Edgarton might prove unfriendly, though she didn't plan on sharing details about how she'd known the woman's son. Calling on her to offer condolences might lead to a conversation. At least, that was Amelia's hope.

She'd worn a black mourning gown for the outing with the thought that her attire would create a connection with Mrs. Edgarton and make her appear less of a threat.

Henry would *not* approve. That much she knew for certain.

She shoved aside the thought as the cab rolled to a halt. After all he had done for her, she wanted to aid him. The sooner Edgarton's murder was solved, the better—and Henry's name would be cleared.

They could both move forward. *Possibly together.*

Though her efforts might not be of any assistance, trying was better than pacing her drawing room, wondering how Henry fared. With that firmly in mind, she followed the maid out of the cab.

"Please wait until we return," she advised the driver, who nodded as he tied the reins. "We won't be long." A lofty promise, when she didn't know how much time it might take to locate Mrs. Edgarton's home, let alone speak with her.

"Where do you propose we begin?" Yvette asked as she eyed the nearby houses warily.

Amelia followed her gaze. The neighborhood appeared safe enough, with modest, well-tended brick homes lining the street. But who knew what lay behind those doors. "Surely those who live in the house directly across the street from Edgarton noticed more than anyone else."

"Right." Yvette nodded. "Much like Mr. and Mrs. Prescott."

The thought of the elderly couple whose home faced her own made Amelia smile. "Exactly. They never fail to note any interesting happenings on our street. We must have kept them quite entertained the last few months."

On more than one occasion Mrs. Prescott had sent her maid over to discover the latest news under the premise of borrowing one item or another. The maid was careful to ask for Yvette as Mrs. Appleton, Amelia's cook, had already made it clear she had no time for such gossip.

Amelia led the way up the walk to the door and knocked. A maid answered and looked between them curiously.

"I am looking for Mrs. Edgarton, but I can't remember which house she lives in," Amelia said apologetically. "Do you happen to know her?"

"She lives about half a dozen doors down the street." The maid pointed in that direction, lowering her voice. "You'll see black ribbons on the door. My mistress says Mrs. Edgarton is quite distraught over the death of her son. He meant the world to her."

"I'm sure." Amelia held back the urge to ask how proud she could be when he'd committed several murders, not to mention other atrocities. Instead she thanked the maid.

"That was easier than I expected," Yvette murmured as they continued down the street.

"Let us hope the next stop goes as well."

"Forgive me for asking, but what do you intend to say to the woman?" the maid asked, curiosity dancing in her eyes.

Nerves tingled along Amelia's skin at the question. "I—I don't know yet. I'm hoping the right words come to mind." She only hoped Mrs. Edgarton would see them. There was always the chance she wouldn't be receiving callers, especially those who were strangers. "If you have an opportunity to speak with the servants, inquire as politely as you can whether they've heard any information about who might have killed him."

Yvette smiled as if enjoying their mission. "I will, madam. You may count on me."

And Amelia knew she could.

The house, built of red brick with black shutters and white columns on either side of the front step, had a boxwood wreath adorned with black ribbons on the door to tell callers the house was in mourning.

Amelia knocked then waited with Yvette for someone to answer. After several long moments passed, she prepared to knock again when the sound of the door opening had her drawing a breath to bolster her nerves.

A large man in a black suit, who looked as if he could have served as one of Edgarton's bodyguards in his younger days, answered the door. "Yes?"

Amelia handed him her card, wondering only in that moment whether anyone in the household would recognize her name. "Mrs. Greystone, to see Mrs. Edgarton."

He studied the card, then looked her over from head to toe. "Allow me to see if she is receiving."

"Of course." To Amelia's surprise, they were left to wait on the front step while he did so.

"Rather rude," Yvette whispered.

"Apparently no one is to be admitted without approval." She had no idea if they would be allowed entrance. It seemed unlikely Mrs. Edgarton knew who she was, and Amelia didn't intend to mention the odd way they were connected. *Your son killed my husband* didn't seem like a good way to introduce herself.

Or did it? Amelia would have to follow her instincts regarding the situation. Taking the woman by surprise might be a way to get her to talk—if she knew anything helpful.

The door opened. "Mrs. Edgarton will see you." Despite the affirmative, the man's tone and demeanor hadn't warmed in the least.

Amelia stepped inside and nodded for Yvette to remain by the door. With luck, she'd have the chance to speak with a passing servant.

The house was nicely decorated with blue and gold striped wallpaper and a dark wood trim. The servant led Amelia up the stairs and down the hall to a small sitting room with sparse furnishings, where a large woman in a black mourning gown sat by the fire. The drapes were drawn, leaving the room dim despite the lamps casting a soft golden glow.

"Mrs. Greystone, madam." The servant stood aside to allow Amelia to enter.

The older woman's eyes narrowed as she looked over Amelia but she made no attempt to rise. Her gray hair was drawn into a tight roll at the base of her head, and she clutched a handkerchief in one hand, her features coarse. "Do we know one another?"

"No." Amelia hesitated, listening to the retreating footsteps of the servant and feeling entirely out of her depth. But if she wanted to aid Henry, she needed to proceed. She needed to be brave. "Please accept my condolences on the loss of your son." She knew the pain of losing a child all too well.

The woman nodded but still didn't seem inclined to be friendly. She had yet to ask Amelia to sit down. "Did you know him?"

"I met him once." *When he held me against my will*. But that wasn't the important part. She held Mrs. Edgarton's gaze, deciding drastic action was required. "You see, he murdered my husband."

Surprise flashed in the woman's eyes, followed by wariness. No protest followed. No shock. Just calm. "Why have you come?"

"To ask if you have any idea who killed your son."

"That is a bold question. The police asked me the same question, but I had nothing to say to them." Her lips tightened. "Why would I tell you if I knew?"

"Surely you want the person punished." Just as Amelia had wanted Matthew's killer caught—but she mustn't think about that.

"My son wasn't perfect." The older woman sniffed. "None of us are."

Anger speared through Amelia. While she agreed, she tended to think the man in question hadn't bothered to try. Still, she held her silence to see if the woman said anything more.

"I pray he asked forgiveness in that church before he was killed." She dabbed her nose with the handkerchief. "That's as much as a mother can hope."

"Yes, it is."

"I saw him briefly a few days ago." Grief tightened the lines of her face as her lips trembled. "He said he...he was working with someone with the police. He thought it ironic. I told him no good could come from it."

Amelia's blood chilled. To think a police officer was involved in the recent murders was unbelievable. Whoever it was seemed intent on causing harm to Henry. "Did he mention a name—or their position?"

"No. No, I don't know anything more. Please go."

Before Amelia could ask more questions, the large servant appeared in the doorway, suggesting the conversation was over. Well, she had tried. "Thank you for seeing me. I hope your memories bring you comfort."

"Do yours?" Mrs. Edgarton asked as her gaze held on Amelia's mourning gown.

Surprise gripped Amelia, but after a moment's thought, she nodded. "Yes, they do."

It wasn't enough, but better than nothing.

Twenty-Nine

*T*HE ROOKERY KILLER STRIKES *Again*!

Henry could already see the headline in tomorrow's newspaper exactly as Stephens had said. His thoughts—and stomach—churned as he, Fletcher, and the constable once again rode the omnibus toward Whitechapel.

"What details were reported?" Henry asked, forcing himself to treat the murder as he would any other. He couldn't allow worries about his career to derail him when he had work to do.

"The constable stated a woman was found stabbed just outside a gin house." Stephens' obvious distress was catching the notice of the other passengers. "Do—do you think it could be the same murderer who killed Edgarton?"

"Think, man," Fletcher demanded in a gruff but quiet voice before Henry could answer. "We don't know enough about the situation to say. And we do *not* make assumptions. There's more than one murderer in this place." He sent the constable a stern look before glaring at their fellow passengers, who quickly looked away.

"Right. Sorry, sir." Stephens shook his head as if trying to gather his thoughts. "Between the newspaper this morning and now this..." He glanced at Henry out of the corner of his eye.

Henry smothered an oath. It was only natural for the younger man to have questions, especially when a few of Henry's fellow inspectors had publicly expressed their own doubts. Stephens' expression made Henry realize he hadn't dealt with the questions as well as he could have, especially not from those lower ranking than him.

"Stephens." Henry waited until the man met his gaze. "I did *not* kill Edgarton. I did not take the scarab, nor did I place it in Edgarton's pocket. I'm determined to find out who did, and I hope you will aid me in that endeavor. It does seem as if the cases, including the prison guard's murder, could be connected, but we must follow the clues wherever they lead."

The constable nodded, eyes still worried. "Yes, sir. I knew that all along, of course, though it's helpful to hear as much from you. I appreciate it, sir." Stephens straightened as if his confidence was restored. "I will do all I can to help."

"Good." Henry glanced at Fletcher, who also nodded. "We will carefully examine the scene and interview those in the vicinity to discover all we can as quickly as possible. We'll take statements, names, we'll find evidence. And there will be no mention of a potential rookery killer."

"Right." Fletcher looked at the passing street. "Be sure to watch your back while you do so. We can't forget the dangers of the area."

"Agreed." Henry remained silent as the omnibus drew to a halt and the three of them alighted.

Stephens repeated the address he'd been given, but none of them knew precisely where it was. An old woman walking past directed them to its location, though with missing teeth and a strong German accent, she was difficult to understand.

Henry looked for Marcus, the young lad who'd proven helpful before, without success.

"Walking these streets is like being in a different city," Stephens said, his gaze darting about at the poverty, the suspicious gazes and the mutinous stares.

"Isn't that the truth," Fletcher murmured.

The crowded buildings, most of which were in disrepair, and the waste in the streets lent a depressing heaviness to the air. Or perhaps it came from the general feeling of hopelessness of those who lived there. A few people sat in doorways, looking as if they didn't have the wherewithal to rise.

One particular young man, with a pale face and ragged clothes that hung loosely on his thin frame, looked especially defeated. Too young to be trapped in the rookery without hope. Henry couldn't bear the despair in his dark eyes, given his youth. He pulled a shilling from his pocket and handed it to the man as discreetly as possible. "Get yourself some food and a bed for the night."

The gratitude and disbelief on the man's face said it all. "Th-Thank ye, sir."

Henry nodded and continued forward, aware of the attention his action had drawn.

"If you're not careful, they'll be mobbing us to see what else is in your pocket," Fletcher warned in an undertone.

"I know." Henry quickened his pace with the hope of avoiding such an outcome.

"And he'll more than likely spend it on drink," Fletcher added.

Henry lifted a brow. "Or he could do as I suggested. If so, he might have the strength to search for work tomorrow."

"Ever the optimist," Fletcher said with a smile.

"You've more than likely turned his life around, sir." A flash of admiration shone in Stephens' face.

"One can hope." And Henry truly did. A few unfortunate events, when strung together, were often all it took for a person to find themselves living on the streets.

Workhouses took some in, but the requirements for staying there often made it prohibitive to do so. From what Henry knew, one had to be without a single coin in their pocket, willing to risk lice and other vermin, eat the slop that passed for food, and be prepared to work the following day at whatever task the workhouse assigned. Henry had heard the tale time and time again from those who had slipped into petty theft; by the time they were allowed to leave the workhouse, daily workers for the businesses in the area had already been hired. That meant another hungry, cold night sleeping on the street until roused by the police and forced to move on, or another trip back to the workhouse. Once in, it was hard to leave.

The cycle was a vicious one. Henry hoped the paltry sum he'd given the poor young man made a difference.

"This must be the place." Fletcher nodded to where nearly a dozen people gathered in a tight knot, suggesting they'd found the location.

"Police. Clear the way," Stephens called and moved some aside to reveal the body of a woman on the pavement with a harried looking constable beside it, obviously relieved by their arrival.

"Impossible to keep order when something like this happens." The uniformed officer shook his head. "I only arrived after it was over and done."

The victim appeared middle-aged, from what Henry could see of her profile, though she might've been younger. Life in Whitechapel tended to age people beyond their years.

Fletcher and Stephens helped the constable push back the onlookers, leaving Henry to have a closer look at the scene. He checked for a pulse but found none and gently turned her over.

"It's Betty Knox," one person announced from the crowd. "God rest her soul."

Henry released a quiet breath, unsurprised to learn her identity.

The woman's blue eyes stared unseeing at the sky, mouth agape in a pale face. She wore a ragged shawl over a worn brown gown. Both hands were coated in blood as if she'd clutched the wound in her abdomen. A slice in the rough, blood-soaked fabric was visible, suggesting she'd been stabbed as reported.

Someone kicked a knife along the ground which landed close to the body. Henry glanced up to find Constable Peters staring between him and the body.

"Sorry, sir. Didn't see it there," Peters said with a sheepish look. "I heard the alarm and came as quick as possible to see if I could help."

"Be more careful," Fletcher said, glaring at the constable before directing him to help hold back the onlookers and give Henry more room.

Henry directed his attention to the knife, even as he wondered how Peters managed to appear at every one of Henry's crime scenes of late. His beat was nearby, but still...

The blade was covered in blood and likely the murder weapon. Interesting that it looked to be about the length of the one used to kill Edgarton. The handle was also spotted with blood.

Faint red smears marked the pavement for several feet as if the woman had crawled the last yard before dying. Henry carefully wrapped the knife in his handkerchief and placed it in his pocket. A look around the body didn't reveal any other evidence.

"Who witnessed the stabbing?" Fletcher asked those nearby as Henry worked.

A series of murmurs rose in response until a woman stepped forward. "I-I saw." Her face was pale as she stared at the body, eyes wide, clearly distraught.

Henry straightened to walk over to her, pulling out his notebook as he did so. "Your name, ma'am?" He wrote it down. "And what did you see?"

"She was talkin' with a man. Over there." She turned to point a few doors down where a gin shop stood. "They was arguin'."

"About what?" Henry wanted every possible detail she could provide.

"She said 'e owed 'er money. He tried to walk away, but she was 'avin' none of it. She grabbed 'is arm and turned 'im back. Then he stabbed 'er quick like." She mimicked a stabbing movement. "Terrible." She shook her head. "It 'appened so fast."

"Can you describe him?" Henry asked.

The woman frowned and gestured to those nearby. "Oh, 'e wasn't one of us." She looked Henry up and down. "Y'know...'e looked a bit like ye."

Henry stilled as those nearby stared at him. "In what way?"

"Same color suit and 'at. Brown 'air, too." Her eyes narrowed. "Might've been a copper like ye cause of the way 'e acted."

"He was," someone else joined in. "I fink 'e 'ad to be, by the look of 'im."

Henry met Fletcher's eyes, the alarm in them matching how he felt. It took only a moment for the sergeant to bring the man closer, and Henry took down what he could tell them.

"Any other witnesses?" Constable Stephens asked.

Another man came forward. Henry spoke with each person, but no one had seen the killer's face.

"I weren't payin' much attention until I 'eard her 'ollerin'," explained one man. "'e 'ad 'is back t'me."

"So someone killed Edgarton's roommate," Fletcher murmured after they'd finished the initial questioning of the witnesses.

"Yes," Henry agreed quietly. "Someone is definitely cleaning up loose ends—but this time, it isn't Edgarton."

Determined to learn more, Henry spoke to the first witness again, taking her through the details one more time. Her recounting remained consistent with her previous statement. No inconsistencies, but no new details.

No one in the crowd had noted where the killer went after the stabbing either, their attention on the screaming woman.

"Odd that whoever killed her left the weapon," Fletcher said quietly to Henry. "Almost like they wanted it found."

Henry nodded. Or he didn't want to be caught with it, so left it behind. "It does seem strange."

Within half an hour they had gathered all the details they could, though the story varied the more people they spoke with. It never failed to amaze Henry how a group could observe the same event and yet tell slightly different versions of what had occurred. But that was humanity, wasn't it? One of the first things one learned on the force.

Henry sent Peters to find a dogcart to haul away the body. The constable not only showed up at pivotal moments but didn't lend much aid. He would keep his eye on the man.

Someone offered a ragged blanket to cover the victim, which helped disperse the crowd. Henry and Fletcher left Stephens and the other constable to watch over the scene, and questioned those in the gin shop where the skirmish had started, as well as the nearby businesses, all without much success. Several had heard parts of the argument about money, along with the screams, but none had investigated. He supposed such cries weren't so unusual around here.

Peters soon arrived with a dogcart and driver, and they loaded the body and took one last look around the scene. Henry couldn't help but wish there was more to be found. Something, anything. A clue that pointed them in the proper direction.

"Let us return to the victim's rooms," Henry advised Fletcher as Peters pulled away to escort the body to St. Thomas'. "Maybe she returned there prior to her death."

The three made their way to the lodging house, Stephens remaining near the entrance of the building while Henry and Fletcher went upstairs. The door was locked, but the sergeant gave it a firm shove with his shoulder at Henry's nod and opened it easily enough. Well, Betty Knox wouldn't be complaining about it. Not now.

The rooms looked much like they had before—still a dump. An empty gin bottle lay on the bed. Had Betty mourned the loss of Edgarton? Or had she been frightened for her own life and drank to ease that fear?

Henry searched under the mattress, which was about the only place to hide anything when the rooms were so sparsely furnished.

"Anything?" Fletcher asked from the doorway.

Henry spotted a piece of paper in one corner under the bed. "Give me a hand."

Fletcher came forward to hold the mattress while Henry reached for the paper. "What is it?"

"A message of some sort." The handwriting was undoubtedly masculine but not Edgarton's, from what Henry remembered.

"What does it say?" his friend asked.

"It's to Edgarton. At least, it has his initials at the top. Whoever wrote it requested him to meet at St. Mary's on the day of the murder."

"And?" Fletcher released the mattress to look over Henry's shoulder. "Who sent it?"

Henry's gaze dropped to the signature, a mixture of dismay and regret filling him as he took in the name. He looked at Fletcher to watch him read it too.

Disbelief widened his friend's eyes. "I—I don't understand." He shook his head and took a step back. "My uncle wouldn't have written it, let alone signed it if he had. He's no murderer—but more, he's no fool."

Henry didn't understand either. Why would a newly appointed inspector send a note to meet a criminal—a meeting that had ended in murder?

Thirty

"Mother. Father." Amelia hugged her parents, thrilled by their midday arrival. "I'm so happy you're here. How was your journey?"

"Uneventful," her mother supplied with a smile as Fernsby closed the door behind them. "Just as we like it."

"Indeed," her father agreed brightly. "I always manage to forget how busy the city is. It appears to have grown every time we return."

"That is a sign you should come more often," Amelia countered with a smile. "Then you wouldn't notice the changes as much."

Her father laughed, the booming sound warming Amelia's heart. Their visit was just what she needed.

"It is truly wonderful to have you both here." She looked between them, pleased they didn't appear overly tired from travelling.

Her mother looked quite stylish in a plaid walking dress with a kilted underskirt. A matching hat in the same shade of green sat atop her brown hair which was rolled into a sleek chignon. She appeared far younger than four and fifty years.

Dapper was the perfect word to describe her father. He was of medium build with a moustache that curled upward at either end. His receding hairline grew a little more noticeable each year, but the twinkle in his brown eyes, so like her own, never changed.

"We're happy to be here," her mother said.

Just as she studied them, they did the same with her. The slight nod her father gave suggested he was satisfied with what he saw. Then he turned to the butler, who stood to one side of the foyer. "Fernsby, it appears you've been taking good care of things here."

"I strive to do my best, sir," he said with a bow before turning to Amelia. "Shall I bring tea?"

"Please do, Fernsby. Thank you." Amelia led the way up the stairs to the drawing room.

The time passed pleasantly as they settled in and caught up on news from home. Master Leopold made a grand entrance, trotting into the room to introduce himself, tail aloft. Her parents lavished attention on him until he decided that was enough and settled into his customary chair by the window.

"And Aunt Margaret intends to call on us tomorrow," Amelia continued, smoothing her hands along her gray skirts as her stomach tightened at thoughts of Henry's impending arrival. She'd already mentioned that he would be coming for dinner in her letter, but speaking of it was proving more difficult.

"Oh, good." Her mother lifted a brow. "How is she faring in London?"

"Quite well, from what I have seen," Amelia replied. "She is busy with her charitable work and has made several friends through those endeavors." She didn't mention the issue with her aunt's former gentleman friend, as she'd asked her not to.

"I'm pleased to hear it. London is a challenging place for a woman living alone, as I'm sure you know." Her mother sent her a pointed look.

"It can be, but it is also home." Amelia was accustomed to fielding suggestions that she return to Birmingham to live closer to them. While she missed her parents, London truly was dear to her heart now. She cleared her throat. It was time to mention Henry, even if she wasn't sure how to articulate the words. "As you may remember from my last letter, Inspector Field will be joining us for dinner this evening."

"Oh, yes." Her father nodded. "I look forward to meeting him after all you've told us."

"He feels much the same." Amelia only hoped no problems arose with the case to interrupt their plans. His frustration must be mounting after the recent news stories. But she didn't intend to mention any of that to her parents. She preferred they form their own opinion before learning about the questions swirling around him and the police at the moment, thanks to the news reports.

"May I ask about the nature of your relationship with him?" her father asked with a lifted brow.

"Now, William, Amelia is a woman grown and a widow," her mother admonished serenely. "It is her business, not ours."

"She's our daughter and always will be," her father countered before Amelia could respond. "Of course it's our business."

"Not until there is news to share." Her mother glanced at her. "And if there were, we would have already heard it. Isn't that right, darling?"

"Yes, you would have." Amelia's cheeks heated, making her feel more like a girl of sixteen rather than well over a decade older. "Henry and I—Inspector Field have become good friends in recent months." That much was true...but she wouldn't deny that she looked forward to the day when she could claim more.

The flutters in her stomach at the admission—if only to herself—didn't do anything to ease the warmth in her cheeks.

"I like the thought of you having a man beyond Fernsby to call on if the need arises, and I look forward to meeting Inspector Field." Her father frowned. "Has the fugitive been caught?"

She'd written to them of Edgarton's arrest followed by his escape, but events had happened so quickly... "He was found dead. Murdered, just a few days ago."

Her father considered the information for a moment, then nodded. "I suppose that is a form of justice."

"True." Amelia was of the same mind. It bothered her that his murder was still unsolved, but surely not as much as it did Henry.

"I hope it provides you with some peace," her father added.

"It does. I'm relieved not to have to worry about where he is anymore."

"Good." Her father stood, seeming restless, as was his nature. "I believe I will stretch my legs while I have the chance after all those hours sitting."

"Don't wander too far, William," her mother said fondly.

"Yes, dear." He smiled and squeezed her shoulder before departing.

The sound of him speaking to Fernsby echoed from the foyer, followed by the closing of the front door.

"Now then." Amelia's mother turned to her with eagerness in her expression. "Tell me everything about your Henry."

Amelia couldn't help but laugh at the gleam of interest in her mother's eyes. "There truly isn't anything more to share. As I said, we are friends. Good ones, I think." She hesitated, choosing her words carefully. "I...I admire him very much, and I like to think he feels the same."

"That is what I wanted to know." Her mother grinned. "Now I am even more anxious to meet him."

"It can't have been him," Fletcher muttered as he followed Henry down the stairs of the Whitechapel lodging house. "It can't be my uncle."

Henry held his silence to allow the sergeant time to work through his thoughts. There could be no question the letter was damning, with 'Clarke' signed at the bottom.

"The moment we return to the Yard, I will demand that my uncle—"

"No." Henry paused on the final flight of stairs to hold Fletcher's gaze. "No, we aren't going to do anything of the sort. Our job is to gather all potential evidence. We don't have enough to confront anyone as of yet."

"Humph." Fletcher's hands clenched with his frustration, but he didn't argue.

"Do you know beyond a doubt if that's his handwriting?" Henry didn't, and he wasn't about to make any assumptions.

His friend considered the question, brow furrowed. "Not for certain."

"So that's something we need to verify before making any accusations."

"Right." Fletcher shook his head. "Sorry. I'm not thinking properly."

"Understandable, given the situation. For now, we keep this information to ourselves until we know more." Henry continued down the stairs. "We have work to do."

"Agreed."

They stepped out of the building to find Constable Stephens speaking with a scrap of a boy—Marcus.

Pleased to see the lad, Henry clasped his shoulder. "Good to see you, Marcus."

The boy dipped his head. "I 'eard you have another murder t'solve."

"We do." Henry lifted a brow. "Happen to know anything about it?"

Marcus shifted his gaze to the upper floor of the building. "Only that it was the lady livin' up there wot we was keepin' an eye on."

"Betty Knox. Yes. Anything else?"

"Not yet. Shall I see what I can dig up?" The lad gave him a hopeful look as if eager to try—or perhaps it was because of the chance to earn some money.

"Certainly. But as always, take care. Don't put yourself in any danger." Henry gave him a stern look to make his point as he tossed him a coin.

Marcus caught it and offered a cheeky grin. "I won't. I wants another shilling." With a tug on his cap, he took off down the street, quickly disappearing around a corner.

Stephens shook his head. "That lad is a clever one. He'll probably be the first to learn more."

Henry exchanged a look with Fletcher but didn't say anything about the letter they'd found. "Stephens, I've kept you long enough. We'll depart Whitechapel together, and if you could take the knife we found to the Yard, I'd appreciate it. Fletcher and I have one more stop to make before the day ends."

The supposed witness to the prison guard's murder had been weighing on his mind, and Henry had a few more questions for the man.

"Yes, sir."

An hour later, Henry and Fletcher were in Camden Town nearing Cobb's lodging house, his heart still heavy and his mind whirling. Clarke? Was the note the proof they so desperately needed?

"What do you have in mind?" Fletcher asked.

Henry had been considering that very question since deciding another conversation with the supposed witness was in order. "I want to see what more we can ease out of this Mr. Jackson. I don't think he's telling us the full truth about what he saw the night of Cobb's murder."

Fletcher nodded and reached for the door, which took two tries to open as it stuck, then held it ajar for Henry.

"Does your uncle smoke?" Henry asked, thinking of the match he'd found outside Cobbs' door.

"No. Why?"

Henry shook his head. "Just curious." The match might not have been from whoever had killed Cobb—or there could have been two men. Or it could have been dropped hours before.

Damn. That was the trouble with evidence. All it proved was that something had happened.

Henry led the way up one flight of stairs and knocked at the door nearest the stairs.

The same man, with a pockmarked face, opened it and frowned as he looked between them with a wary expression. "What?"

"We have a few more questions for you, Mr. Jackson," Henry began, foregoing the reassuring smile he'd offered last time.

"Oh?"

Once again, Henry was following his gut. Whether it resulted in any new information remained to be seen. "We need a description of the police officer who advised you how to answer any questions you were asked about the night of the murder upstairs."

"What?" The man acted confused, but that didn't cover his blatant alarm. "I—ye're the only copper I've spoke to."

"I don't think so." Henry took a step closer, hoping a little intimidation might loosen the man's tongue. "Sometime prior to ten o'clock on the night Cobb died a police officer, possibly in plain clothes, knocked on your door. He paid you to make a statement if asked about what you saw and heard that very night." Henry felt the weight of Fletcher's stare, suggesting he was surprised by the statement. Ignoring him, he kept a steady gaze on the supposed witness. "If you'd prefer, we can have this conversation at the police station."

The man's mouth gaped.

The truth came out in bits and pieces with much prodding from Henry while Fletcher remained silent. From the description the witness reluctantly gave, it sounded as if Clarke had been the one to advise him of what to say, though the details were vague enough to fit others in the department.

It took only a glance at Fletcher to see he thought Mr. Jackson had just confirmed his uncle's duplicity. The gray expression of horror was potent. Sympathy for the sergeant rose, but Henry was relieved not to have to be the one to tell him what the witness had said. Better he heard it firsthand—and even better that Henry had another officer to confirm it.

"Don't tell anyone that you've spoken with us," Henry advised the man once the story came to an end. "Your life may depend on it."

"Y-Yes, sir."

"And don't leave the city," Henry added. "You may be called on to give testimony later."

"I don't want no trouble," Mr. Jackson protested.

Then you shouldn't have lied, Henry wanted to say but held back. Being ordered by a police officer to do so would be intimidating enough, but the added bonus of a payment would make it nearly impossible to refuse.

Had made it impossible to refuse.

The silence was heavy as Henry and Fletcher made their way back to the Yard, evening quickly approaching.

"Why?" Fletcher asked at length. "*Why* would my uncle pay the man to lie?"

Henry didn't have an answer. "I don't know. That is a piece we need to solve. Do you think Clarke is having financial problems?"

"Not that I've heard." He shook his head helplessly. "To break your word as a police officer, to lose your honor—for money?"

"Desperation comes in many forms." Henry couldn't imagine what the inspector might be going through that would make him think breaking the law was his best option. Fear? Greed? A desire for control? His actions could be for many reasons. Power of the criminal variety, perhaps. Money, almost certainly.

"I can't believe he would've killed Cobb." Fletcher shook his head. "To come at him from behind, squeeze his neck until the life flows out of him. It doesn't match the man I know."

Henry couldn't offer an opinion, when he barely knew Clarke.

"I still want to blame Perdy," Fletcher added at length.

The gruff words were almost enough to make Henry smile. "Perhaps we will find he is partially to blame."

"One can only hope." Fletcher heaved a sigh that sounded as if it came from the depths of his soul.

Henry felt for him, but no words of comfort came to mind. "Are you certain you want to return to the Yard? Conversation with your uncle could prove awkward if he happens to be there."

"Awkward for him, I hope." Anger colored his friend's tone.

"Fletcher," Henry began, glancing at him. "As a friend, and as an inspector, I would ask you not to hint that anything is amiss. We don't know enough to accuse him, or anyone else yet. The note we found and the word of a witness who already admitted to lying...it's hardly enough to press charges."

"Right." Fletcher nodded with reluctance. "I'll take care."

"Good. I'm going to see if Mr. Taylor has had a chance to examine Betty Knox, and come morning, we'll make another trip to Holloway Prison."

"To talk to Cobb's fellow prison guard again? The one who'd been drinking with him at the pub the night of his murder?"

"No. I want to speak with whomever else the warden suspects of aiding Edgarton's escape."

"I thought the prison was conducting their own investigation."

"As did I," Henry said heavily. "But nothing seems to be coming of it. Might be time to ask a few questions of our own."

Where else could Henry press to untangle the knots of the investigation? The question would have to wait; he had dinner with Amelia's parents to enjoy.

Thirty-One

TIME PASSED EVER SO slowly as evening approached. Amelia's father had returned from his walk only half an hour before voices in the foyer suggested Henry had arrived.

Amelia released a relieved breath that not only had he come but was punctual, a trait her old-fashioned father appreciated.

Fernsby announced Henry formally, which amused her since the butler never bothered to do so any longer.

Henry's gaze sought her first, sending awareness along her skin, before his attention shifted to her parents. "Good evening."

"I'm so pleased you could come, Henry." Amelia rose, gesturing to her mother and father who also stood. "May I introduce you to my parents, Mr. and Mrs. William Crosby. Mother, Father, this is Henry Field." She deliberately left off his position as an inspector. They already knew that, after all, and Henry was so much more than his work.

"It is a pleasure." Henry stepped forward to shake her father's hand, then dipped his head in greeting toward her mother.

"We've heard so much about you," her mother said, clearly taking his measure as she looked him over from head to toe.

"Likewise." Henry glanced at Amelia with a smile. "I appreciate having the opportunity to meet you both."

Amelia also studied Henry to gauge how his day had gone. His hair was neatly brushed to one side as if he'd taken the time to comb it, and the black suit was more formal than he usually wore. He didn't appear distraught, but the man was adept at hiding his emotions. Had there been any breakthroughs in the investigation?

As if sensing her question, his expression tightened briefly, making her wonder even more. Perhaps she could manage a moment alone with him later to get an update.

"Whiskey?" her father asked. "You'll forgive me for offering, we're rather relaxed with our daughter."

At Henry's nod, he poured them each one and glasses of sherry for the ladies.

"I suppose the murder business has been busy of late, eh?" her father asked as they took their seats.

"It has, unfortunately." Henry paused to take a sip, making Amelia think he was deciding how much to say.

"I appreciate your efforts to help keep my daughter safe." Her father lifted his glass in Henry's direction. "Thank you."

"Of course." Henry lifted his glass in return, then sent Amelia a rueful look. "I am only sorry it was necessary."

"Yes, I don't remember you encountering so much trouble before you moved to London, dear," her mother said.

"It isn't as if life here is always fraught with peril," Amelia countered, not continuing to say that the blame for any danger she'd faced these last few months lay partly at Matthew's feet.

He'd been the one who chose to sell illegal antiquities and to become involved with Edgarton.

However, she didn't say any of that. She had intended to tell her parents more about what she and Henry had discovered regarding her late husband's business in person rather than putting it in a letter, but this wasn't the time.

"Amelia tells us that you come from a line of successful inspectors," her father said.

Henry hesitated, making Amelia wonder why, though the moment was so brief that she didn't think her parents noticed.

"I do," he said at last. "My father and grandfather were with the Metropolitan Police and retired as chief inspectors."

"How impressive." Her mother sent a look of approval toward Amelia.

"His grandfather was friends with Charles Dickens," Amelia added, knowing her father would find that as interesting as she had.

Henry sent her a warm look and shared a couple of his grandfather's amusing stories, the pride in his voice undeniable. He then asked her father about his work as an apothecary and how his interest in the field had developed.

Amelia could only shake her head as her father told Henry stories of her as a young girl in the shop, mixing one concoction after another.

"I feared an explosion might result from one, so I was obliged to teach her about the properties of the substances. Much to our surprise," he said, sharing an amused look with his wife, "she remembered all of it and soon started reading every book I had about remedies and chemistry. Before long, she knew more about them than I did!"

"That isn't true," Amelia corrected with a laugh. "I will never know as much as you do."

Her father looked at Henry with a wry expression. "Don't let her pretty face fool you. She's razor sharp."

Henry smiled. "I've learned that firsthand, sir. When I realized she could perform the test for arsenic poisoning, I was nearly beside myself. Quite impressive."

Amelia's heart swelled at Henry's praise and the admiration in his eyes. Aware of her mother's continued scrutiny, she quickly stood when Fernsby arrived to announce that dinner was served—and was delighted to see Henry politely offer his arm to her mother even as her father took her own.

The meal was truly enjoyable, and she was thrilled by how well Henry and her parents got along. Knowing they saw what she did in Henry pleased her. They'd liked Matthew, too, having known him for much of his life; he'd been raised in the same town as she had. But somehow this felt different.

A sense of anticipation filled her as they settled in the dining room: not for what might happen in the next few hours but rather the days and weeks ahead.

She took a sip of wine, her gaze meeting Henry's for a long moment.

Dare she hope he felt the same?

Soon after dinner ended Henry stood to take his leave, stating he had an early morning ahead of him. Her father offered his hand again as they said goodbye, a sign he genuinely liked Henry.

"Why don't I see you out?" Amelia suggested after he said goodbye to her mother warmly.

She led the way to the front door, pleased Fernsby was nowhere in sight, allowing them a few minutes of privacy. "Thank you for coming, Henry."

"I appreciate the invitation. Your parents are delightful."

"I'm pleased you think so." She bit her lip. "Is all going well with your investigation?"

He drew a slow breath as if to collect his thoughts. "A woman associated with Edgarton was killed in Whitechapel earlier today."

"Oh dear." Amelia frowned as she considered what that meant. "Someone is tidying loose ends."

"So it seems." His expression grew taut. "A few clues have arisen. Discomforting ones. I can't help but feel we will discover who is behind all this soon."

"I'm pleased to hear that." She hesitated on how best to tell him what she'd done, but their shared honesty was something she treasured, something they'd agreed on. "I called on Edgarton's mother yesterday."

Henry's eyes widened in alarm. "Amelia!"

She glanced over her shoulder to make certain her parents hadn't emerged from the dining room. "I took Yvette with me—I didn't think there could be much danger since her son is dead."

He shook his head firmly. "I'd rather you kept your distance."

"I know, but I had to try."

"How did you know where to find her?" Henry asked, eyes narrowed with curiosity.

"I inquired at the house across the street from Edgarton, and a maid was able to tell me."

"Hmm. Your cleverness never fails to amaze me." He lifted a brow. "And did she offer any helpful information? She refused to tell us anything prior to his death."

"She said he was working with someone with the police but didn't know who." As she'd anticipated, Henry didn't seem surprised by the news. "I have to think you already guessed as much, with the missing evidence and all."

"Unfortunately, yes." Shadows darkened his brown eyes. Clearly the issue weighed on him.

"I hope you can get to the bottom of it soon."

"As do I." He hesitated, then took her hands in his, causing her heart to skip a beat. "I'm honored that you invited me this evening. I enjoyed meeting your parents."

"They like you already," she whispered with a smile, appreciating the feel of his strong hands clasped with hers. "That's a good thing...as I also like you." She waited, hoping she hadn't said too much.

His slow smile caught her breath. "A very good thing, indeed, as you hold a special place in my life."

Warmth filled her at the admission, but she was still unprepared when he leaned close to briefly kiss her cheek, the faint scent of his cologne catching her notice. "Goodnight, Amelia."

"Goodnight, Henry."

With one last lingering look, he released her hands and took his leave.

Amelia locked the door behind him and leaned against it for a moment, holding the precious moment tightly. It was one worth remembering.

Thirty-Two

Henry's spirits were high the next morning as he and Fletcher returned to Holloway Prison. He couldn't help but feel the tides had turned with the case. Slowly, the pieces were coming together.

Discovering the message under Betty Knox's mattress was a significant breakthrough, even if it potentially involved Fletcher's uncle. Henry had taken the opportunity to compare the handwriting to the notes in one of Clarke's case files, and they were similar enough to cause concern.

Henry felt certain they would soon be able to answer the questions pertaining to everything from Cobb and Edgarton's murders, to the evidence that had been taken, as well as Betty Knox's death. It was all coming together.

And then there was Amelia...

Dinner with her and her parents had been wonderful; it couldn't have gone better as far as he was concerned. He liked Mr. and Mrs. Crosby and hoped they felt the same. Traits from them both were visible in Amelia, from her father's warm, brown eyes to her mother's chin. She had her father's curiosity and her mother's practicality.

And he admired *all* of her.

"You seem rather chipper, considering recent events," Fletcher remarked as they alighted from a hansom cab.

"I had an enjoyable dinner at Mrs. Greystone's last evening with her and her parents." Henry rarely spoke of his personal life, but if he was going to trust Fletcher and deepen their friendship, sharing such details would be expected—especially if he wanted his sergeant to do the same. It wouldn't hurt to distract the man from the concerning issues with his uncle.

"Oh?" Fletcher's dark brows nearly rose to the brim of his hat. "I didn't realize you and she were..." He paused, clearly uncertain how to complete the thought.

As was Henry.

The fact that she'd invited him to meet her parents was enough, for now. It served as another subtle indication of a potential future. Henry hoped he hadn't been too forward by kissing her cheek, but after such a wonderful evening, he'd been unable to resist.

In truth, he couldn't be happier with how their relationship was developing. Surely it would grow more quickly once he solved this case, when doing so would help to finally put her husband's murder behind them.

"We are coming to be good friends," Henry offered. "Where that might lead remains to be seen."

Fletcher nodded. "She is a nice lady with a good heart."

High praise from the gruff sergeant. "I couldn't agree more," Henry said with a smile.

They walked in silence for a few minutes before Fletcher cleared his throat. "I have thought long and hard about the note we found."

"Oh?" Henry still didn't know what to make of it. If Clarke had written it, why would he have signed it?

"There has to be some mistake." Fletcher shook his head, his expression troubled.

Henry's chest tightened with sympathy. It would be difficult to learn someone he'd trusted and respected had a dark side. "There is more information to uncover. That is for certain." Based on what they knew thus far, it seemed Clarke was involved in something untoward, but Henry didn't think he was the only guilty one within the department.

His stop at Scotland Yard that morning had been brief, and he'd caught Fletcher before the man had gone inside, deciding the less time he spent with his uncle, the better. Bringing him along that morning held some risk. If Fletcher had to choose between loyalty to family and his fellow officers, what might he do? Would Fletcher be tempted to warn Clarke of the evidence mounting against him?

It was better for Fletcher to continue to discover the truth along with Henry. That was what he would prefer if in the sergeant's position.

He didn't dare forget that his own reputation was at risk and that he needed to proceed cautiously. Whoever was guilty would likely place the blame elsewhere if given the chance. They'd already attempted to do that to Henry by forging his signature on the evidence log and possibly feeding the reporter information.

How complex was this criminal web?

"We will keep an open mind and continue to gather all evidence," Henry advised Fletcher cautiously. "To begin with, someone other than Cobb had to have helped Edgarton. One prison guard on his pay wouldn't be sufficient to allow him to escape—and I want to know who."

Fletcher cocked his head as he looked at Henry, sending him a knowing look. "Trusting your instincts?"

The sergeant was aware of how reluctant Henry was to do just that, even if he didn't understand the reason.

"I'm allowing them to point me in a direction at any rate." Most police officers had hunches, Henry reminded himself.

"And do those instincts tell you my uncle killed Edgarton?"

The quietly spoken question took Henry aback. He didn't know how to answer. While it was a definite possibility, he had yet to determine a motive.

Why would a newly appointed inspector, a position which had taken years of hard work and long hours to obtain, stoop to help a notorious criminal like Miles Edgarton, only to double-cross him? To what end?

It didn't make sense. Not yet anyway.

"I don't know." The silence drew long as they walked along the bustling street. "But I fear *someone* at the Yard did."

"And they'd like nothing more than to pin the blame on you," Fletcher suggested.

"So it seems." Henry was relieved Fletcher saw that, too. Between the temporarily missing evidence and the news story, he knew the Director was watching him closely.

The sergeant heaved a sigh. "Or pin it on my uncle. I fear that no matter who is to blame, the situation isn't going to end well."

The statement dampened Henry's mood; he had to believe Fletcher was right. "No, it isn't. But our job is to keep moving forward and follow every lead to a conclusion." And to the guilty party, no matter who they were.

"Right."

Holloway Prison was as gloomy as ever and Henry hoped it wasn't an omen. He did his best to ignore the heaviness that pressed on him as he and Fletcher entered the building.

Though he should've spoken with Director Reynolds before meeting with the chief warder who ran the prison, at times it was better to plow ahead and hope for the best. He hoped this was one of those.

A guard escorted them through a heavy door that led to several offices. A clerk manned a desk near a small waiting area where Henry explained what they wanted, telling him as little as possible.

"You say it's regarding the solving of Cobb's murder?" At Henry's nod, the clerk stood. "Wait here while I see if Chief Warder Alcroft can see you."

"Thank you." Henry resisted the urge to pace the narrow space.

"Do you think he'll tell us anything?" Fletcher asked when the door closed behind the clerk, doubt coloring his tone.

"I have no idea, but it can't hurt to inquire."

Henry thought it concerning that Scotland Yard hadn't been notified about the results of the prison's investigation into the escape, considering the cases were connected. He might be over-stepping, but the prison officials should have completed their examination by now, shouldn't they? He needed to know what they'd found.

After several long minutes had passed, the clerk returned. "Warder Alcroft says he can spare a few minutes to speak with you." He turned away to lead them down a narrow hallway to the warder's office.

"No doubt he's anxious to hear what you have to tell him about Cobb's murder investigation," Fletcher whispered to Henry with a wry look.

"How terrible he has the wrong impression," Henry murmured, refusing to feel guilty about misleading the clerk.

The Chief Warder's office was a spartan one, not so different than a prison cell, with minimal furnishings and a large desk. A small window placed high on the wall allowed in daylight, but the bars across it were a vivid reminder of the building's purpose.

Henry had met Chief Warder Alcroft on several occasions. He was a large man with thick, gray hair clipped short and muttonchops that lined his jaw, who answered only to the governor of the prison and was proud of his position.

"Field." The Chief Warder nodded politely at both Henry and Fletcher. "Good of you to come by to provide an update." He gestured to the simple wooden chairs before his desk. "Have you discovered who killed Cobb?"

"Actually, I am here to inquire as to how the investigation into Edgarton's escape is proceeding, since the crimes are closely tied to one another."

"You mean you haven't yet found the murderer?" Alcroft frowned, his displeasure clear.

"The investigation is ongoing." Henry wasn't about to mention it might involve a police officer. "Any information you've learned could aid us."

The Chief Warder scowled. "The prison is not an arm of the police force."

"I'm well aware." Henry kept his tone firm but respectful. "However, since your investigation into the escape is underway, and cooperation is advantageous to both the prison and the department in situations like this, we would like to hear what you've discovered. Surely, you agree that communication between us is important."

Alcroft held his silence, his glare suggesting otherwise.

Henry waited for the man to decide whether to show them the door or answer his inquiry.

After a long moment, the Chief Warder cleared his throat. "I suppose it wouldn't cause any harm to advise you...we have dismissed a guard for his potential part in the escape."

"Potential?" Fletcher interjected before Henry could.

"He refused to confess, despite the suggestion of guilt based on his proximity to the situation." Alcroft sighed. "It isn't the first time a guard has succumbed to the temptation of a bribe, and I fear it won't be the last."

"No evidence was found against him?" Henry asked curiously.

"Only the testimony of another guard who claimed to have overheard Cobb and this guard whispering about the matter. The man also had extra money in his pocket which was unlikely to have come to him honestly."

"Huh." Fletcher shifted in his chair.

Not exactly iron-clad evidence, in Henry's opinion, but he kept the thought to himself.

"When he refused to cooperate, we were forced to dismiss him."

"Can we speak with him?" Henry asked.

"I suppose, but based on his responses to our questions, I doubt it will result in anything helpful."

"We would still like to try." Most definitely, Henry thought.

"I'll have the clerk provide you with his address." The Chief Warder lifted a brow. "Quite the turn in the case to have your main suspect turn up dead, eh? Sounds as if several problems plague Scotland Yard these days."

Irritation struck Henry. "Any murder is a problem, even that of an escaped prisoner," he said in clipped tones before he could stop himself. He certainly didn't care to discuss any of it with the warder.

"Who else could be responsible for Cobb's death, if not Edgarton?" Alcroft shook his head. "I'm rather surprised you haven't announced his guilt. That would make for an orderly end to the investigation."

"I prefer the truth over tidy solutions." Though in the past more than one inspector had found a likely suspect and declared him guilty rather than having an unsolved case on their hands, Henry refused to follow suit.

He liked to think those days were behind the force, even if not all the other inspectors were as conscientious as Henry. Perdy, for one, seemed to prefer easy solutions whenever possible.

"While I applaud your efforts, sometimes it's important to provide an answer—right or wrong—in the court of public opinion," Alcroft advised in a dry tone.

"That will have to wait until we have the right one in this case." Henry refused to consider any other possibility.

"If you say so." The Chief Warder stood, signaling the meeting was at an end. "Good luck with the former guard."

"Thank you for your time." With a nod at Alcroft, Henry and Fletcher departed.

Within a quarter of an hour, they'd left the prison with the former guard's name and address in hand and found a hansom cab to hire. The distance to the address wasn't far, but Henry felt compelled to hurry.

"That went better than I expected," Fletcher advised with a shrug after they settled inside.

"Let us hope a conversation with this Howard Brooks does as well." Henry tapped a finger on his knee, thinking they couldn't get there quickly enough. Whether Brooks would be at home or willing to answer their questions remained to be seen.

And of course, there was the ever looming threat that he might not still be alive...

"Ever the optimist." Fletcher's lack of a smile was a reminder of who they were gathering evidence against—not that Henry had forgotten for even a moment.

"Brooks might lead us to someone other than Clarke." In truth, Henry would prefer that, even if Fletcher's uncle owed them an explanation for the note.

"Now that is something I will be hopeful about."

The rest of the brief drive passed in silence.

"Here we are." Fletcher reached for the door latch when the cab halted.

"Shall I wait?" the driver asked after they'd stepped out.

"No need." Henry had no idea what to expect from this visit and didn't want to pay the cabbie to wait.

"Must be this building." Fletcher pointed to a lodging house similar to the one Cobb had lived in. "He might have found another job by now, might not even be home."

His friend seemed determined to find the glass half empty today. "Perhaps," Henry agreed and started inside.

Their knock on Brooks's door was answered by a man who appeared to be the person they wanted to speak with, based on his age and demeanor.

"Yes?" He glanced between them, eyes narrowed in his grizzled face, clearly taken aback to find the police on his doorstep.

"Howard Brooks?" Fletcher asked.

"Y-Yes?"

Henry showed his warrant card, which the man peered at as if in need of spectacles, before glancing back at him.

"Scotland Yard?"

Henry nodded. "We have a few questions for you regarding Miles Edgarton's escape from prison."

The man's lips tightened. "I don't have anything to say about that."

"We only want to confirm some information we've received." Henry acted casually, hoping that would convince the man to talk.

"Holloway Prison already asked me. Talk to them." The man tried to shut the door in their face but Fletcher was too quick, sticking his booted foot in the doorway.

"We did," Henry continued blithely. "We're also investigating Rupert Cobb's *murder*." He emphasized the word, wanting Brooks to understand he, too, could be in danger.

The man tugged at his shirt collar. "And? D-Do you know who killed him?"

"We have a few leads." Henry nodded, then leaned forward as if imparting confidential information. "The sooner we can announce who did it, the safer you will be."

Brooks slowly nodded, seeming to ponder that. "Safer. Right. That would be good." He looked up and down the hallway. "I confess...I'm watching my back."

"Excellent idea." The sergeant gave him an approving look. "Might be worthwhile to keep a weapon at hand, if you know what I mean."

"Do you think?" The man's eyes widened, clearly alarmed to think danger might lurk around the next corner.

"Wouldn't hurt," Henry added brightly. "Now then, we have received a description of the person who bribed Cobb and would like you to verify it."

Brooks blinked as he seemed to consider how best to answer. "How would I know?" he asked at length.

"Surely you...saw him." Henry nodded encouragingly, not directly accusing him of accepting a bribe from the same man. "Our understanding is that he approached Cobb outside the prison. We only need you to confirm the details. Pale hair or dark?"

The man licked his lips, obviously torn about whether he was incriminating himself. "Dark."

"My height or shorter?" Henry continued, not bothering to get out his notebook. There was no possibility of him forgetting these details.

"Shorter by a couple of inches."

"What color eyes?" Fletcher asked reluctantly.

Again, he hesitated. "Blue."

Henry shared a look with Fletcher, noting his upset. Thus far, the description matched Clarke perfectly.

The evidence against the new inspector was mounting…yet Henry still had more questions than answers.

Thirty-Three

A MELIA WAS DESCENDING THE stairs directly after luncheon when someone knocked on the front door. Fernsby arrived from the depths of the house to answer it, and she drew nearer to see who was calling. The day looked to be a fine one, the first in over a week that hinted at spring.

Her mother and father were in the drawing room and they intended to visit the British Museum with her shortly, something she looked forward to. The natural history exhibits were among her father's favorites. While she enjoyed going to museums, she didn't care to do so alone. It was more fun to peruse exhibits with someone else and share impressions and interests. She also looked forward to Aunt Margaret joining them for dinner that evening. Their visit was going perfectly.

Fernsby opened the door to reveal Constable Peters with his hat in hand.

Amelia's heart leapt to her throat at the sight of him, fearing bad news—that Henry had been injured...or worse.

"Good afternoon." The uniformed officer smiled broadly, his blue eyes darting between them. He dipped forward, an awkward cross between a bow and a tip of his head. "I hope the day finds you well."

"Constable." Relief flooded her with his smile, certain he wouldn't be offering one if something serious was amiss. Yet neither could she imagine the reason for his visit. "What brings you by?"

"I wanted to make certain all is well here."

Amelia frowned, surprised. She didn't miss having a police guard and certainly didn't miss Constable Peters. "Quite well. Thank you."

"That's good to hear. Very good." He nodded, glancing around the inside of the house.

She couldn't imagine what he was looking for.

"No...unusual occurrences?" he asked with a lift of his brow.

Amelia shared a puzzled look with Fernsby. "None. Why do you ask?"

The constable drew himself up smartly. "It pays to remain on guard during these troubled times."

"My understanding is that the threat to our household ended with Edgarton's death," she countered, even as unease crawled along her spine. Henry hadn't mentioned a specific concern the previous evening—and he certainly would've taken the time to advise her if anything was worrying him.

"Of course." Peters nodded. "But he's not the only criminal in the city." He took a step forward. "In fact—"

"Amelia, are you ready?" Her father stood at the top of the stairs, frowning at the sight of the constable. "Oh. I didn't realize you had a visitor."

"I will only be a minute." She returned her attention to Constable Peters. "You were saying?"

The man's gaze held on her father for a long moment, then he took a step back, his smile returning, though not as broad as before. "Nothing—I'm pleased to hear all is well. I wish you a good day."

With that, he placed his hat on his head and hurried down the front steps.

"How odd," Amelia murmured as she watched him go.

"Odd indeed," Fernsby said. "I can't imagine why he would take the time to call without a reason."

"Nor can I." She considered the man's strange behavior as Fernsby shut the door. "I believe I'll mention it to Inspector Field next time I see him."

"Excellent idea, madam."

"Is all well?" Her father sent her a puzzled look as he joined them. "Who was that?"

"One of the constables who watched the house after the prisoner escaped. I'm not certain why he came by." Amelia couldn't imagine his purpose.

"Kind of him to check on you, don't you think?" her father asked approvingly.

"Hmm." For some reason, Amelia didn't think it was kindness that had caused him to knock on the door. Though Constable Peters had always acted friendly, there was some underlying issue that bothered her about the man, even if she would be hard-pressed to name it. "I hope he doesn't make a habit of doing so."

"I would be happy to discourage him if he does so again, madam," Fernsby offered.

"I believe that would be for the best, but I will mention it to Inspector Field to be certain." What had the constable intended to say before he saw her father? She dearly wanted to know.

"Shall I send for a hansom cab?" Fernsby asked.

"Please do." Amelia turned to her father. "I believe we are ready to depart, are we not?"

"Yes. Allow me to make certain your mother is prepared."

In a short while, they were on their way to the museum, but Amelia couldn't set aside the uneasy feeling that had descended since the constable's visit.

At the very least she would keep a watchful eye out, and knew her father would as well during his stay. He was always wary in the city, determined to ensure a pickpocket or the like didn't get the best of him.

She hoped Henry would come by again soon, so she could mention Constable Peters' visit. Somehow she didn't think he'd like it any more than she had. She debated whether to send him a message but decided against it, not wanting to bother him with something so minor when he had yet another murder to investigate. Besides, if his concerns that there was a police officer involved with Edgarton were true...no. She would wait to see him, and then tell him of her concerns.

Their arrival at the museum proved the perfect distraction. Her father led the way toward the exhibits, leaving Amelia and her mother to walk side by side a short distance behind him.

"I know you claim to be only friends, Amelia," her mother said quietly as they paused to study the fossilized skeleton of a dinosaur. "But I have to say, I sense more between you and Inspector Field. Am I correct?"

Though she'd expected her mother to mention it, she still felt unprepared to answer. How to put into words what they shared? "We enjoy one another's company. I won't deny a certain attraction to him, though it's too soon to say."

His unexpected kiss the previous evening had her beginning to think otherwise.

"It's only too soon if you feel it is." Her mother's gentle smile eased Amelia's concern. "There is nothing wrong with seeing where that attraction leads."

"True." Relief flooded Amelia.

"He seems like a fine man. Honorable, intelligent, kind. And it's been nearly a year and a half since Matthew's death," her mother continued. "A painful year and a half. You've mourned long enough, you should feel free to move on with your life." Her mother paused as her gaze swept over Amelia's gray gown, then took Amelia's hand. "You know better than most, life is fleeting. Reach for happiness, my dear. Anyone who looks down upon you for doing so can look the other way."

Amelia squeezed her hand. "Thank you, Mother. I appreciate hearing that." She liked to think her relationship with Henry was progressing, and it felt quite freeing to hear her mother approved.

They continued forward as her mother leaned close. "For what it's worth, your father and I discussed the inspector at length last evening. We both believe him to be a good man with honorable intentions."

"I'm pleased to hear that." There were times when Amelia wasn't certain she could trust her own opinion, given her blindness to what Matthew had been doing. Her parents' support eased that concern.

"You mentioned you've met his parents?" her mother asked.

"Yes, and they are delightful." It was clear they adored Henry, his father proud to have his son follow in his footsteps.

While Henry had seemed uncomfortable with their praise, he was too humble in her opinion. At times he appeared to almost doubt his own skills.

Though she'd thought for certain that Edgarton must've killed the prison guard, Henry hadn't believed so, and it looked as if he'd been right. He was an excellent detective. She didn't understand why he questioned his abilities, but perhaps it made him a better, more thorough detective.

"That's wonderful." Her mother smiled. "Perhaps one day we'll have the pleasure of meeting them as well."

Amelia only smiled, not ready to confirm or deny any hopes of the sort.

There was no rush; no danger stalked either of them now. She'd know when the right moment arrived, wouldn't she?

Thirty-Four

H ENRY AND FLETCHER STOPPED for a quick bite to eat before returning to the Yard. Neither had the urge to linger over their late luncheon with so much on their minds.

"I...I just can't believe it. There must be some sort of explanation," Fletcher muttered yet again as they entered the building.

Henry wasn't sure what to think either. As he'd already told his friend, they needed more evidence before any accusations could be made. They had to tread carefully, given it involved a police officer.

"What do you intend to do?" Fletcher asked quietly.

"Share what we know with Reynolds and determine how to proceed with his approval."

The heartfelt sigh the sergeant heaved made Henry wish he could offer something to reassure him, only to have his friend nod. "Very well," he muttered.

A quick look around the office showed Clarke working at his desk. Only a few other officers were in attendance at the moment. Perhaps it was better that way.

Henry led the way to Reynolds' office and tapped on the open door. "Sir?"

The Director set down the report he'd been reading and gestured for them to come in. "What do you have for me?"

Henry closed the door behind them, which caused Reynolds to lift a brow. His superior would understand the reason soon enough.

The pair took a seat and Henry pulled out the note they'd found to hand it to the Director. "Yesterday we found this under the mattress of Betty Knox, the woman Edgarton had stayed with. The woman murdered in Whitechapel." He paused to allow Reynolds time to read it before continuing, "We also questioned the witness in Cobb's building again. He has changed his statement and confirmed that a police officer matching Clarke's description told him what to say if asked."

The Director glanced at Fletcher, clearly wondering how he felt about the news. "This is very concerning."

Fletcher cleared his throat. "There's more. A second prison guard is suspected of helping with Edgarton's escape. He's been let go, but we spoke with him."

"And?"

"He saw who supposedly bribed Cobb, and that description also matches Clarke," Henry said quietly.

Reynolds removed his spectacles to clean them on his handkerchief, as if needing time to process the information. "These are serious accusations and include multiple murders. Are you sure?"

After a quick glance at Fletcher, Henry sighed, wishing he knew for certain of Clarke's innocence or guilt. "No. Neither of the witnesses could provide a distinguishing mark or detail that absolutely confirms the person's identity. Height, dark hair, blue eyes, it's not definitive. And I have yet to determine a motive. As Fletcher will tell you, none of this matches the man he knows."

"That's right, sir. My uncle wouldn't do any of these things."

"Hmm. Well, if this is true, it would seem likely that Clarke is also responsible for the missing scarab and its subsequent return," the Director suggested.

Henry nodded. "Whoever killed Edgarton might have placed it in his pocket to be found." *By me,* but he didn't say that.

Yet he had to think whoever had stolen it meant to make it appear as if Henry himself had not only taken the scarab but returned it when the search for it became too intense. The officer who'd stolen it and forged Henry's signature on the logbook used it to make another attempt to cast doubt on Henry by making sure he was the one who found the scarab. Once that failed, had the guilty person decided to place blame on Clarke for recent events?

Despite the evidence pointing to the new inspector, Henry still had doubts.

Fletcher shook his head. "I can't believe it of him."

"I would rather not believe it either." Reynolds replaced his spectacles. "Of him, or any of us. Let's speak with him and see what he has to say before we take this any further." He studied Fletcher. "Sergeant, if you'd prefer to remove yourself—"

"If it's all the same to you, sir, I'd like to stay. Hear his explanation."

"Very well." Reynolds looked at Henry. "Request that he join us."

Clarke showed only puzzlement, not nervousness, to Henry's request to join them in the Director's office.

"We have some concerns we need to address, Inspector Clarke." The Director leaned his elbows on his desk and held the other man's gaze.

"Oh? What might those be?"

Henry was surprised by how collected Clarke appeared, considering the note with his supposed signature rested on the Director's desk in clear view. Either the man was an incredible actor, or he wasn't guilty.

Damn.

Then who was, Henry wondered, as Reynolds stared at Clarke, allowing the silence to grow heavy.

"Do you recognize this?" Reynolds turned the note so Clarke could better see it.

"No." The reply was immediate before he started to read it. He scoffed at the sight of his name on the bottom. "I didn't write it, and I certainly didn't sign it."

"It looks similar to your handwriting," Henry advised, keeping his tone even.

"Perhaps it docs, but I didn't write it." The man's exasperation was evident. "Where was it found?"

They went through each piece of evidence, but Clarke had an answer or an alibi for much of it, including the days Edgarton and Betty Knox had been stabbed.

"I don't know who those witnesses you mentioned saw, but it wasn't me. I've been working on the theft case on Arlington Street." Worry tightened his expression as Clarke looked between them, the severity of situation seeming to finally sink in.

"I—I've kept you apprised of it, sir, along with Inspector Perdy, just as you suggested."

Reynolds nodded, shifting his focus to Henry, clearly waiting to see if Henry had any other questions.

Henry shook his head, holding silent as the Director told Clarke that none of this was to be discussed with anyone inside or outside of Scotland Yard.

"Yes, sir," Clarke agreed, his blue eyes flashing with temper as he glared at first Henry, and then Fletcher, as if he couldn't fathom that they'd believe him capable of what the note inferred.

"Clarke," Reynolds said in a sharp tone.

"Sir?" The inspector forced his attention back to the Director.

"They are doing their job, just as I expect you to. Do I make myself clear?"

"Yes, sir." Clarke lowered his gaze as if uncertain he could keep his anger in check.

"That will be all." Reynolds waited until the newest inspector departed, closing the door behind him before looking at Henry. "Well? He certainly had an answer for much of the evidence you presented."

"He's not our man," Henry confirmed, his heart nonetheless still heavy. While pleased for Fletcher's sake, he couldn't deny wishing they'd found the guilty party.

"Agreed." The Director scowled. "Well, we can't march every man with dark hair and blue eyes into here, we'd never get any other work done, and we'd ruin morale in the process. We need to determine who the rookery killer is before the Home

Secretary decides to restructure the entire force and we all lose our jobs. Is that understood, Field?"

"Yes, sir." Anger sparked at the hint of a suggestion that he wasn't already doing all he could. Did the Director think Henry shouldn't have told him what they'd learned thus far? That they should've pushed for more before coming to him?

In a typical case they would have, but not one involving their own. In Henry's opinion, that required his superior's oversight.

He turned to Fletcher after they left the Director's office. From his expression, his friend appeared significantly relieved by the outcome. Surely his uncle would realize Fletcher had no choice in the matter, and they would soon reconcile.

At least, Henry hoped so.

"I need some air," Fletcher advised curtly and took his leave.

Henry returned to his desk, sitting heavily in his chair, somewhat relieved that Clarke was nowhere in sight. He'd prefer not to work with the other inspector glaring at him for the remainder of the day.

Allowing the relative quiet of the office to settle around him, Henry opened a case file, his thoughts circling on the evidence they'd just presented.

It hadn't made sense that Clarke would sign the note if he'd written it. At most he would've used his initials or even just one initial, not a full signature. Perhaps Henry should retrieve the note from the Director and attempt to compare it to the handwriting of the other officers to see if there were any similarities.

And what of the descriptions they'd received from both the witness in the murdered prison guard's building and the fired guard?

Those were vague, though they had matched Clarke. Who else did they match?

Perdy's eyes were hazel, if he remembered correctly. And, as Henry had thought before, Perdy seemed neither clever nor motivated enough to commit murder. He might have helped to take the scarab, but not the rest.

Whitlock, then? Henry frowned as he tried to remember the color of the man's eyes. He was of a similar build to Clarke, whereas Perdy was heavier.

Duncan had unusually bright green eyes, suggesting he couldn't be to blame, nor did Henry have any reason to suspect him. He might not have been able to gather much information to aid Henry as of yet, but that didn't make him guilty.

Henry ran through his mental list of the other officers at the Yard in any way involved with all this, with little success. Peters was a potential match, but surely if he hadn't been walking his beat, it would've been noticed. He refused to consider Constable Dannon or Stephens as he'd worked closely with them on numerous occasions and knew them to be trustworthy.

Or did he? Did he know anything about any of them?

Frustration welled as he jotted notes in a few other case files that required his attention, but soon he, too, felt the need to escape. Perhaps some fresh air, or whatever version of that London could offer, would help clear his thoughts.

In short order he was walking in the crisp spring air, the faint sunshine helping to ease his distress. He allowed his thoughts to drift, amused by how quickly they went to Amelia. Had she and her parents ventured to the museum as planned? The thought nearly had him smiling as he imagined the three doing just that.

Amelia seemed to enjoy museums. Perhaps he could find one she hadn't already visited to take her to.

But first, he needed to solve the case.

A conversation with his father might help him shake loose an idea as to who had committed the three murders, and why. Given the last terrible news article about the police's ineptitude, which had mentioned Henry specifically, he hoped his father didn't feel as if Henry had brought shame to the Field name. The worry was a sobering one, something he needed to address to ease his mind and his heart.

His footsteps changed direction and soon he was entering his father's study.

"Henry." His father's beaming smile and obvious pleasure at Henry's unexpected appearance eased his worry.

"Father. How has your day been?"

He offered a wry look. "Better than yours, I would guess." When Henry frowned in confusion, he held up the news sheet.

The Rookery Killer Strikes Again! Exactly as Henry had feared.

"I didn't have a chance to look at it this morning." He'd been too distracted by other things to read the latest news, and he had known he wouldn't like it. He sighed. "It's been a challenging week."

His father nodded, nothing but sympathy in his expression as he moved around his desk to sit in the chair next to Henry. "It sounds like a complicated case, from what little I know. How is the investigation progressing?"

"Not very well, in all honesty." Henry cleared his throat. "I hope the news reports haven't caused you and Mother distress." He braced himself, willing his father to say it hadn't.

"Please." He waved a hand to dismiss the idea. "Their job is to sell papers. Yours is to solve crimes. The two do not always agree." His father leaned forward in his chair, holding Henry's gaze. "I can't begin to tell you the number of times some reporter or other said terrible things about me."

"Truly?" Henry couldn't imagine such an occurrence. His father had always seemed successful and confident.

"Oh, yes." He shook his head. "I would advise you to ignore them, but you're too much like me for that to be possible."

Henry's heart ached at the words. Was he? Given his adoption, he'd always had doubts. Serious ones. The temptation to tell his father that he knew the truth had him pressing his lips tight.

Should he mention his true parentage? Or would that only hurt his parents when that was the last thing he intended?

His father's attention shifted to the view out the window. "I was constantly compared to your grandfather, and not in a favorable manner."

"Oh?" Henry had always considered them two of a kind. They had been well-regarded, each man incredibly capable of any challenge presented to them, even if a case had involved a fellow officer or took place in a rookery.

His father's focus returned to Henry. "Surely you don't think I felt capable of following in the steps of the great Charles Field? Nor did most reporters think I was. Living up to the reputation of a man who was bigger than life proved impossible, and it was something I struggled with frequently."

The notion was logical, yet something Henry had never considered. Not when his father had received so many accolades over the years. "I didn't realize that."

"Ask your mother." His father gave a rueful look. "There were times when I was certain I'd chosen the wrong career."

"I had no idea." Henry paused before adding, "I confess to feeling the same."

Frequently.

His father reached to place his hand on Henry's knee, the gesture both familiar and heart-warming. "Henry, you are more than your last name. Your skills have enabled you to become a successful detective, able to sort through information with logic and precision. Your observation skills are remarkable, and I am constantly impressed by your patience and determination. Your grandfather would be very proud of you, as am I."

Henry could only blink in response. While his father had offered praise before, Henry had brushed it aside as what any father might say. But now the compliments, considered and caring, touched him deeply. "Thank you."

His father nodded and sat back. "I am sincere. I remember all too well the cases I didn't think I'd ever solve. And some I didn't. It's a terrible feeling and leaves you with doubt. But you can't let that hold you back. Not every person has the calling we do, and your job matters. Every step, regardless of how small, is progress. You mustn't forget that."

"You're right." Henry shifted in his chair, already feeling better. "Since this investigation points to someone within the police itself, it feels especially difficult."

"And distressing, I would imagine." His father sighed. "We had our share of scandals of one form or another. Bribery on numerous occasions, too. It's always disappointing to learn someone you thought you could trust proves otherwise."

"Henry, I didn't realize you were here!" His mother's greeting had him rising to kiss her cheek, the warmth in her tone a reminder of how lucky he was to have both of them.

"I wanted a quick word with Father."

"Of course." She searched his face, and he hoped she couldn't sense his recent worries.

Her perusal made him pleased he hadn't said anything about his adoption. Somehow he was certain she'd prefer he didn't know the truth.

"And I assume your father had words of wisdom to offer?" she asked.

"He did." Henry shared an amused look with his father. "As always."

"Good. Can you stay for dinner?"

"Not this evening as I have work to do—but soon." He needed time to think further about the case, and that meant spending the evening alone.

"We look forward to it." Her smile suggested she wasn't offended in the least.

"I had dinner with Amelia's parents last evening," he shared, certain the news would please her, even if he was a little uncertain why the news spilled out of him.

"Oh?" Delight shone in her eyes. "And? Did you like them?"

His heart pinched at her question. She hadn't asked if it was the other way around, most likely because it didn't cross her mind. Her faith in him never wavered.

"I did." Henry nodded with a small smile. "I think you will as well." That was more than enough of a hint at his hopes for the future.

His mother's eyes brightened with excitement as she grinned. "I look forward to that day."

So did Henry...even if it felt a long way off.

Thirty-Five

THE MESSAGE AWAITING HENRY when he returned to his lodging house that evening alarmed him. Amelia had written to advise him that her parents had enjoyed meeting him *and* that Constable Peters had stopped by, the conversation cut short when he saw her father and abruptly departed. She went on to say she nearly didn't mention it as she didn't want to alarm him but decided to share it since the visit had felt odd.

Unease crawled along Henry's spine at the news. Something was amiss with the constable, and Amelia's note solidified that belief. He jotted a quick reply, requesting she not allow Peters' entry under any circumstances and that he had enjoyed the dinner, too.

The night was a long one as Henry tossed and turned, unable to sleep, bits of the investigation flowing through his mind—an image of each victim followed by the potential suspects. The only connection seemed to be Edgarton, but the identity and motive of the rookery killer remained elusive. However, he felt certain Peters was somehow involved. Perhaps Duncan had uncovered something useful. It might be worthwhile checking with him in the morning.

By the time dawn arrived, he'd already risen, washed, and shaved, anxious to begin the day. Peters was the first one he intended to speak with, and he hoped the conversation would lead to some answers.

Director Reynolds' warning echoed in his ears. *We need to determine who the killer is before the Home Secretary decides to restructure the entire force, and we all lose our jobs.*

If only the Director knew how badly Henry wanted to solve the case. What had made anyone within the force choose to commit not just one murder but three, among their other crimes?

Had they taken a small, meaningless bribe, and events progressed from there? Perhaps an encounter with Edgarton had changed the course of the guilty officer's future. It might have tempted them by offering a taste of a better life with access to money and power.

The wages of an inspector were nothing to brag about, and the pay for a constable was even less. If a person had other obligations pulling at them, an unexpected debt or a family member's illness, the promise of extra funds might prove too tempting to turn aside—not that Henry considered any circumstances, no matter how dire, to excuse murder.

Once entangled in Edgarton's web, escape might be nearly impossible. It would be a slippery slope with no purchase to halt oneself, especially with money to grease the fall. Unfortunately Edgarton was dead and couldn't help answer the questions, not that he would have willingly done so.

Henry's thoughts continued to circle as he walked to work. He neared Scotland Yard, slowing his steps at the sight of Constable Peters speaking with someone.

Who was it? Unfortunately, Peters blocked his view. Though too far away to hear anything, from the way the constable leaned forward and the abrupt gestures he made, the conversation was a heated one.

Henry lingered unobserved from the corner of a building across the street, willing the constable to move aside so he could see with whom he was speaking. He didn't have to wait long, as the constable spun away as if in frustration to reveal—

Whitlock.

A sense of knowing swept over Henry, along with excitement. *Whitlock and Peters.* It made a terrible sense.

Whitlock's knowing smirk when Henry realized the scarab was missing.

The gold watch Whitlock had held, suggesting his pockets were flush with money.

The way Peters appeared at the crime scene soon after each of the recent murders.

The mention of the officer's blue eyes by more than one witness—and Peters had blue eyes.

And Amelia's concerning message from the previous night.

Henry had to assume, at least for now, that he was right about the identity of those involved—Whitlock and Peters. He couldn't know the motive for certain, but most likely a series of events that presented the men with a terrible opportunity. Greed might have been the only reason behind it. And they'd chosen the darker path.

Now he needed solid evidence rather than speculation to prove the case against them.

The men continued the conversation before an angry Peters stomped into Scotland Yard, and Whitlock strode down the street in the opposite direction.

Who to follow?

Whitlock, Henry decided, starting forward. He didn't believe the bumbling constable with his nonchalant manner and disarming smile was in charge of anything the two were doing. Peters was more likely to be taking orders rather than giving them.

As Henry passed near Scotland Yard, Fletcher emerged. *Perfect timing.* Henry gestured for the sergeant to join him, urging him to be quiet.

"What is it?" Fletcher whispered after he crossed the street, his pace quickly matching Henry's, eyes alight with interest as if he sensed the urgency of the situation.

"I think Whitlock and Peters are the ones we're in search of."

"Really?" Fletcher's steps faltered. "I just passed Peters. Should I—"

Henry shook his head. "Whitlock must be in charge, given his age and experience. Peters doesn't seem like he'd have it in him to do something on his own."

"That makes sense," Fletcher agreed, his attention fastening on Whitlock. "Let us see where the inspector is going this morning."

Whitlock took a winding route along several streets, and Henry and Fletcher were careful to keep their distance. Then he hopped on an omnibus, causing Henry a moment of panic.

Luckily, Fletcher caught a passing hansom cab, and they instructed the driver to follow the other conveyance.

"What fer?" the cabbie asked with a puzzled look.

"Because he's paying you to," Fletcher advised with exasperation while Henry kept his focus on the omnibus to make certain Whitlock didn't alight without them realizing.

The driver grumbled but did as requested, slowing his horse once or twice when the cab drew too close for Henry's comfort.

When the bus rolled to a halt Whitlock was the first passenger to emerge, a pipe clenched between his teeth.

Henry waved for the cabbie to stop as well, and quickly paid him.

"Headed toward Whitechapel, isn't he?" Fletcher murmured.

"It appears so." The destination made Henry even more relieved to have his friend at his side. He couldn't help but touch his neck, remembering all too well what could go wrong in the rookery.

Edgarton might be dead, but that didn't reduce the peril, especially if Whitlock was as dangerous as Henry suspected.

"We'll take care and watch our backs," Henry advised, and Fletcher nodded.

The oppressiveness of the desperate, crowded streets weighed on Henry once again, but perhaps that was only his own nerves taking hold. Whitlock glanced back with narrowed eyes, and Henry quickly tipped his head down as Fletcher, more visible in his uniform, stepped behind Henry to hide. Surely the passersby also helped to keep them out of view.

After a moment Whitlock continued forward, much to Henry's relief.

Aware of the curious glances of those they passed, Henry noticed only a few paid any attention to Whitlock. Was the man so familiar to those in this area? One more strike against him.

Whitlock rounded a corner, leaving them to hurry to catch up. Henry located him in time to see him enter a shop. A faded wooden sign near the door had a jug and juniper sprigs carved into it.

Just like the one where Betty Knox had argued with her attacker...

"What business does he have in a gin shop?" Fletcher asked with a frown.

"Good question." Henry waited, rewarded when Whitlock soon emerged only to enter the next shop, which sold tobacco.

The inspector exited that one quickly, too, stuffing something in his pocket, before he moved toward the next shop.

"He's on the take." Henry held Fletcher's gaze for a long moment. It was a betrayal of all the Metropolitan stood for.

"Offering protection from the very threat he arranged," Fletcher added with a scowl.

"Exactly. He doesn't need Edgarton to run this racket. Not anymore." Henry tipped his head toward the first shop. "See if you can convince the owner to talk. Tell them we're putting an end to the scheme this very day. Promise them whatever you have to in exchange for their testimony against Whitlock."

Fletcher didn't wait to be told twice, hurrying into the first shop as Whitlock headed to a fourth one. Henry waited in a doorway to see Whitlock emerge yet again, a satisfied look on his face, deepening Henry's anger.

Next, Whitlock approached a rag and bone man with a barrow, who scowled at his approach, someone he surely had little in common with. But Henry could guess at the conversation, even if he couldn't hear it. Everyone had to pay, even the rag and bone man.

Patience and determination. His father's words echoed in his mind. He needed those qualities now more than ever. To know his father had struggled with the same doubts as Henry was oddly reassuring—yet he preferred to question his investigative skills and strive to improve them rather than having the arrogance of Perdy.

Sensing a presence at his side, Henry glanced down to see Marcus grinning at him.

"Fancy meetin' ye 'ere."

Henry's gaze darted to where Whitlock still spoke with the rag and bone man. "Do you have anything for me?"

"From what I 'eard yesterday, there's a copper on the take." Marcus shook his head. "He makes 'em pay to keep the bad uns away. Can ye believe that?"

Just as Henry had suspected. Was that very scheme the way Whitlock and Edgarton had met? Had Whitlock thought the criminal was necessary and so helped him escape prison, only to realize he didn't need him after all? Perhaps Cobb and Betty Knox had been nothing more than unfortunate casualties once Whitlock's association with Edgarton ended.

"Is 'e the one?" the boy asked as he watched Whitlock. "I 'eard 'im and the other bloke who got stabbed in St. Mary's were thick as thieves," Marcus continued in a low voice with a nervous look around. "They also 'ave a brothel or two. The copper 'elped the dead man stay outta prison fer years." The lad looked back at Henry, a gleam of admiration in his eyes. "Til ye came along and caught 'im."

The list of Whitlock's crimes was quickly lengthening. What else had they done? Had Whitlock also been involved in the illicit artifacts that Edgarton had sold with Matthew Greystone? Or the lottery scheme? How many years had this been going on?

No wonder Edgarton's activities had remained hidden from the police for so long.

Whitlock had made sure of it.

"How did you discover all this?" Henry asked.

Marcus grinned as he rocked on his heels, clearly proud of himself and rightfully so. "I 'ave my ways."

"I need proof, Marcus." Urgency swept over Henry as he offered a coin to the lad. "Someone willing to testify against the officer." The more evidence they had, the better.

The boy considered the request even as he pocketed the coin. "I reckons a few are tired of him leanin' on 'em and might be willin'."

Henry looked over to see Whitlock take something the rag man handed him before moving down the street. Apparently, Henry and Marcus weren't the only ones exchanging money. The odd parallel somehow made him feel dirty—tainted. But not for a moment would Henry forget which side he was on. "Get me a name or two, Marcus, and I will happily put an end to all the schemes *and* make it worth your while."

"I'll do wot I can." The lad took off with a bound, gone as quickly as he'd appeared.

Henry had the feeling that once he yanked out a brick, the whole house would fall, Whitlock along with it. He dearly hoped Fletcher would return with proof, but if Marcus could find someone to add to it, the case against Whitlock would be even tighter. If these people had been under Whitlock and Edgarton's thumbs for years, they might not all be willing to confess to it. Henry wanted as many to testify as possible, the more the better.

He turned to look for Whitlock, only to realize he'd disappeared.

Damn.

Thirty-Six

H ENRY CONTINUED FORWARD, NERVES stretched taut, certain Whitlock must've stepped into another shop. But which one? He walked slowly, keeping a careful eye out for the other inspector and for Fletcher's return.

As he moved past one shop, then another, he worried if Whitlock had gone inside one and would soon emerge to spot him. Henry preferred that didn't happen. Not until they had a better idea of how many businesses the man was extorting money from.

Where was he?

"Field."

Henry stiffened, then slowly turned, masking his irritation as best he could. "Whitlock. What brings you to Whitechapel this morning?"

The inspector's eyes narrowed with suspicion. "I would ask you the same."

Henry feigned surprise, willing Fletcher to arrive. "On the hunt for the rookery killer, of course. What of you?"

Whitlock glanced around with a familiar smirk. "Expect to come upon him as you stroll along the street?"

"You never know who you might encounter." Henry drew a shallow breath of relief when Fletcher quietly approached Whitlock from behind. Henry was careful not to look at the sergeant. For once, for the first time in his life, Henry was going to follow his instincts even without evidence in hand. Now was the perfect time to test the waters for Whitlock's reaction. "Murderers come in all shapes...and occupations."

Wariness flashed in Whitlock's eyes and excitement rushed through Henry. "What are you suggesting?"

The sight of Fletcher nodding out of the corner of his eye told Henry he was right, and Fletcher had proof, so he pressed forward. "It means we know everything."

The other man paled, only to offer what was surely supposed to be an easy smile. "Everything? Everything about what? You're not making any sense, Field."

"We know about your long relationship with Edgarton. The bribes, the prostitution, the illegal goods. All of it."

Whitlock scoffed, his gaze darting about. "You've lost your mind."

Now to see what he could provoke the man into saying. "Peters has been quite helpful in providing details."

Fear pinched Whitlock's face even as he stiffened. "Peters? What does he have to do with anything? The man is worthless."

"Not much of a constable, I agree, but a believable witness. He jumped on our offer to reduce the charges he's facing...in exchange for testifying against you." Though it was a lie, Henry had the feeling Peters could be convinced to do precisely that.

If only he could get a confession...

"You must be desperate to solve all those open murder cases if you're stooping so low as to accuse a fellow inspector of what—all of them?"

"The evidence speaks for itself," Henry countered.

"Not coming from you. Your reputation is in tatters. First, the escaped prisoner, then the missing evidence, and now not one but three unsolved murders on your hands. You've become a joke of a detective."

"I think you're behind all those events," Henry suggested, aware of Fletcher listening to every word. "Clever of you."

Whitlock chuckled, chest puffing out as if he were proud of himself. "I suppose there's no harm in admitting as much when no one will believe you. I've been with the department for nearly a decade. Given them my heart and soul, and for what?" Anger tightened his expression. "Do you know how many opportunities have passed me by since your arrival?"

"So you took a bribe from Edgarton to look the other way. And then it wasn't so difficult to do it again. Or to become involved in a scheme offering protection to shops in exchange for money. Then, your association expanded into a brothel or two."

Whitlock's scowl suggested he didn't like the fact that Henry knew as much as he did. "It wasn't fair that Edgarton had more than me, considering he was on the wrong side of the law."

"What of the illegal antiquities? Were you involved in that?"

"I'm done talking to you, Field." Whitlock leaned forward to hold Henry's gaze. "Too bad that name doesn't mean what it used to."

"It means everything to me." Henry smiled at that truth.

"You'll feel nothing but shame when Fleet Street runs their next story about you." Whitlock took a pipe from his pocket and lit it, his hand trembling ever so slightly as he shook out the match and tossed it to the ground.

Henry bent to pick it up. "Thank you for this." He held it up and smiled before tucking it into his pocket. "I will have this tested to confirm that it matches the one found on Cobb's doorstep." Though he didn't know if that was possible, Whitlock probably didn't either. And Henry knew Amelia could work miracles if necessary.

The other man's eyes flashed with concern, his breath coming quickly. "Give that back." He held out his hand, further tipping the scale of his guilt.

Finally.

At Henry's nod, Fletcher stepped forward. "You should thank Inspector Field for picking up the rubbish around here, starting with you, Whitlock."

The inspector gasped and spun around as if wondering who else had heard the conversation.

"Douglas Whitlock, you are under arrest for the murders of Rupert Cobb, Miles Edgarton, and Betty Knox, as well as for extortion, bribery, and prostitution, and perhaps a few other crimes, as well."

Panic shimmered in the man's eyes as he stiffened, seeming frozen with indecision—then he gave Fletcher a mighty shove and tore off down the street, hurling people out of his way as he ran.

Henry was directly behind him, leaping over a broken cart, and darting around those in his path, his heart hammering.

"Halt! Police," he shouted—not that he expected anyone to aid him when the law wasn't looked kindly upon by those who lived and worked here, but it helped to clear the way. "Halt! Police!"

Fletcher's whistle pierced the air from behind them as Henry closed in on the fleeing man. Henry reached out to grasp his shoulder and forced him to halt.

Whitlock jerked free and spun to face him, a knife flashing in his hand, and his chest heaving. "Get back, Field. You've gone mad, threatening a fellow officer."

"Drop the weapon!" Henry held out his hands, prepared to slap the blade from Whitlock's grasp if given the chance. "The game is over. You are the rookery killer, Whitlock. There is no escape."

"Yes—yes there is." The other man looked about frantically in search of a route to freedom.

Henry lunged for the knife, hoping to catch Whitlock off guard—but the man was quick, pricking Henry's forearm. The sharp sting only made Henry more determined.

He kneed the other man in the thigh, hard enough to send him off balance, and Fletcher arrived to grab one arm. Henry caught the other and squeezed Whitlock's wrist with both hands, willing him to drop the weapon.

Several onlookers gathered around them, shouting encouragement, though Henry couldn't tell which side they were on.

"Get 'im!" "Watch out!"

"Drop it," Henry ordered again, pressing his thumbs into the underside of Whitlock's wrist until the man cried out in pain, and the knife clattered to the pavement.

Whitlock tore free from Fletcher's grasp to throw a wild punch, hitting the sergeant in the nose. The man struck out again, this one landing on Henry's jaw. Henry returned the favor even as his head rang and landed a blow to the inspector's stomach, then the side of his face, dropping Whitlock to his knees.

Fletcher reached for the flailing man once again, cursing as he tried to grab him, but Whitlock scrambled away. Henry slammed a booted foot in the center of his back, flattening him to the pavement.

Between the pair of them, Henry and Fletcher managed to wrench Whitlock's hands behind his back and cuff him.

The murmur of the crowd drew Henry's notice. In an attempt to calm them, he called out, "This man is under arrest for multiple murders."

"He's the rookery killer," someone in the crowd shouted as similar comments followed. "They've arrested the murderer!"

Yes, they had. It was done. Finished.

Whitlock didn't go quietly. Throughout the entire process, he cursed Henry and Fletcher as he struggled against them. "Release me! I am an inspector with Scotland Yard—unhand me!"

"That doesn't make you above the law," Henry said through gritted teeth as they hauled the handcuffed man to his feet.

A constable soon arrived in answer to Fletcher's whistle—one Henry had never met—and lent aid. It took nearly a quarter of an hour before a police wagon appeared to haul them to Scotland Yard.

By the time they arrived at the office, Henry longed to gag Whitlock, who continued to make his displeasure known.

Henry ignored the threats to both his career and his manhood as they marched Whitlock past an astonished Sergeant Johnson at the front desk and through the office.

"Here now!" Inspector Perdy jumped to his feet. "What is this about? Field, have you lost your mind?"

"Tell him to release me," Whitlock demanded, his lip still bleeding.

Duncan stood from behind his desk, giving Henry a nod of approval. "Clearly, I'm a day late in sharing what I learned."

Constable Peters emerged from the back only to halt abruptly at the sight of Whitlock in cuffs, eyes wide and face going pale.

"Blast you, Peters!" Whitlock shouted desperately. "You are not innocent in all this. You were the one to kill Cobb, not me."

Fletcher took hold of Peters, and the constable appeared too shocked to put up a fight. In the blink of an eye, he'd restrained Peters, the constable's customary smile nowhere in sight.

"Put him in an interview room," Henry ordered harshly, needing to separate the two men to prevent them from coordinating their stories.

"Yes, sir." Fletcher quickly hauled away Peters while Whitlock continued to hurl insults and demands.

Director Reynolds emerged from his office, his glare at Whitlock enough to finally silence him. "Damn you, Whitlock, for bringing disgrace to yourself and this force."

Inspector Clarke moved to Henry's side and took hold of the now motionless Whitlock. "It would be my pleasure to put this one in the second interview room. Seems like the least I could do, given the trouble he put me in." He glanced at Henry's bleeding arm. "Looks like you need some medical attention."

Before Henry could respond, Clarke hauled Whitlock toward a second interview room, jerking on the cuffs and managing to shove the prisoner into the wall along the way, causing more cursing. Perdy continued to stare at them with a dumbfounded expression.

Henry flexed his hand, the pain of the wound at last penetrating his thoughts. He pulled out a handkerchief and pressed it against the injury, deciding it was a small price to pay for putting a stop to the rookery killer—to finding and digging out the rot in the very heart of his police force.

Director Reynolds nodded at Henry. "Excellent work, Field."

"Thank you, sir." Henry drew a relieved breath, pleased he'd trusted his instincts and bluffed Whitlock into confessing as much as he had and even happier that Fletcher had heard every word.

The sergeant returned, his nose red from where Whitlock had struck him. He clasped Henry's shoulder in support, before tying the handkerchief over the wound. "Well done, but you've ruined another suit. You're giving too much business to your tailor with these last few cases."

Henry grinned, despite his sudden exhaustion. "Very true. I need to work on that."

"Your sergeant has a point," Reynolds agreed with the hint of a smile. "Now then, I want to hear what you learned. Next, we'll see what Whitlock has to say, followed by Peters."

"Hope you have plenty of time on your hands, sir," Fletcher added. "It's a bit much to take in."

Henry nodded and followed the Director to the interview room where Whitlock waited, eager to see what else they might learn. Yet Henry paused outside the door and drew a slow breath, allowing satisfaction to flow through him.

At this moment, he did not doubt that he was a true Field in every way that counted.

He'd longed for an end to this case for some time now, since Matthew Greystone's death. Justice didn't always take the form he expected, but it had come full circle, providing an ending, but also hopefully a beginning—for him and Amelia.

Epilogue

Three days later

AT THE END OF yet another very long day Henry waited for Fernsby to answer the door, his heart thudding and palms damp. He'd used up all his patience over the course of the past three days and was eager to see Amelia.

Luckily the butler opened the door before the urge to do so himself overcame him. "Good evening, Inspector."

"I hope it finds you well, Fernsby." Henry stepped inside, glancing up the stairs before he'd even handed his things to the butler, anxious to speak with Amelia.

It had taken hard work and long hours for Henry, Fletcher, and other members of the force to compile the testimony and evidence against Whitlock and Peters. There was more to do, but the pair would soon stand trial for their crimes.

The rot within Scotland Yard was gone, cleansed thanks to the efforts of more than just Henry.

He'd sent a message to Amelia to advise her they'd solved the case, but had only shared a few details. Though the urge to update her in person had nearly overtaken him several times, he'd wanted the details uncovered before he called on her.

After all, this was a milestone he'd been waiting for.

But now that he stood in the doorway of the drawing room, his mouth was dry, and his stomach twisted with nerves as he wondered how the evening might end. Before he could tap on the doorframe to announce his presence, Amelia looked up.

"Henry! What a wonderful surprise. It's so good to see you." Amelia laid aside her book and rose. She wore a deep purple gown; it had been some time since she'd worn anything but gray. Did he dare take that as a good sign? The color brightened her face—along with her smile, her beauty stealing his breath.

"You enjoyed your visit with your parents?" he forced himself to ask as he drew closer, remembering they'd departed the previous day.

"I did, yes." She moved to the sideboard to pour them drinks without inquiring, and soon they were seated before the cheerfully burning fire. "I wish they had stayed longer, but they promised to come again soon."

"Good." He sipped his drink and gathered his thoughts. "I wanted to share news of the investigation with you."

"Please do. I've been quite anxious to hear more since receiving your message." The avid interest in her eyes made him smile.

"It's quite the tale," he began as he sat back in his chair. "From the information we've gathered, Edgarton and Whitlock came to know one another when Edgarton paid the former inspector to turn a blind eye to his activities, including the lottery scheme and the operation of several brothels. Their association expanded from there. Soon, Edgarton's men threatened shops in Whitechapel while Whitlock offered protection in exchange for a fee, which the two men split. They expanded the scheme into other neighborhoods, which was when Peters became involved."

"Unbelievable," Amelia murmured.

"It gets worse." Henry shook his head. "Once Edgarton was arrested, Whitlock thought to take over his business dealings, but not all of Edgarton's men were willing to answer to a crooked police inspector."

"So Whitlock helped to arrange Edgarton's escape," she suggested.

"Yes, by bribing a couple of prison guards, including Cobb. But once Edgarton was out, he wasn't of much help since he was busy evading the search. Without Edgarton's contacts, Whitlock couldn't reestablish the import-export business, which brought the illegal antiquities into the country. Nor could he get the lottery scheme going or the other businesses Edgarton had run without the criminal and his network."

"Interesting. Does that mean Whitlock is the one who took the Egyptian scarab from the evidence room?"

"Yes. He hoped to use it in the illegal antiquities trade, but when he realized that wasn't possible, he grew frustrated and arranged to meet Edgarton at the church to discuss matters. The argument grew heated, and Whitlock killed Edgarton, then stuffed the scarab into his pocket, not wanting to be caught with it."

"I assume Inspector Whitlock also killed the woman in Whitechapel?"

Henry nodded. "Edgarton had told Betty Knox of Whitlock's identity, and after Edgarton's death, she demanded money from Whitlock in order to keep quiet, so he killed her too."

"My goodness. What a tangled mess." Amelia's eyes narrowed. "You were right then. Edgarton had no reason to silence Cobb, so who did?"

"Whitlock and Peters were both involved, but Whitlock insists Peters was the one who did it. They paid a man in Cobb's building to describe Edgarton as the one who'd killed him when we asked. However, he later identified Peters as the man he actually spoke with, which meant Peters was there the night Cobb was killed."

The dismissed prison guard had also confirmed Peters was the one who'd bribed Cobb. Henry had also uncovered hints of sex trafficking in addition to prostitution. There were definitely holes to fill in the story, but only shambles remained of Edgarton's empire, and Whitlock and Peters were both in prison.

"You were right not to trust Peters," Henry said, his blood chilling once again to think Amelia might have been in danger because of the constable. To know Peters was capable of murder and had been supposedly guarding her made his stomach turn.

The constable had been quick to offer to testify against Whitlock in exchange for a lighter sentence, something that frustrated a few of the men in the Yard. Though the constable's account was necessary to confirm Whitlock's involvement, they still wanted Peters to pay for what he'd done.

"I thought there was something odd about the man, as did you." Amelia pressed a hand to her chest. "I can hardly believe it all. Thank goodness you sorted it out, but how terrible for a fellow inspector and a constable to be guilty of such crimes." She gestured toward her desk. "I saw the headline, of course, but the full story is even more distressing."

The Rookery Killer is Caught—Scotland Yard Inspector to Blame.

Henry had seen it as well and didn't care for the poor light it cast on the force. The Director hadn't either, and neither—according to the rumors—had the Home Secretary. But such things were out of their control.

He preferred to focus on the fact that they'd put an end to it. "I am certainly relieved to have found those guilty so the investigation can be closed and justice served."

"What makes someone choose to commit such crimes?" she asked thoughtfully.

He sighed, having spent far too much time wondering the same thing. "Whitlock mentioned his frustration that Edgarton, a criminal, had so much more than he did, and that he didn't appreciate being passed over when opportunities for advancement arose in the force." Henry didn't mention that Whitlock blamed him. "The former inspector confessed to many of his actions. As for Peters, he claimed to need the money to help his family after they'd suffered a few setbacks."

"That is no excuse for murder," Amelia suggested.

"On that, we agree." As they did on most subjects.

"You must be exhausted after everything that's happened." Amelia's warm look was a reminder of the true reason for his visit.

"The last few days have been long but productive," he agreed with a smile even as his pulse quickened. Henry set aside his glass and wiped his palms as subtly as possible on his trousers. "Amelia," he began, working hard to keep his voice level. "I know it has been a trying few months, but I hope you feel some measure of relief that justice has prevailed."

"I do." She reached to take his hand and gave it a gentle squeeze, much to his delight. "I'm sure you feel much the same since Edgarton has been a thorn in your side for some time now."

"And yours." Henry rubbed the pad of his thumb over her hand, appreciating the touch and the way it steadied him. "I'm even more grateful to have had the chance to become better acquainted with you. I...I'm sure it's no surprise for you to hear how much I care about you, and I hope there is the chance for a future between us." He forced out the next question, desperate to hear her reply, needing to know even if the answer might cut deep. "May I call on you, to that end?"

The delight in her eyes was all the answer he needed. "Yes. Yes, I should like that very much." Amelia leaned closer as if to tell him a secret. "But Henry, it will be just the beginning."

"I quite agree with you." As he so often did.

"Good," she whispered, a lovely blush rising in her cheeks.

Henry stood, pulling Amelia to her feet, and then gently kissed the back of her hand. "You've made me very happy." He pressed his lips to hers as his heart sped its pace, unable to resist cupping her soft cheek, enjoying the moment more than he could possibly say.

The sound of footsteps on the stairs had them easing apart.

Yet Henry's focus held on Amelia's flushed face and sparkling eyes, delighted to think the kiss had meant as much to her as it had to him. He couldn't remember the last time he'd felt such joy, such hope, all because of the lovely lady whose strength and determination, along with her curiosity and a certain stubbornness, had caught his affections.

"Pardon me for the interruption, madam," Fernsby said from the doorway where he held a silver tray with a letter on it. "But a message arrived for you, and the lad who delivered it claims it's quite urgent."

"Oh?" Amelia frowned as she took the letter from the tray. "How curious." With a wary glance at Henry, she opened it and quickly skimmed the contents. "Oh, dear."

"What is it?" Henry asked, unable to resist when her expression showed more than a little concern.

"It's from a woman who requested I interview her for the periodical. She claims to be in touch with the spirits and serves as a medium for divination. And she says she knows where the body is of the young lady who's missing." Amelia pressed her lips tight before holding it out for him to read.

A chill ran down Henry's spine. "What young lady might that be?"

Ready for the next Field & Greystone adventure? Look for *The Cursed Divination*!

When a self-proclaimed medium contacts Amelia Greystone with chilling knowledge of a corpse's location, she

turns to the one man she can trust—Scotland Yard Inspector Henry Field...

Henry has no patience for mystics or séances. He believes in evidence, not whispers involving a dark prophecy. But when the medium's cryptic letter leads to the discovery of a young woman murdered in an abandoned tunnel, even he must question whether there's more to divination than he thought.

Amelia, haunted by tragedies of her own, is wary of the woman who claims to commune with spirits. Yet the medium's dire prediction fills her with unease...and when the body is found exactly where the woman foretold, Amelia fears something—or someone—is reaching out from beyond.

Drawn together by a case steeped in death and deception, Amelia and Henry must navigate fog-choked streets, forgotten tunnels, and the lure of a darkly compelling medium whose intentions may not be as selfless as they seem...before another victim is claimed.

Order your copy of *The Cursed Divination* today!

Author's Notes

I hope you enjoyed *The Rookery Killer*, Amelia and Henry's latest adventure. For those of you who like a peek at the research behind the book, I've compiled a few historical notes you may find interesting.

A 'rookery' is defined as a colony of birds, particularly 'rooks', members of the crow family, which are often noisy with nests crammed together, but is also used as a term for a crowded and dilapidated area. This version was first used to describe densely populated tenements or slums by poet George Galloway in 1792. The more famous rookeries in London included Whitechapel, St. Giles, and many others

Jack London, author of *The Call of the Wild*, also wrote *The People of the Abyss*, published in 1903, where he wrote of his own experience of living in disguise in Whitechapel for a few weeks. His account is very interesting and creates a vivid picture of not only the conditions but the people he encountered.

In 1884, the Metropolitan Police issued whistles instead of clackers to help constables and other officers warn the public of potential danger and to aid in crowd and traffic control. The whistle had a pocket-chain and hook clasp for easy access. As always seemed to be the case, the change was welcomed by some but not by all.

A 'rag and bone man' was someone who roamed the streets with a barrow, collecting bottles that he sold to merchants, bones for fertilizer, and rags for paper mills. Seems like an interesting way of recycling!

Thank you again for reading this book. Reviews are much appreciated and help authors more than we can tell you. Watch for the next book in the Field & Greystone series, *The Cursed Divination*.

Other Books by Lana Williams

The Field & Greystone Series

The Ravenkeeper's Daughter, Book 1 Also available in Audio

The Mudlark Murders, Book 2 Also available in Audio

The Gravesend Murder, Book 3 Also available in Audio

The Rookery Killer, Book 4

The Cursed Divination, Book 5

The Mayfair Literary League

A Matter of Convenience, Book 1

A Pretend Betrothal, Book 2

A Mistaken Identity, Book 3

A Simple Favor, Book 4

A Christmastide Kiss, Book 5

A Perilous Desire, Book 6

A Sweet Obsession, Book 7

The Wallflower Wager, a novella connected to The Mayfair Literary League and the Revenge of the Wallflowers series

A Secret Seduction, Book 8

The Wicked Widows Collection

To Bargain with a Rogue, a novella

The Duke's Lost Treasures:

Once Upon a Duke's Wish, Book 1
A Kiss from the Marquess, Book 2
If Not for the Duke, Book 3

The Seven Curses of London Series

Trusting the Wolfe, a Novella, Book .5
Loving the Hawke, Book I
Charming the Scholar, Book II
Rescuing the Earl, Book III
Dancing Under the Mistletoe, a Novella, Book IV
Tempting the Scoundrel, a Novella, Book V
Romancing the Rogue, A Regency Prequel
Falling For the Viscount, Book VI
Daring the Duke, Book VII
Wishing Upon A Christmas Star, a Novella, Book VIII
Ruby's Gamble, a Novella
Gambling for the Governess, Book IX
Redeeming the Lady, Book X
Enchanting the Duke, Book XI

The Seven Curses of London Boxset (Books 1-3)

The Secret Trilogy

Unraveling Secrets, Book I
Passionate Secrets, Book II
Shattered Secrets, Book III

The Secret Trilogy Boxset (Books 1-3)

The Rogue Chronicles

Romancing the Rogue, Book 1
A Rogue's Reputation, a Novella, Book 2
A Rogue No More, Book 3
A Rogue to the Rescue, Book 4
A Rogue and Some Mistletoe, a Novella, Book 5
To Dare A Rogue, Book 6
A Rogue Meets His Match, Book 7
The Rogue's Autumn Bride, Book 8
A Rogue's Christmas Kiss, a Novella, Book 9
A Rogue's Redemption, a short story, Book 10

A Match Made in the Highlands, a Novella

Falling for A Knight Series

A Knight's Christmas Wish, Novella, Book .5
A Knight's Quest, Book 1 (Also available in Audio)

A Knight's Temptation, Book 2 (Also available in Audio)
A Knight's Captive, Book 3 (Also available in Audio)

The Vengeance Trilogy

A Vow To Keep, Book I
A Knight's Kiss, Novella, Book 1.5
Trust In Me, Book II
Believe In Me, Book III

Contemporary Romances

Yours for the Weekend, a Novella

If you enjoyed this story, I invite you to sign up to my newsletter to find out when the next one is released. I'd be honored if you'd consider writing a review!

About the Author

Lana Williams is a USA Today Bestselling Author with over 50 historical fiction novels filled with mystery, romance, adventure, and sometimes, a pinch of paranormal to stir things up. Her latest venture is in historical mysteries.

She spends her days in Victorian, Regency, and Medieval times, depending on her mood and current deadline. Lana calls the Rocky Mountains of Colorado home where she lives with her husband and a spoiled rescue dog named Sadie. Connect with her at https://lanawilliams.net/.